TOUCHED BY FATE

A PSY-IV Team Novel

JAMI GRAY

Publisher: Celtic Moon Press Revised edition, 2018
ISBN: 978-1-948884-05-1 (ebook) ISBN: 978-1-948884-04-4 (print)

First edition, May 2016, MuseItUp Publishing ISBN: 978-1-77127-807-2 (ebook)
ISBN: 978-1-77127-848-5 (paperback)

Sign up for free reads from Jami!

Join Jami's newsletter to be the first to hear about new releases, free books, special prices and other nifty events.

Sign up at: https://www.subscribepage.com/jami-gray-books

What Readers Say...

About Arcane Transporter:
"Taking a refreshing approach to fantasy magic, this fast-paced, economical thriller is told from a highly likable perspective." —Red Adept Editing

About PSY-IV Teams:
"This story is an emotional roller coaster, from betrayal, anger, fear, love…" —InD'tale Magazine

About the Kyn Kronicles:
"…a fantastic paranormal action novel is quite possibly the best book I've read this year. I could not put it down, and had to exercise serious self-control to keep from staying up all night to finish it." — The Romance Reviews

About Fate's Vultures:
"…if you like your characters with a bit more bite, with secrets, with hidden agendas, and all those sorts of things, and your worlds are a far more deadlier place, then this is for you." —Archaeolibrarian

<u>Also by Jami Gray</u>

ARCANE WONDERLAND

Last Call

Bitter Spirits

Rune & Tonic

ARCANE TRANSPORTER

Ignition Point (*Prequel Novella*)

Grave Cargo

Risky Goods

Lethal Contents

Collision Course

Blind Spot

Terminal Drift

THE KYN KRONICLES

Shadow's Edge

Shadow's Soul

Shadow's Moon

Shadow's Curse

Shadow's Dream

Shadow's Fall

Tangled in Shadows (*Short Story Collection*)

FATE'S VULTURES

Lying in Ruins

Beg for Mercy

Caught in the Aftermath

Fear the Reaper

PSY-IV TEAMS

Hunted by the Past

Touched by Fate

Marked by Obsession

Fractured by Deceit

Linked by Deception

BOX SETS

PSY-IV Teams Box Set I (Books 1-3)

The Collapse: Fate's Vultures (Books 1-4)

The Kyn Kronicles Box Set (Books 1-6)

Arcane Transporter Box Set I (Books 1-3)

Arcane Transporter Box Set II (Books 4-6)

To my critique partners, my Knight in Slightly Muddy Armor and my Prankster Duo who taught me to treasure those who dare to see beyond my dints and dings, and for every well-worn nook and cranny is well-earned and well loved, thank you.

Acknowledgments

As with every book I write, there are a great many people who take the time to respond to my strange questions without calling the authorities. So all my military, firearm experts, and first responders who took the time to help me out, I give you a big thank you, and proclaim any errors solely mine.

Contents

Chapter One

Why, when you finally think you have your chosen path hammered out, Fate, the fickle bitch, always, I mean always, manages to knock you on your ass?

Let's just check out where my ass was currently. Hunched behind a mammoth RV, the massive house on wheels kind that tended to flock southward every winter. Unfortunately, this particular one was perched in a parking lot, a stone's throw from my lovely, air-conditioned condo in downtown Las Vegas. Not only was the baked asphalt burning said ass, but I was watching another daring ass of the male variety, dangle off my top-floor balcony before dropping to the one below.

What the hell?

Maybe the July heat was playing tricks with my mind. It was either that or last night's ugly events had finally broken my tenuous hold on sanity. I was currently leaning toward the second option because sanity and I had a very contentious relationship. One in which it threatened to take a hike on a regular basis, while I tried to lure it back with lofty promises even I knew I wouldn't keep.

Promises such as, I would never again question that gut-tugging sensation that screamed things were about to take a very drastic downturn. The same warning that erupted last night when I waltzed into my home, confident that the building's security wouldn't allow for an ambush, only to discover I was wrong.

Arrogant, maybe.

Careless, not usually.

Distracted, definitely.

Instead of kicking off my gorgeous lavender Jimmy Choo's and enjoying the possible end of a difficult assignment, I was met by Lawrence Rawlings, the egomaniac behind Aether Industries and his hulking sidekick in my own (albeit rented) living room.

And that wasn't the end of it. It got better. Or worse, depending on your point of view.

While I sipped a Booker Noe neat and tried to disguise my internal freak out, Rawlings decided to explain how he was going to get what he wanted—my endorsement of Aether's upcoming contract with the Department of Defense and me. If he didn't, he would happily exploit what I believed, until he laid out his threat, was a very well-hidden secret.

The DOD paid me good money to vet their civilian contracts, money which allowed my penchant for expensive footwear, a skyline view of the Vegas strip, and a closet full of indulgences. That same money kept my troublesome secrets six feet under. Secrets Rawlings shouldn't have been able to unearth. But whoever he set to digging up my past, had dug deep.

So deep, in fact, that by the time Rawlings left with his smarmy smile and menacing shadow, I found myself between a rock and a hard place, wishing I had something a hell of a lot stronger than whiskey at hand. A couple more shots of whiskey to already ragged nerves triggered my desperate attempt at leveling the playing field. Which, in turn, led to my current position, crouched behind an RV watching someone spider-man his way out of my condo.

It was such a death-defying stunt even my lungs were stunned. And until whoever that was dropped safely onto the balcony below mine, they couldn't remember how to function. For a long moment, all I could do was stare at where the whole surreal thing went down, my very tired and battered brain trying to figure out the who and why, only to come up empty.

One thing was clear. Going home was not an option.

Damn, but fate was having a hell of a good time at my expense, and she was racking up quite the bill while she was at it. A black eye, check. Bruised ribs, check. A bullet graze across my shoulder that stung like a bitch, check. Nerves strung razorwire tight on exhaustion, double damn check.

Sweat trickled down my spine, and the muscles in my legs trembled. Not just from their uncomfortable position, but because I spent the last fourteen hours running more than I'd ever run in my life. Despite being blessed with a hyperactive metabolism, I had never considered running a worthy pursuit. Well, not until last night. And if things didn't change soon, there would be more mad dashes in my future as I tried to stay ahead of the rolling mounds of crap hurtling toward me.

I should probably call Colonel Delacourt, seeing how it was her fault I was in this mess to begin with. As the colonel's information collector, my job allowed me to play some very exciting, sometimes dangerous games. Generally, I didn't mind because the heady rush of danger was almost as good as the paycheck. But not this time. This time the adrenaline rush left my nerves frayed to tiny shreds. I wasn't sure the DOD or Delacourt could pay me enough to repair the emotional and physical damage incurred by Rawlings's blackmail.

Rawlings came to the DOD's attention initially because his communications company had managed to find a newly discovered weak spot in the government's encrypted communications program known as the Boyau Project. Once he had pointed out the DOD's pet project's little problem, he spent three years perfecting his proposed solution. He called it Aether, and when he requested one of the many U.S. acronymned agencies make Aether's prototypes proprietary, the DOD decided to send me in to evaluate Rawling's creation.

Then Delacourt, mistress of manipulation and guilt trips, called. She shared that it appeared as if someone had managed to hack into some very delicate files in some hush-hush agency and were now prepared to market them to the highest bidder. For reasons known only to her and those above my pay grade, her suspicious eye turned to Rawlings and his new, nifty toy. Since my job just *happened* (heavy on the sarcasm) to put me in the perfect position, would I mind poking around for her? Stir in a subtle tablespoon of "you owe me" and a dash of guilt, and I teetered. When she offered two paychecks for one job, I tumbled right over the edge and agreed.

Caught up in the current mess, I was regretting that decision. There was one slim lifeline I might be able to pull. Delacourt had a team, a kick-ass team, with unusual talents who might be able to save my ass. Two things held me back from making the call. One, a favor from Delacourt carried a high repayment value, and two, I was working hard to avoid one particular team member.

Not because he carried the plague (if he did, it would make things much easier) but because he messed with my head at the most inopportune times. It was mortifying really, especially since I was pretty sure my preoccupation was one-sided.

Yet skulking in a parking lot in Vegas's late afternoon sun with dried blood and other things I tried not to think about, decorating my black cargos and T-shirt, calling Delacourt was quickly turning into my only viable option. Tenuously armed with a new plan, I straightened, and simultaneously winced and groaned as my injured shoulder woke up. A reminder of the too-close call with a bullet that resulted from my attempt to level the playing field. An attempt that not only failed, but tilted it decidedly out of my favor.

I looked around and prepared to move out, but life reached out and slapped me upside the head. The late-afternoon sun seared across my retinas that were safely ensconced behind dark lenses, and the world began to white out in a distressingly familiar warning. I slammed both palms against the RV so I wouldn't fall, ignoring the burn of metal against my skin. "Dammit, not now, please not now."

My plea fell on deaf ears as the world wavered, the edges turning too bright, and shadows danced in strange forms. Then sanity twisted sideways and the whispers started. Frustration and maybe a smidgen of fear rose, but I refused to listen, refused to see. My forehead joined my hands. I set my waning patience, desperation, and anger against the sense of impending doom, and shoved against what waited.

It backed off, but I knew the reprieve wouldn't last long. It never did. And when it returned, it would bring reinforcements. *Fun times.* My breathing was overly loud, but the sounds of approaching voices and footsteps managed to get my attention. I slowly raised my head, trying not to aggravate the soft pounding in my skull.

At first, all I could make out was a moving blob, but then it morphed into a small group of people exiting the condo and crossing through the parking lot. As they got closer, something —no, someone—caught my attention. It took a moment for the image to register. When it did, I didn't know if I should jump for joy, or just sit down and bawl.

At least I now knew who was spider-manning from my balcony, and possibly courted a death wish. Because walking out the front doors, and standing above the crowd of casually dressed executives, was the last person I wanted to see.

Thomas Anderson Gunderson. Tag.

Oh. My. God. Life really had a hard-on for me.

Chapter Two

My feet were moving before my brain had a chance to quit wailing and gnashing its teeth over this mortifying turn of events.

It wasn't hard to follow Tag's progress as I wove my way around the parked cars. The man stood out in more ways than one. First, his hair was this strangely attractive mix of blonds and burnished browns that obviously didn't comprehend the logic behind a comb. Second, he was built. Not hulking muscles built, but lean and mean built.

Tall, broad shoulders, narrow waist, long, long legs, and an ass no breathing woman could fail to appreciate. Not only did I appreciate the finer things in life, and he was F-I-N-E, but the last I checked, air still circulated through my lungs. When his genetics gathered, they produced a boy-next-door-with-a-secret gorgeousness. Not a run-of-the-mill type secret, but a come-walk-on-the-wild-side-with-me secret. And did I mention tall?

See, at five foot seven in bare feet, one of my main requirements for any man is that he must be tall enough for me to wear three-inch heels. I could get away with four and still have two inches to spare with Tag.

Of course, being that close in height meant I couldn't miss the revealing flashes of his reaction that sparked in his hazel-shot eyes every time we had a run-in. Or, if truth be told, ninety percent of the time we spent together. I could never figure out if it was lip-curling disdain or contempt, but either one guaranteed he wasn't impressed with my ass—sets.

He was one of the few. My genetics were a toss of Caribbean and Argentinian by way of the good ol' U.S. of A, and they served me well. When you chose to play in a male-dominated industry and uncover dirty little secrets, appearances were the difference between success and failure. I found that men were easily lulled by beauty, and if used correctly, that same beauty could get you access to places and people intelligence alone couldn't.

I assumed Tag didn't like me because I could pull off stilettos and the fine art of deception with equal skill. It wasn't something he said, but it was apparent in the very obvious way he avoided touching me. Every man I'd ever met made a point to touch me. A hand at my elbow, a quick brush against my back, or the ones who tried to take it too far; they all wanted to touch.

Tag didn't.

While I would never admit it out loud, his lack of physical contact stung. It wasn't until much later when I realized the truth. Tag avoided physical touch from everyone. Yet his apparent distaste of me was made clear in other, more hurtful ways. Like his barbs about the way I dressed. Something about my preference for nice things just didn't sit well with him.

Tough luck.

I firmly believed that if a woman wanted to dress to the nines, she had every right. Especially since the best way to pull off confidence was to dress for the part. For me, too many years of wearing other people's clothes had engendered a fierce need not to wear anyone's castoffs. So when I was able to afford nice things, I indulged, and my wardrobe reflected that.

Tag's snarky asides on my lifestyle weren't much better. In fact, those pissed me off the most. His life growing up might have been all fishing poles, family dinners, and fucking lemonade stands, but mine were drafty, shitty apartments where roommates came with multiple pairs of legs and nice family dinners involved ramen noodles. My mom worked her ass off after my dad bailed, and managed (barely) to keep a roof over our heads and something edible on the table. Now, I made sure roommates, two or multiple footed, weren't required to make the rent or mortgage payments. And I did that by earning two paychecks with one job.

The faint sound of a horn broke through my musings. Tag stopped and scanned the parking lot. *Double damn.* If he saw me, his reaction would be obvious to anyone watching. Not good for me. I ducked behind a car, waited twenty seconds, then peeked around, and watched him head to a dark SUV a few spaces away.

Now or never.

Decision made, I slipped through the last three spaces in time to hear the SUV's locks disengage. I came up along the passenger side and kept low to avoid the mirror. The driver's door slammed shut and the engine revved to life. I yanked open the passenger door, and then, ignoring my protesting ribs, I crammed my ass into the SUV's foot well. As I pulled the door closed, my shoulder scraped along the seat. I winced and twisted to face Tag, only to come nose first to a gun barrel. My heart stopped, and my hand froze on the door handle.

"Dammit, Risia!" His words were no less than a growl. The gun jerked up. "Are you looking to get killed?"

"Not particularly." My near heart attack made my voice breathy. I let go of the door. "We need to leave." I couldn't tell what shook more, my hands or my voice. He was scary fast with that gun.

"Want to tell me what's going on?"

His dark sunglasses made it difficult to read him, but his clenched jaw indicated he wasn't happy. That made two of us. "If you start driving, I'll start talking."

For a long moment, tension stretched in the SUV's interior, making the air fairly vibrate. Then, as if coming to some internal decision, he shifted in his seat and the gun disappeared. I let a small, hopefully undetectable sigh of relief loose. He shifted into reverse and jabbed a finger at the seat. "Get up and put the belt on."

His gruff command loosened one or two knots roiling in my stomach, and whatever air remained in my lungs escaped in an explosive gush. At least he wasn't tossing me out. Yet. "Get us out of here first."

Tag backed out of the parking space, and silence filled the interior as he turned onto the road. He made turn after turn, subtly checking his mirrors. He nodded to the empty seat. "We're clear."

I took him at his word and uncoiled from the floor with a grimace. I got in the seat and secured the belt with a reassuring click. Safely ensconced in a moving vehicle, my mind spun, trying to figure out how much to share because an explanation would be demanded.

Between the heavy quiet and frigid blasts of AC, it wasn't long before small quakes took over my body. *Delayed reaction. Adrenaline drop.* Whatever name it went by, it sucked. What sucked more was no matter how hard I tried, I couldn't stop it. It had been a long damn night and even longer day.

"I'm driving, but I don't hear you talking."

"Not sure where to begin."

"Begin with the outfit. What gives?"

"What? You don't like it?" Okay, so when stressed I tended

to gravitate to sarcastic-bitch mode. Sue me. I brushed a hand over the definitely odiferous, sweat-dampened black T-shirt streaked with dust and…things. "It's the latest fashion statement."

The tremors continued their rampage and I dropped my hands to my lap. I plucked nervously at my cargos. A ragged end of a broken nail caught against the fabric, and a hiss escaped at the slight sting as it tore.

There was a soft curse from the driver's seat, and then Tag reached behind the passenger's seat and dug around. A moment later he came back with a water bottle and shoved it in my face. "Didn't know urban cat burglar was your style."

I took the bottle and unscrewed the top, draining half of it in one shot. The water hit my stomach at the same time as the world decided to take a sharp left. The sickening spiral dragged me down without remorse. I must have made some sort of noise, because the vehicle's smooth ride jostled. I didn't get a chance to find out why because my world went white, the edges bleeding to black.

Black like the blood pooled around vacant eyes. Hands trembling. A gun falling to the floor. Fear, sour and acrid, coating my mouth.

The air around me shifted, and something brushed against my face. I tried to bat it away.

"I don't lose." Rawlings's voice, cold and elegantly lethal echoed around me, freezing me into terrified stillness.

The echoes expanded, and so did the darkness. Changing, morphing, impatient, demanding to be seen.

"No, no, no…" The future was coming, and demanding bitch that she was, there would be no stopping her this time. My body jerked, trying to escape her greedy grasp. The protest from my ribs merged with the sting of the seatbelt cutting into my chest. Neither could stop my instinctive physical reaction to her presence.

"Breathe, Risia." Tag's voice, solid and unbreakable, snuck

under the nightmare. Something warm cradled my face, the touch both strangely intimate and disconcerting, even as it somehow granted me much needed space between what was coming and my battered psyche. "C'mon. Slow. In. Out. In. Out."

I tried to follow his direction, but every time I inhaled, everything stuttered, leaving me nothing to exhale with.

Suddenly the warmth disappeared, and the impending vision surged forward. A whimper escaped before I could call it back. The pressure on my chest loosened, and a weight forced my head down and forward, putting my face too close to my disgusting jeans. My ribs screamed in protest, but I couldn't escape.

The baseball cap capturing all my curls tumbled off to land at my feet. I focused on it, desperate to stay in the here and now. Warmth ran down my spine, as if I was being petted. The touch was light, but definitely there, and chased the horrors in my head back.

"Breathe, Duchess." Tag's voice cut through the looming vision and anchored deep, giving me something real and present to hold on.

I struggled to sync my breathing with the pattern of his stroke.

Up, suck in air. Down, push it out.

"That's it."

I tried to hold the vision back and maintain the rhythmic breathing, but it was futile, the attempt too little, too late.

Tag's voice wavered between too loud and too soft, and the rise and fall of undecipherable words joined the tsunami bearing down on me. Everything crashed in at once, the vision dragging me under, forcing me to watch.

To see.

An ear-piercing shriek of a hunting bird tore through the air and yanked my attention up. Unnaturally bright blue sky stared down, a tiny shadow expanding across the horizon until feathers filled the sky. Stunned, I stared and raised my arm in a futile attempt to ward off the huge-ass, lethal talons coming my way. A savage wind whipped my hair across my face, blotting out the surreal scenery and veering the damn bird off course.

Thank God.

A child's laughter spun me around. The sound lacerating my heart. I knew that laugh. I know I did. Where? Where was it?

A dead man stood in front of me. "He won't lose."

"He can't win," I shot back, not understanding, but knowing beyond a shadow of doubt I uttered the truth. Sometimes the dead argued. This one didn't.

Another avian scream split the air, the long drawn-out shriek morphing into the squeal of brakes. The scent of burnt rubber assaulted my nose, making me want to gag.

A muted pop, then a spider-web of cracks fractured my world, bleeding a viscous ebony.

A pained grunt sounded nearby. I turned, giving the dead man my back, and saw Tag's SUV parked along a road, and behind it, in reverse colors, like some psychedelic negative, my condo rose.

I didn't hesitate and rushed to the truck, until I was standing next to it. For a moment what lay before me didn't make sense. The windshield morphed, lines growing from a small white center.

A bullet hole. At head height.

Tag!

My heart stopped, fear clutching me in a cold grip. My arm rose, my hand outstretched to grasp the handle right there.

More cracks formed as the lines in the windshield continued their relentless journey.

Behind the shattered glass, in the driver's seat was a crumpled body. Everything twisted sideways, this scene disappeared, only to be replaced by a mud splattered truck racing toward Tag's SUV, gaining speed instead of slowing down. It slammed into the driver's side, the horrendous metallic shrieks filled the air, while glass rained down in a sickening counter note.

Unable to stop what was happening, all I could do was watch as Tag's vehicle shuddered and his body wrenched forward, painting the spreading cracks in the windshield red. Bile crawled up the back of my throat.

Another spiraling scene shift and now Tag's SUV was surrounded by police crouched by their car doors, their guns spitting shot after shot into Tag's vehicle. The bullets sliced through metal and tore through skin.

"NO!"

My scream blended with the shrill cry of the circling bird above as the shadow of its wings blotted out the sun. I ignored the deadly hail and finally reached the door, yanking it open, desperate to get to Tag. To keep him safe.

Too late. Always too late.

Blood decorated the interior. The seats. The windows. And when I finally managed to turn him over, he stared at me, the light in those hazel eyes slowly dimming.

"Risia, stop! You're going to hurt yourself." His yelled at me, his voice hard and unyielding.

How could he yell at me without moving his lips?

Solid heat enclosed my face, holding me still. "Risia, duchess, look at me. I'm right here. See me."

The last was an order I couldn't fight. Didn't want to fight.

Tag's face changed, death retreating, life coming back. Deep-set eyes, filled with flashes of green and gold, and framed by thick lashes. The shadow of a beard dusted along his angular jaw. His sunglasses almost lost among the mess of wild hair.

We were so close we were breathing the same air.

Breathing—we were breathing.

He was alive, not full of holes. Not dead.

Not yet.

Relief, so huge it left me shaking, washed through me, but I refused to look away. I clung to his steady gaze, using it to anchor me in the here and now. There was something different from his normal lip-curling disdain lurking there. I had no idea what it was, except something in me liked it. A lot.

"You with me?"

I dipped my head, only then realizing he cradled my face, the heat of his touch burning just below the bruise under my eye. Somehow, he had twisted around until he was looming in front of me without getting out of the car, and my hands were pressed against his chest. His heart beat a rock-solid rhythm under my palms.

The scary fact that we were touching disappeared as urgency took over. Sometimes I could outrun what I saw, and I needed this to be one of those times. "We need to leave!" I tilted my head back until our gazes met and held. "Now, Tag."

Whatever he saw in my face, or heard in my voice, made him pull back. I curled my hands into fists to keep from clinging like some deranged, needy woman. Deranged may be accurate, but needy, never.

"Who's coming?" His voice changed, gaining a granite edge, but it didn't wipe out the suspicion lurking behind it.

I shook my head, frustration overriding my fear. "Everyone, no one, I don't know, but we need to leave. NOW!"

I think the last part may have escaped a little too forcibly considering that strange whatever it was in his eyes quickly morphed to his more familiar stony, distance. The atmosphere in the cab took on a new, unknown intensity. He leaned forward.

I pressed back against the seat, ignoring the pain in my shoulder because I wasn't sure exactly what he had planned, but I knew I didn't want to find out.

A snick drew my gaze down to my lap. He'd refastened my seatbelt. Then a water bottle came into my peripheral vision. "Drink."

Not about to argue with that tone, I took the bottle.

He sat back, settled his sunglasses, grabbed the steering wheel, shifted into gear, and drove.

Chapter Three

I held my tongue as Vegas disappeared in our rear-view. Our passenger, Silence, grew into monstrous proportions, and in no way did I want to tempt its teeth. Instead, I worked on draining the water bottle. This task lasted about ten minutes.

Then, because it so often worked, I closed my eyes, hoping to forestall any further conversation until I got my damn nerves under control. Or figured out what answers to share that would satisfy the man beside me. The fact it gave me a chance to regain my footing in reality was a bonus.

The sound of rubber spinning over pavement provided a hypnotic lullaby. Not really asleep, I drifted in a pleasant arena where neither past, present, or future could catch me.

The past, present, and future walked into a bar, it was tense.

I choked back a hysterical giggle as a familiar joke ran through my mind. Strange and wondrous are the things that traipse through your mental vaults when you're trying to patch the cracks with duct tape. My silent, mini-breakdown lasted until Tag turned off the highway. The change in our traveling melody brought me blinking back into the present.

The familiar buildings of Henderson, a small city outside of Vegas, took shape. Instead of taking the left to Hoover Dam, Tag made a right and navigated his way through the streets until he pulled into a parking lot guarded by a sign that read, El Gardeña.

Silence still dominated our conversation, so I didn't interrupt.

The engine shut off and he turned to me, nothing remotely friendly lurking in his face or voice. "Stay put." Then he slammed his door closed and strode to the door with the word OFFICE stenciled on it.

Normally this would be my cue to get the hell out of dodge. Being told to stay like some recalcitrant puppy did not engender sweet feelings toward Mr. Gunderson. As a matter of fact, now that I had a moment to catch my breath, it made me want to slap his arrogant face into next week. However, that particular action would need to wait until after I managed to outrun the other trouble chasing me.

Instead, I found my ball cap (tossed in the backseat) and my sunglasses (in the center console) and reapplied my rather meager disguise. I snagged another bottle of water from the back and managed to down half its contents before Tag made a reappearance.

He didn't go to his side, he came to mine. He stood there, hand on the handle, staring at me through the window. Or at least I assumed he was staring. Hard to tell with his sunglasses. We sat there for a few moments, staring at each other through the glass. His lips twitched, and then he was tugging on the door handle. It rattled but didn't open.

Snapping out of my strange haze, I hurriedly flipped the locks, a slow heat rising under my face. God, he could make me feel foolish without trying.

He pulled it open. "Room number eight."

He waited by the door as I swung my legs out. It took a

little longer than expected to get upright, mainly because my muscles decided to go on strike and freeze all further movement. This meant bracing myself against the SUV for a moment before getting my legs to agree to move. The whole damn time, Tag stood there, never once offering a hand.

I straightened my spine and left him standing in all his disapproving glory. Only when I stepped up on the sidewalk in front of the long line of doors circling the parking lot to wait for him, did he close the truck's passenger door, beep the locks, then take the lead, a small pouch or something in his hand. While his attitude may be shit, I had to admit following behind him was not a hardship. Seriously, the man had a fine ass.

Oh for the love of God, girl!

I blew out a hard breath in exasperation at my weirdly inappropriate reaction. We made it to room eight without incident, and my hormones sat in the corner pouting.

Tag wouldn't let me enter until he checked it out, only motioning me in once he was satisfied. He closed and locked the door as I took in the room. Dresser, two chairs, a small table, small fridge, coffee pot, bathroom, bed.

One bed. One.

I looked for a couch. Nope, just two chairs and one bed.

Okay then.

He brushed by me and went to the big window facing the parking lot to pull the curtains closed. I turned, watching him. With the room in shadows, my sunglasses became a hindrance, so off they went.

He grabbed one of the chairs, moved it near the bed, and pointed to it, his silent order loud and clear.

Really not up to arguing, as there was now a door between me and trouble, I carefully sat down. It didn't take long before I realized that was the wrong move, because everything began to catch up with me and i could feel myself starting to shake.

He sat on the edge of the bed facing me. He leaned in, his

fingers tracing a feather-light touch around the bruise around my eye. It was so unexpected, those betraying shakes froze. His lips thinned, and something moved behind his stony facade. "Any other injuries besides the shiner and the ribs?"

Knowing what his touch could do, besides give my hormones false hope, I pulled back gently. "What? You're a mind-reader now, too?"

His hand dropped, and he pinned me with a look. "You're moving slow, and you wince every time you turn."

My gaze fell, and I realized the pouch he brought in was a first-aid kit. I wondered if he'd let me take it to the bathroom and deal with my owies on my own?

"Risia?"

The demand behind my name answered that question. "Bullet graze on my shoulder," I muttered.

He stood up and motioned for me to do the same.

Cautiously, I did.

He stepped in close, and before I could do more than blink, he had one hand between my shoulder blades and the other just under my breast, pressing gently.

Caught off guard, I sucked in a breath and held it, even as my spine stiffened. If I dared to exhale, his hand and my breasts would become fast friends. I wasn't sure I was ready for that friendship. "What are you doing?"

"Checking your ribs." His hand moved, and I managed the tiniest of exhales, mainly because I didn't want to go "ow-ow-ow".

Finally, he said, "Nothing's broken or cracked, as far as I can tell. Just take it easy, and those should be fine." He dropped his hands and turned to the bed. "Take your shirt off and let me see your shoulder."

His abrupt order required a snippy response. "A please would be good."

He folded his arms across his chest. "Take it off or I'll do it for you."

Now he was seriously pissing me off. "You get laid with that attitude, Tag?"

He leaned in close and my pulse sped up. "All the damn time. Want a turn?"

Shitdamnfuck. Walked right into that one, Risia girl.

With no ready response I did what any self-respecting cornered woman would, I kept my mouth shut and glared. He didn't crumble into a pile of ash, more's the pity. Instead he just held my glare. Waiting. Since my shoulder hurt like hell and tending it myself was out, I didn't rip into him on his crappy bedside manner.

Sucking it up, I pulled off the baseball cap and set it on the table next to my sunglasses. Then I grabbed the hem of my T-shirt and awkwardly pulled it up, only to have it get stuck halfway. Frustrated tears rose, the stupid T-shirt finally managing to do what a dead body, getting beaten and shot, then running for my life hadn't. Biting my lip hard so Tag wouldn't know I was falling apart, I gave another sharp yank to the T-shirt.

My ribs clamored, and a breath escaped on something close to a sob. Then other hands were there, helping. The shirt cleared my head, leaving me in a tank top and jeans. I could feel Tag standing next to me, but kept my head down. "Thanks." Not exactly gracious, but manners were a necessary evil.

He brushed my hair over to my opposite shoulder, then leaned in to inspect the damage. Goosebumps erupted as his breath fell over my neck. He sat back and studied me. "Graze is long, but not deep. What happened?"

Avoiding his gaze, I gathered my curls in one hand and kept them from springing back over his way. They were unruly like that. "I kind of stumbled into a murder."

Really, there was no other way say it.

I heard the zipper as he opened the first-aid kit, then rustling as he pulled out whatever supplies he needed. "Stumbled into a murder? How exactly do you do that?"

Not quite ready to tackle that question, I asked one of my own. "Did Delacourt tell you what I'm working on?"

He continued to unpack pieces from the first-aid kit, laying them out neatly on the bed. "Nope, just sent me over to get you."

"Great," I muttered. Because now I'd have to dance around an explanation. Fine, then, I was light on my feet. "It was recently pointed out to the DOD that their encryption program may have a flaw. Lawrence Rawlings and Aether Industries believe their prototype program will solve the DOD's problem. The DOD sent me in to evaluate the company."

"Do they want you to evaluate Rawlings as well?"

"Rawlings is Aether, so yes."

"Is that all you're doing?" He rummaged in the first-aid kit and pulled something free. "Or are you playing with him, like you do most of your targets?"

And there was the contempt I was used to hearing from him. "First, I'm damn good at my job. Second, contrary to your low opinion, sleeping with my targets is not in my job description."

His jaw flexed, but he didn't look up. "Never said it was."

"Seriously?"

He slid a sideways glance my way. "I asked if you're playing him, not fucking him."

The urge to slap him left me gritting my teeth. "After last night, the only one who's being fucked with is me."

He stilled, and his gaze met mine. "Explain."

"Rawlings paid me an unexpected visit last night. Which is what started this whole mess."

"Is your cover blown?"

"No." At least not completely, but again, not something I

felt like sharing. When the energy around Tag took on a dangerous edge, it became obvious I wasn't successful at making that no convincing.

"Was he the one who trashed your apartment?"

Even after my horrific night, his question managed to catch me unawares. "My apartment's trashed?"

He studied me, a muscle flexing in his jaw, then he gave a slow nod.

"How—" I had to stop and cough to clear the rough rasp from my voice, before continuing, "How bad?"

A flash of pity was there and gone. "There's not much to salvage."

Even though a barely discernible gentleness edged his tone, the images his answer invoked gripped my stomach in a cruel fist and twisted. My home, my things, gone. My legs began to buckle, but reaching behind me, I used the table to brace myself.

Tag caught my other arm. "Duchess, take a breath. It can be replaced."

Maybe, but still… Instead of concentrating on this newest wound, I answered his earlier question. "He's not the type to stoop and get his hands dirty." Lawrence had plenty of peons to do that for him.

Tag had no problem resuming his inquisition. "But he made threats?"

Big scary ones but I wasn't sharing that with him, because if I did, he would drag my butt right back to Delacourt. I couldn't let him do that. Not yet.

"Risia?"

My name from Tag, made me realize I'd been staring in silence at the carpet. I lifted my head.

He watched me closely. "He threatened you." A statement, not a question.

Oh yeah, threatened me with things he shouldn't have

known. Which was why fear took the upper hand last night. Swallowing, I answered, "Implied." I didn't think it was possible, but Tag's face got even more grim. His expression had me stumbling quickly through the rest. "He wants the contract with the DOD, enough that he's willing to offer me whatever I want to get my endorsement."

My answer obviously didn't put him at ease, because that dangerous energy took a drastic spike. My pulse went along for the ride when he gritted out, "Did he find your price?"

Guilt and resentment clashed, caught between his assumption I could be bribed, and because Rawlings had found a weakish spot to poke at. I bit my lower lip and looked away.

Not a good move because Tag's spine stiffened, and I could feel the weight of the glare he directed at me. "What did he promise you?" He snagged my chin and forced me to meet his accusing gaze. "What did you give him?"

His questions shattered a fragile hope I hadn't realized, until then, existed. "Not a damn thing," I snapped, letting my fury bury the hurt. I ignored the aches and pains of my battered body, and yanked my chin out of his grip. Then, I shoved my hands against his chest and pushed. He barely budged, but it didn't matter, because I got right in his face and hissed, "What is your problem?"

"Someone is selling the names of Delacourt's team to the wrong side."

My shock sank under a sickening wave of nausea as I searched his face. "And you think it's me?"

His expression remained cold, and he didn't bother to answer, didn't need to because his suspicion was easy to read.

"Fuck you, Tag!" It came out harsh with betrayal, but it didn't take long for fury to strengthen my voice and turn it into a harsh whip. "Just because you think I'm shit, doesn't make it true."

His eyes narrowed. "I never said you were shit, Risia."

"You've always believed the worst of me. But this..." I shook my head, ignoring the way it woke up the throbbing that had barely begun to settle. "This is bullshit."

He folded his arms across his chest and met my anger with icy disdain. "It's not bullshit if it's buried in truth."

Bull-headed, conceited jackass! "Well, why don't I just clear the shit off and make this crystal fucking clear then, Thomas," I snarled. Before he could react, I wrapped my hand around his wrist and yanked his arm up between us. "You're a touch empath, which means if I touch you, you can tell if I'm lying or not. So pay close attention." I leaned in, my fingers tightening against his skin and my ragged nails digging in deep. Anger, fueled by disillusioned pain, swirled through me, and I didn't bother to hide it.

Let him read what he wanted. It no longer mattered. He no longer mattered. I wouldn't deal with his constant condemnation any longer. But no way would I let him doubt where my loyalties lay. "I didn't make a deal with Lawrence. I would never do anything that would hurt Delacourt or her team."

His eyes burned, and his mouth thinned, but he didn't pull away.

Churning fury gave me the strength to hold his gaze. "Any other accusations you'd like to throw at me?"

A handful of seconds passed, neither one of us backing down, before he gave a small shake of his head. Deliberately, I uncurled my fingers, one by one, from his skin. Raking him from head to toe with my most scathing look, I turned and made my way around the bed to the phone sitting on the nightstand. I snatched up the receiver and began punching in numbers to call a taxi. No way in hell was I sticking with him, I'd find my own damn hotel room.

"Who are you calling?"

Ignoring him, I hit the last number. On the other end, the phone began to ring.

"Risia."

I kept my back to him. A voice in my ear chirped, "AAA Cab."

"Hello, I need a pick up from—"

The receiver was yanked from my ear and slammed back into its cradle. Then he grabbed my shoulder, the non-injured one, and forced me to face him. "Where do you think you're going?"

"As far away from you as I can get."

His hands dropped to his side and curled into fists. "You can't run away because you're pissed at me."

"First, I'm not running away, and second, I passed pissed awhile ago."

He turned and stalked back around the narrow confines of the room. By the bathroom, he stopped, ran a hand through his hair, then wrapped it around his neck. Finally, he turned to look at me. "Look, I was being an asshole, I'm sorry. It's just..." he trailed off, something strange running across his face.

"Just what?" *Argh, why was I still talking to him?* I was such a glutton for punishment.

"Nothing."

I wanted to argue that this was a hell of a lot more than nothing, but kept quiet. No doubt he'd find some other heinous deed to lay at my feet.

"Right now, I'm your backup." He came back and rummaged through the first-aid kit.

Watching him set up cotton pads, stere-strips, and disinfectant, I murmured, "I'm better off on my own."

He didn't look up, but his jaw tightened. "Too bad Delacourt's the one giving the orders then." He poured liquid onto one of the cotton pads. "And you need me." He didn't wait for me to respond, but ordered, "Turn around, we need to treat your shoulder."

I didn't move. "I don't need you."

"Yeah, you do. You can't treat yourself, you have no money, no transportation, and no home to go back to. So your only option is me. Now, turn around."

"Lucky me." I grudgingly gave him my back.

He came up behind me, and with a care I knew he would never really feel, began to clean the bullet graze. The minutes ticked by, only the rustles of his ministrations breaking the quiet. A question kept poking at me. "Why were you spider-manning from my balcony?"

The careful wiping against my shoulder paused. "Spider-manning?"

"The stunt you pulled, dropping from my balcony to the one below."

"I was avoiding the cops."

"Cops?"

"A detective was getting ready to enter your apartment. Having him find me in a trashed apartment and unable to answer his questions, I choose to use an alternate exit."

"By jumping from balcony to balcony on a ten-story building? Are you nuts?" Either that or he had a standing date with the Grim Reaper.

"It's no different than rock climbing, easier actually." He tossed a bloody pad on the bed next to the small growing pile.

The stinging in my shoulder was amping up to a full-on dull razor blade. Gritting my teeth, I managed, "If you seriously believe that you need therapy."

That brought his head around. "Said the kettle to the pot."

Another bloody cotton pad hit the bedspread. He picked up a clean one and the small brown bottle. He combined the two, then went right back to my shoulder.

"I'm not the one with a death-wish, here."

"Neither am I, Duchess." Obviously tired of our conversation, he changed it. "What happens if you don't give Lawrence what he wants?"

"Like you really give a damn." I sucked in a sharp breath at the sting of antiseptic. "Dammit, Tag, watch it."

He flicked a glance at me then went right back to torturing my shoulder.

Fine, whatever. "He'll figure out a way to get it."

"Which involves what?"

Answering that question would reveal more than I wanted, so, time to pick and choose my answers. "The normal." It came out tight as he wiped across my wound and another cotton pad joined the pile.

"With results similar to what you stumbled across?"

Not appreciating his sarcastic lean on the word "stumbled", I snapped, "Probably."

Unfazed, he continued to poke and prod, probably getting off on causing me pain. "Who was it?"

Tangled up in my seething thoughts, his question proved too difficult to decipher. "Who was who?"

He finally lifted his hands, leaving my poor battered shoulder alone. Of course, he then shot me a disgusted look. "The dead body. I'm assuming, since you mentioned stumbling over a murder, there's a body lying around somewhere."

Oh, right. "Curtis Trammel. He does contract negotiations for Aether. We were hammering out various contingencies over the last week and were almost done." And I almost had the information I needed. It was why I had walked blithely unaware into my apartment last night and right into Rawlings's sticky-ass web. Didn't share that, but did manage to hold Tag's gaze with a studied casualness.

His lips tightened, and he shook his head. "Poor bastard, you were using him." He ducked back around and resumed his not-so-gentle ministrations.

"It's a job, Tag." Something I shouldn't have to remind him, of all people, about. You did what you needed to get an assignment done. Of course, considering his opinion of me was probably one step up from a hooker, I'm sure his mind was swimming in the cesspools of possibilities.

What would he do if he knew the last person I let that close was over three years ago? Probably call me a liar, then I'd have to kill him and explain to Delacourt how she wouldn't mind missing one irritating male from her team.

I turned away and focused on the wall behind the dresser. "To get the files I needed, I had to exploit an access point. Most of the files were copied in previous runs, but during my last foray I uncovered a cluster of encrypted files. Unfortunately, there wasn't enough time to copy them over. After Rawlings's visit, I decided it was time to get the hell out of dodge. Which meant a late-night run to Curtis's office. Less security on his computer."

"Did you get what you needed?" He spread something cool and slightly moist over my shoulder, then laid a gauze pad over it. "Hold this for me," he instructed.

Reaching back and over awkwardly, I held it in place as he applied the steri-strips. And here was another sticky spot. "I did."

In the midst of applying the last piece, he stopped and looked at me. "I hear a 'but' in there."

I bit my lip. "It's all on a flash drive."

"And the drive is…?"

"Back in Curtis's office."

A long slow blink. "Of course it is," he muttered, setting the last tape in place. "Let me guess, we need to go back and get it."

"Might be a bit difficult with it being a crime scene and all."

He turned and collected all the bloody materials. "Ya think? Especially since your last attempt nearly got you shot." He stalked around the bed to the bathroom, tossing the medical mess into the trash.

I snagged my T-shirt, wondering if it was at all salvageable.

Nope, it was a complete loss. *Damn.* "As if you'd shed a tear if I died," I said under my breath.

"One, maybe two," he shot back, the sharp tone jerking my head up, only to be greeted by what I was coming to believe was Tag's go-to expression with me. He stood at the end of the bed, his hand extended with two white tablets. "For the ribs, since we can't do much else."

Blessed aspirin! Unwilling to let his disapproval eat away at me, I tucked my battered emotions behind steel-reinforced doors and snatched the tablets from his hand. My fingers brushed across his palm. "Do you have a T-shirt I can borrow?" So much easier to get the hell away from him with a shirt than running around beaten to shit in a tank top and gross cargos.

He yanked his hand back like it was burnt, and his jaw went rigid. Instead of answering, he spun on his heel and stormed out of the motel room.

Chapter Four

I blinked at the door. *Well, all righty then.*

Really not up to dealing with Tag's temper tantrum, I wadded up my shirt and made my way to the bathroom. Tossing the shirt away, I made use of the facilities and washed my hands. What stared back from the mirror wasn't pretty.

One eye resembled a puffy survivor of a run-in with a mosquito on steroids. Grimy streaks of sweat and, leaning closer because my image was a tad blurry, yep, blood, decorated my skin. Normally a golden caramel color, it currently carried a seriously pale undertone. The dark circles under my non-puffy eye made the sky blue brighter, and my crazy, spiral curls were…well, insane.

I splashed water on my face, then tried to scrub away the nasty reminders of my night from my hands, face, and arms. Using one of the scratchy hand towels to dry off, I stepped back into the room to find Tag waiting.

"Here." He threw something at me.

Unprepared, I dropped the towel and caught the object hurtling through the air. After catching it, I discovered it was a

T-shirt and shook the soft material out. Since it was one of Tag's, it would hang to my thighs. *Better than nothing.*

Careful of my shoulder, I pulled it on. When the uniquely spicy scent I always associated with him surrounded me, I dragged it deep into my lungs, and lost myself for a brief moment. A dangerous lapse. *Can't forget who you're dealing with, girlie.* With the shirt on, I freed my hair from the collar. "Thanks."

Completely forgoing good manners, he grabbed one of the chairs, turned it around so the back faced me, and straddled it. He folded his arms along the back. "You're in the office after hours, downloading files that aren't yours. What happened next?"

I carefully perched on the far side of the bed. "I was downloading the last file, when things went to hell." In a damn hand basket, truth be told. I dragged a hand through my hair, and tried not to focus on the memories crowding in. "Curtis came back to the office unexpectedly. Which left me with very few options."

"Yeah, not a lot of good hiding spots in an office."

So I found out. When Curtis began unlocking his office door my heart had nearly leapt from my chest and made a break for it. Who the hell came back to an office after two in the morning?

Tag wasn't finished, his voice taking on, dare I say it, a teasing note. "Unless you lucked out with an executive who feels the need to have his own john, you're pretty screwed."

My lips twitched, because he was so right.

"So where did you go? Under the desk?"

Yep, it was humor in his voice. Humor, which quickly disappeared when I nodded.

His jaw dropped. "You're shitting me? Seriously, Risia?"

Mortified, because he had every right to be flabbergasted, I went to shrug, only to stop when my shoulder declared that a very bad idea. "I didn't have much choice."

He shook his head. "Damn fool, Duchess."

Duchess? What the hell did that mean? Wait a second... "Did you just call me a fool?"

Unfazed, he matched my temper with controlled frustration. "You're lucky you're still breathing. You went in without backup, no contingency plan, all because Rawlings rattled you."

"Excuse me?" Seriously, what was his problem? Besides being a dick.

He had the audacity to raise his hand, palm facing me. "I'm just saying, you went in without a plan. That's an engraved invitation to shit hitting the fan."

I fought not to roll my eyes at his statement of the obvious. "I had a plan. Get the info. Get out. It did not involve being an eyewitness to an execution and catching a murderer's attention."

"Execution?" The word came out sharp.

Oh shit...

Nibbling on my lower lip, I stared at the stained beige carpet at my feet wondering if there was any way to rewind the last few moments and get a do-over. Considering the heavy, expectant silence descending like the final curtain on a stage performance, my chances seemed minuscule. Why was he so upset? It wasn't like he cared. Perhaps if I kept my mouth shut, he'd let it go. It worked, for about fifteen seconds.

"Risia..."

How in the world did he manage to make my name sound like a threat? Too entranced by the strange wavy dance of the worn rug at my feet as it crept closer, drifted away, and then crept back, I didn't answer. Would he leave me alone if I just tilted to the side and took a nap?

"Explain."

Nope, he was determined to keep me talking, the bastard. Heaving an unmistakable put-upon sigh, I took my sweet time raising my head, and made sure to express my displeasure in a one-eyed glare. "Explain, what, Tag?"

He cleared the distance so fast, I didn't have a chance to blink. Instead, I found myself leaning precariously backward, even as my ribs and shoulder protested, while Tag got in my face. Literally.

"Let's start with the execution part," he bit out. My tired brain focused on his mouth as it moved. "Then move on to catching the attention of a murderer."

Giving my head a small shake, I tilted it back. My balance shifted backward, and I wrapped my hand around the nearest anchor, which happened to be Tag's bare arm. Heat seared my palm and chased away a chill I hadn't felt creeping along my bones. "There was a guy with Curtis. They came into the office arguing."

I lost track of what I was saying because I could feel the shift of his muscles under my hand. It was distracting. And strangely comforting as last night's drama began to replay in my head. My fingers tightened, not wanting to lose even this small connection. Something in the back of my brain tried to interrupt, but I was enjoying the moment too much.

He pulled back a bit, but I didn't let go of his arm. Warm, calloused fingers cradled my chin, lifting my head. "About what?"

"Unpaid debts. The man told him it wasn't enough to pay what he owed. Curtis argued, told him it was more than enough, any more would cost more than he could afford to pay."

Repeating the conversation brought it all rushing back. Huddled under the damn desk, trying not to hyperventilate or choke on my own fear. Half listening to the argument raging on the other side of the flimsy desk and praying to anyone who'd listen they'd be too involved with each other to look down and notice me.

"Wide toe, hand-tooled leather shoes," I blurted, images collided in my head, crowding out Tag's face. "The other guy was wearing hand-tooled shoes. Hand Tooled moved so close he almost stepped on Curtis's shiny black shoes. Curtis was scared shitless."

And so was I. Memories of the menace hanging thick and heavy in that office left me sucking in a lungful of much needed air.

"Then what?" The question was soft, as if afraid of pushing me over some unseen edge.

Then what? "Hand Tooled said there were other payment options available. Curtis kept saying he didn't have anything else to give." The poor man had been so frightened his shaking left his pants quivering as if blown by a strong a wind. I had stared in horrified fascination as his shoes began a stuttered dance in front of the desk. "Hand Tooled did something and told Curtis if he didn't have anything else to give, then he was of no use." Curtis had started sobbing and babbling. The sound of a grown man crying hadn't just been uncomfortable, it had been terrifying.

"What did he say?" Strangely gentle, Tag's voice provided a bit of space from the choking memories.

Blinking, I tried to regroup, using his gaze as my focal point as he crouched in front of me. "Curtis offered more, begging for a couple more days to get it together." But his offer was too little, too late. Even if the sense of impending doom hadn't been tightening its dreadful noose around my heart, there would've been no escaping the final outcome. I swallowed around the lump in my throat. "Hand Tooled slammed him into the desk and told him he'd take option A."

Puzzlement furrowed Tag's brow. "What was option A?"

Hours later, far from that damned office, safe with Tag, I

should've been fine. But I wasn't. Tears burned against the back of my eyes, the pressure built in my sinuses, and tremors began to take over. "He shot him." The report of the gun still echoed in my head. The rest of the nightmare tumbled out. "I wasn't expecting that, and I think I made some sort of noise. He jerked me out from under the desk."

He had wrapped his hand in my hair and slammed me face down on the desk. Right next to Curtis's sightless eyes. Right in the pool of blood and things I couldn't think about without wanting to scream. I could still feel the warmth of the blood seeping through my T-shirt. For a moment, the feeling returned, so real I let go of Tag and began brushing at my chest.

Warmth wrapped around my hands, stilling their frantic movement. "You're okay. You got away."

I gave a jerky nod, holding tight to his hands, using his steady gaze to find my footing. "There was a metal name plate on the desk. Sharp edges. I jabbed it into his leg. He dropped his gun. I got around the desk hoping to get to it first, but he was on me before I could find it. The damn gun must have been way under the desk because even as we struggled I couldn't see it. Then he punched me."

Which momentarily laid me out on my back, not my first, second, or third choice in a ground fight. When I went to protect my head, he managed two more hits to my ribs. Asshole. The shock of being hit had quickly been replaced by training and fury. "He was dragging me toward him by my ankle, but I smashed my other foot into his face. Think I may have broken his nose. Didn't stick around to ask though. I got the hell out of there."

"He followed you?"

I gave a short nod, despite Tag's fingers still cradling my chin. "The bullet graze happened on the way down an emergency stairwell. I hit the parking garage and managed to lose him once I hit the streets."

"Did you recognize the guy?"

"Never saw him before." The emotional and physical toll piled up and without my permission, my body leaned forward until my forehead rested against Tag's chest. I closed my eyes. "Hope never to see him again."

"Does he know who you are?" A strange intensity vibrated behind Tag's question.

Too damn exhausted to care, I answered, "Doubt it. We didn't exactly introduce ourselves."

For a long moment, quiet descended between us. Not the heavy, uncomfortable silence I was used to. It was nice. Obviously, Tag didn't like it. "After the parking garage, where did you go?"

"Stuck to the streets. Too dangerous to head home."

"Have you spoken to Delacourt?"

"Not yet," I mumbled, leaning in a little more. For once, he wasn't pulling away. "Was going to call her."

"When?"

"When I got home."

Under my head, his chest rose and fell as he sighed. "I'll call her." A warm weight cradled the back of my head. "Lie down, take a couple of hours."

As much as I wanted to follow his directions, I had a job to do. "I need to get back to that office and get the flash drive."

"Can't waltz up in daylight, so we'll have to wait until tonight. Rest. I'll touch base with Delacourt and make sure Rabbit's on stand-by once we have the files." His hand fell away from my head. "Then we'll figure out our next steps."

Exhaustion, physical and mental, crowded in, weighing me down. "Just a couple of hours, then." I pushed back from him, my hand going to the waist of my pants. "Can't sleep in these, and they're gross."

"I've got it." Tag took over from my fumbling fingers, unbuttoning and unzipping, before going to my hips to tug them down. He followed the pants and ended up kneeling in front of me. He brushed my left knee. "Lift."

Okay, I did not expect to ever have this man at my feet, but it was strangely appealing. Moving on autopilot, I balanced a hand on his shoulder and followed his directions. It mere moments I was standing in his shirt sans shoes and pants, blinking.

He tossed my pants aside, grabbed the loose material of the T-shirt, and tugged me to the bed. Pulling back the covers, he held them up. "In."

I crawled in.

He tucked the sheet over me, his fingers brushing my chin. "Sleep. I've got you covered."

Letting my eyes close, I did what I was told.

Chapter Five

TAG

It didn't surprise me when Risia dropped into sleep as soon those curls of hers hit the pillow. What did surprise me was that after her misadventures the night before, she managed to stay upright for as long as she had.

I settled into one of the chairs at the table, slouching down until I could rest my feet on the foot of the bed and keep watch. Taking in the yellow bruising around her eye reminded me of how carefully she moved thanks to her bruised ribs, and anger surged. Never would I understand how any man could raise a hand to a woman. Granted, if one was aiming a gun at my head, then yeah, discouraging her with a well-aimed blow was definitely an option. Yet I was all too aware of how many dickless wonders got off on beating someone smaller and infinitely more fragile.

Of course, Risia would rip me a new one if she thought I connected her with small or fragile, but for all her superficial attitude, there were a hell of lot more levels to her than what she showed the world. Unfortunately, I missed all the clues, until she threw my angry words back in my face. And when her temper finally snapped, I finally got a peek at the real Risia.

If I hadn't been touching her, no way would I believe how deep my comments sank. Not that she let me catch more than a glimpse, but that glimpse ignited a hollow ache in my chest.

I owed her an apology. One she probably wouldn't take. Hell, she was more likely to throw it back in my face. Still, she deserved more than my shit attitude.

The blessing and curse of being a touch empath. You didn't so much read people's minds, thank God, but their intentions. For a moment, you weren't you, you were them, with a ring-side seat to who a person really was, what demons rode them, or, on really special occasions, you got to relive the nightmares with them. Unfortunately, the demons that drove people weren't all tripping sunshine. Nope, they thrived best in the blackest pits of hellish needs and twisted desires.

I grew up hating to touch anyone and went out of my way to avoid it. Thank God I finally managed to hook up with people who didn't think I was crazy. Even better, they helped me create a mental block, which meant I could endure casual touches most people never thought of, a brush of a hand, a pat on the back, a hug from my mom. Before that, well, let's just say that courting death comment Risia threw at me may have had some merit.

Once.

Too much darkness lay hidden inside people, covered in layers of forced happiness and acceptance. There was enough darkness crawling through my head to discourage adding the shit ton of misery of others, thank you.

But with Risia, it was different. Always had been. The few times we touched, there wasn't an avalanche of shit barreling toward me. Instead, there was determination to see things through, no matter the cost. As if she was the one chatting it up with death. No regard for what would happen to her, if the decision she made turned out to be the wrong one.

And it was pure chance I caught the elusive fascination she

had with me. It happened during her last case with Delacourt. It required her attendance at some political shindig, which in turn required an escort. So, I donned the monkey suit, complete with tie, and spent the night holding temptation wrapped in dangerous curves in my arms.

It was after her target interrupted our dance that I finally clued in. Busy wrestling with my body's reaction to her, I don't even remember what I said when handing her off, but her hidden reaction as she was taken away snuck under my guard and softly settled into a little-used corner of my mind. Her whimsical need to continue dancing. The whispered sense of discovering something fascinating. Her need to belong. And finally, her disappointment at being let go.

Knowing her job and what it entailed, it was hard to believe in what I picked up. No way would such a confident beauty ever feel as if she didn't belong, nor was she one to be some man's possession. Certain she was playing a part, I fought against my need to delve further and did my best to convince myself it couldn't be real. No matter how much I tried to pass the strange connection between us off as a lie, it was a struggle to keep out of her head and to keep her out of mine.

I thought I was doing a pretty good job, until today when she lost her temper. She hadn't given me a choice, or time, to block her out. The glimpse I got had burned through every frustrated misconception I held. It showed me the possibility of something more, something I wanted to explore.

And that was a problem.

Risia was neck deep in danger, and if I didn't keep her at arm's length, she'd be under me while I exorcised the need crawling under my skin. Hard to protect a body when you're busy fucking it.

Of course, getting her out of my system also meant escaping the drama that was Risia Lacoste, and I wasn't sure I wanted that. The woman was a mind trip. That glimpse her touch gave me didn't jibe with the image she portrayed. She was a fucking walking, talking fantasy for anything with a dick, good at tempting and teasing, and making a man believe if he played his cards right, she could be his.

She was an intriguing package wrapped in those classy clothes that cost more than my rent, her sexy as shit heels, all that honey-colored skin and caramel curls. And under it all, buried so deep was a need so bright it hurt to see. Layers, the woman was made of fucking layers. And it would take a damn determined man to dig deep enough to touch that beauty, because she made staying out of reach an art form. Of course, as she pointed out, it was just part and parcel of her job.

Her job was shit.

Intelligence operatives didn't know dick when it came to defending themselves. No real experience in ducking that knife in the back or the bullet that could tear through skin and bone. Smart, she may be, but the woman didn't possess a single self-preservation gene.

Waltzing into a damn office at oh dark thirty with no backup? What the hell was up with that? Not to mention, the whole situation with Rawlings made my skin crawl. Then there was the fact there was something she wasn't sharing.

Not that I thought she'd betray the team. No, I took in the half-moon marks her nails left in my arm. She made sure that came through loud and clear. It was the quickly hidden sense of shame and guilt at the mention of Rawlings before her temper sparked that made me wonder. But that wasn't the only emotion that troubled me. She was worried, really worried, and for Risia that meant trouble.

Even more so now, since I managed to blow up whatever fragile connection existed between us. I hadn't missed that either. My damn temper ran my mouth, and I landed some destructive hits. Hits Risia wouldn't forget any time soon. Not that I blamed her.

Then there was that episode in the SUV. Now that freaked my ass out. Considering I worked with a group of people with very unique and unusual abilities, that was saying something. But the whole thing came on so fast; one moment she was fine, the next, not.

Her skin went pale and clammy, her breathing erratic, and her pulse under my hand had skipped. Fear slithered in without warning. She was dying in my arms for fuck's sake and there was nothing I could stand against, all I could do was try and get her to breathe.

I dragged a hand through my hair, and wrapped it around the back of my neck to squeeze the taut muscles. Never fucking again did I want to stand witness to shit like that. When her body began that distinctive jerky dance, I almost lost it. It was something I saw repeatedly during my tours overseas when bullets tore through flesh. It wasn't something you ever forget.

Maybe it would be best to drag her ass back to Delacourt, hand her over, and walk away. *Ah hell, who was I kidding?* I could no more walk away from her than let her walk out that damn hotel door all by her sexy little lonesome and back into the danger barreling down on her. She expected me to, though. Was probably even hoping I would. Too bad, she was doomed for disappointment because I wasn't passing on a chance to uncover the real Risia Lacoste.

Next to me, on the table, my phone vibrated a summons. Checking the display, I recognized the number. I dropped my feet and took my phone into the bathroom so not to disturb Risia. I answered as I softly closed the door behind me. "Colonel."

"Gunderson," the distinctive rasp of Colonel Delacourt's voice filled my ear. "Did you find her?"

I settled on the toilet seat. "Yeah, but we have a situation."

"Explain."

I didn't waste time and laid out what I knew about Risia's situation. "You still want me to bring her back to Phoenix?" Back to where other members of my team were currently working on flushing out a monster.

There was a pause. "No. Stay there, help her recover the flash drive. We need to find out what's on it that's causing such a stir. You two keep it safe until I can get Rabbit up there."

I ran a hand through my hair. "Fine. Do you want me to ask her about Rouser?" Megan Rouser, Delacourt's administrative assistant, who'd been missing for over a week. The initial reason Delacourt sent me off on this errand.

"No, I'm more concerned with what's on those files." The colonel's sudden change in mission objectives made me wonder what was happening down south. "Finding Megan won't stop what's coming."

Her dire tone of prediction sent my internal warning system flaring into life. "What's coming?"

On the other end of the phone, her sigh was quite clear. "A hell of a storm, is my guess."

As if the current situation was a day at the beach. "We could ask Risia to tell us what we're facing." Maybe get some clear idea of the who behind the shit hitting the team.

"It's too early to ask Risia anything. Too many possibilities are in the wind." Delacourt went on before I could dig deeper. "We caught a local lead. I'm sending the team to check it out tonight. If we're lucky, we can net our murderer and stop the arms sale in one shot. Maybe even find out what happened to Megan."

Luck hadn't been sticking around much lately, and I wasn't sure she was going to put in an appearance now. Frustration of not being part of the take-down made my voice sharp. "So you want me to babysit Risia?"

"Not Risia, the drive. It may hold confirmation of the

rumors floating around. Any chance you can break through the encryption?"

"Without seeing it, I couldn't say. But I'd rather not chance damaging it if we can wait on Rabbit." He was a damn electronic genius, and my computer skills weren't even in the same zip code.

"I don't know that we can afford to wait."

Her unusually grim statement caught me off-guard, because Delacourt's focus, while legendary, was definitely on those damn files when it should be on hunting down the man killing off team members and organizing a sale of illegal weapons. "What's going on, Colonel?"

This time her pause was noticeably longer. "Rumors are growing that something huge is coming on the black market."

"Huge in what way?"

"If we could confirm that, or where it was coming from, we'd know where to start looking."

"But you think it's connected to these files. Why?"

"Timing. Rawlings has always been a slick bastard, but this time his proposal to the DOD tripped alarms. I asked Risia to investigate Lawrence Rawlings because intel suggests he may be in bed with Falcon."

Holy shit.

Delacourt headed up the PSY-IV teams, a group of covert operators with psychic abilities. Falcon had the same makeup, except their crew was strewn with psychopathic killers. Money and power were their gods, and I wasn't the only one pretty damn certain they were behind the string of deaths haunting our team.

Pieces started falling into place and the emerging picture wasn't a pretty. "If Rawlings controls the sole solution to the government's communication weakness, it means he could sell the workaround to Falcon. Which will compromise every agency's communication lines. Including black and covert ops."

"Including ours." The bleak note in Delacourt's voice echoed the tightening in my stomach.

"That's not good." Understatement of the century. It was a fucking mess.

"You need to watch out for Risia. I don't like the fact that someone seems to be targeting her. If it's not Lawrence, it could be Falcon."

"Or just a loan shark who doesn't want to go away for murder." But somehow, I didn't think it was that easy.

"Get the drive. Keep it and her safe until I can send Rabbit your way."

"Roger that."

Chapter Six

I woke to find not only had Tag managed to talk to Delacourt, but he also found me some clean clothes. Groggily staring at the faded jeans (with tags) and the T-shirt (also sporting tags), I blurted out the first question that popped into my mind. "How'd you know my size?"

"Rabbit." Tag's one-word answer cleared up the mystery. Rabbit was another member of Delacourt's team, and an electronic genius, liberally doused with good ol' boy charm. Uncovering my size wouldn't even make him put down his coffee.

I gathered up the clothes. "Um, thanks?"

Tag sat at the table by the window, a laptop screen lighting his face. "He's working on getting you replacement IDs, cards, and phone. He'll bring them when he and Jinx come up."

My brain decided three hours was not enough time to function properly. "Wait? What?"

My question pulled his attention away from the computer and to me, giving my brain another hurdle to stumble over as the weight of his gaze landed on me. I bundled the clothes tight to my chest, and my toes curled into the tight weave of carpet.

His distracted tone disappeared, and his voice took on a deeper hue. "Rabbit and Jinx will head up as soon as they're done in Phoenix. Probably be a couple of days. Rabbit said it would be easier if he was here to work on the file."

I leaned against the bathroom doorjamb and ran a hand through my hair, fingers tangling in the snarl of curls. "Phoenix? Doesn't the team work out of San Diego?"

"We work from wherever Delacourt sends us. Right now, she has the majority of the team stationed in Phoenix."

Ah yes, the whole ex-military mindset of command and follow. While I admired those who found the strength to put country before self, I'd spent my younger years pushing against any sort of authority. Well, at least until Delacourt waltzed into my life and showed me a way to focus my talents. "Majority?"

"All but Doc."

If six of Delacourt's eight-person team was gathered in one spot, whatever was happening in Phoenix had to be bad. And that worried me. "What's going on, Tag?"

He studied me for a moment, his hand rubbing over the side of his shadowed jaw. "Go take a shower, then I'll bring you up to speed over dinner."

The mention of possible food made my stomach perk up. "You said there were cops at my place, so going out to eat may not be the best idea."

He smiled, and for once it reached all the way to his eyes. "You shower, I'll grab food, bring it back, and then we can talk while we eat. Deal?"

I nodded.

He stood up and stretched. "Good."

Even after he made his opinion of me quite clear, all that

long and lean still made me stare. I tore my gaze away and turned to the bathroom.

"Hang on, Duchess." He pulled me up short.

Looking over my shoulder, I watched him round the end of the bed.

He stopped by the closet next to me and opened the door, reached in, then came out with a plastic bag for dry cleaning. "Let's get your shoulder covered."

"It's a shower, Tag, not a bath."

He crowded close and my arms tightened on the bundle of clothes in a desperate attempt to fight the urge to reach out and lay my hands against his chest. "We're covering the bandage."

"Fine. Whatever." Yep, brilliant comebacks were my specialty.

He herded me into the bathroom and had me sit on the toilet while he made quick work of cutting a square section from the plastic bag. A few stere-strips later and his makeshift covering was ready to go. "Move your hair so I don't get it caught."

Unwinding one arm from my protective barrier of denim and cotton, I managed to gather most of my hair and get it out of the way. There wasn't much room, so he came in close, so close I shut my eyes so I could remember how to breathe. He stood in front of me and leaned over to work on my shoulder, his touch whisper light.

There was no escaping him in this position. His scent rolled over me, the warmth of his body curled around me, and every nerve came on point, quivering in self-destructive anticipation. Closing my eyes only made it worse. I bit my lip. *He thinks you're a traitor, you idiot.* My hormones were freaking deaf, because the harsh reminder didn't stop them from scrambling for attention.

"Have a question for you."

Caught up in my own mental weirdness, I jerked at his rumbled question and opened my eyes. T-shirt and chest greeted me, and I swallowed. "I might have an answer."

"What did you see in the SUV?"

"See?"

"In the SUV," he prompted. "Right before you yelled at me to get moving."

"I didn't yell."

"Mmm-hmm." His fingers pressed carefully along the edges, the crinkling of plastic sounding over my desperate attempts to gulp in some non-Tag-scented air. "What did you see?"

"Why?"

He finished with the covering and dropped to crouch in front of me, his hands resting on the lid next to my thighs, not touching, but so very close. It also put his face level with mine. Those gold green eyes moved over my face with a strange intensity. "It scared you."

"Lots of things scare me." My whisper escaped without permission from my brain. I tried to cover it. "Spiders, bullets, men with death wishes, I just try to stay out of the way. Yet they still pop up everywhere."

"Maybe you're a magnet for trouble."

Flinching, I leaned back. "Yeah, you've made your opinion of me loud and clear, I don't need a reminder."

He frowned, and something akin to remorse moved over his face. "An apology isn't going to work, is it?"

Confused, I studied him for a moment before giving a small, negative shake of my head. Nope, an apology wouldn't fix what he broke. Experience taught me words said in anger were generally forged in truth, no matter how painful.

His mouth tightened, and his chin dropped in a small nod. "Yeah, didn't think so. Still, for what it's worth, I'm sorry, Risia. More than you know."

Okay, maybe it wouldn't fix the hurt, but it still found a spot somewhere. And once it settled, I had a choice to make; hold on tight to my anger and hurt because it'd keep him away from me, or let it go and move on. Life, as it was so wont to remind me, turned on such seemingly small decisions.

While nursing my grudge might work in the short-term, it took a lot of emotional energy I didn't have right now. Besides, it's not like I'd forget what he said, fall into bed with him, and give him my heart. That would be stupid, reckless, and foolish. I wasn't stupid. But reckless and foolish?

Maybe, answered a little pesky voice.

In danger of falling down that particularly intriguing rabbit hole, I decided to hop to a safer topic. "Your death."

Confusion replaced his seriousness. "What?"

I shifted uncomfortably, wishing he'd back up and give me some room. "What I saw? Your death, three different scenarios."

Finally, he rocked back, not much but it was something. Still, I could see when it clicked for him. A considering light entered his eyes. "And it scared you."

Shitdamnfuck. Now I was in trouble. I had backed myself into a proverbial corner. With no safe answer, I kept my mouth shut.

It didn't help, because he started to grin. "It did."

God save me from arrogant males. I raised an arm and pointed at the door. "Get out. I want to take my shower."

His grin grew wider and he chuckled.

I wanted to scream in frustration. *How in the hell had he turned this around?* "Out, Tag."

He leaned forward, pressed a quick kiss against my forehead, and then stood. "Only because you asked nicely." He left, closing the door behind him.

After a few seconds, I stood, locked the door, turned on the shower so the water could heat, and then set my clothes on the counter. I looked up into the mirror and whispered, "What the hell are you doing, Risia girl?"

But I already knew, I was getting into trouble. Deep trouble. Because outside my bathroom door was a battle-scarred, ex-Marine, who had the ability to read my every emotion with one touch and just happened to be part of a government-sanctioned group of covert psychic police.

They called themselves PSY-IV Team. The name had a certain panache—Psi-four, cipher—but since his teammates could read minds, move objects with their minds, set fire to anything combustible, and other things I tried not to pry into, the fact I saw the future didn't freak him out. Maybe that's why I couldn't walk away. Outside of Delacourt and the team, only one other person knew what I could do, and they didn't call me crazy. Not that Tag thought I was nuts, stupid, shallow, and a bitch, maybe, but not nuts.

A sharp knock at the door, followed by Tag's "I'm heading out for food" rattled me out of my own head. Steam clouded the mirror, reminding me if I wanted to take advantage of the hot water, I'd better get a move on.

So, I did.

Dinner was sandwiches and chips. Tag was at the table, his feet propped in the other chair. I sat cross-legged on the bed, back propped by pillows shoved against the headboard, and my hair still damp from my shower. I nabbed another chip. "So, what's going on in Phoenix?"

He wiped his mouth with a napkin. "Did Delacourt share much about what she's been working on lately?"

"The last time we spoke was in May."

He looked at me. "Before or after I came to see you at that party?"

"After." I balled up the sandwich wrapper and put it inside the now empty chip bag. "A military prisoner escaped from Pendleton, killed two guards. Two men from one of her teams were killed in similar fashion. She sent you and Kayden to track him down, but wasn't having any luck. I studied the files and tried see what his next move was but couldn't get much."

His mouth tightened, and he tossed his napkin toward the trash bin by the door. "Master Sergeant Reeve Ellery. He was selling information on a weapons delivery system. The mission went sideways."

"Sideways?" Something warned me to tread lightly here. For once he was sharing something real, and I didn't want to shatter it.

"It was my last mission with MCIA."

Wow, color me impressed. "You served with the Marine Criminal Investigations Agency?"

He nodded. "We had two teams set to take down Ellery, but somehow he knew we were coming. When it was over, half my unit was dead, and I was in the base hospital at Landstuhl for two months."

The thought of him lying in a hospital hurt something, but I kept that hidden. "And the other team?"

"Belonged to Kayden, and now he's all that's left of his team."

The import of that hit me hard, and a sickening fear left me leaning against the pillows at my back. "So this Ellery is picking you all off one by one."

Tag didn't mistake my statement for a question. "He's a psychopathic killer and a Syphon."

My fear ratcheted another notch, leaving me shaky. "Aren't Syphons psychic sponges?"

"Yeah," he answer was grim.

My stomach churned. "Last time I spoke to Delacourt, he'd taken out a telekinetic, a healer, and a pyrokinetic."

"The bastard's killed three more people. One of which was psychic. A pre-cog."

"Oh God." Nausea rose because if Ellery was a true Syphon, the psychics he killed wouldn't have had an easy death. It would've been brutal and terrifying.

Since Syphons tended to go insane the longer they hunted, the deaths would become more and more vicious. Mainly because as psychic abilities varied in strength, each came with its own set of drawbacks. A healer could heal, but at serious personal cost. A strong touch empath, like Tag, may choose to not physically touch people to avoid the emotional landslide it invoked. A pre-cog could see an individual's immediate future, where as someone like me, a seer, could see multiple futures. Too many at once and it could result in a Cassandra Spiral, a descent into a maddening world where "what-if" was a lethal question. Throw all of that into one person and they'd burn the world to escape. It was a scary thought.

"Add the abilities of a pre-cog to the rest of the mix and his mental state has to be near a breaking point," I pointed out. Hell, Ellery would be a nightmare even nightmares would fear. "If he hasn't broken already."

"I'm thinking he broke awhile ago." Tag wiped a hand over his drawn face and continued, "Considering yesterday he killed his second non-psychic."

"Yesterday?" Tag was in Phoenix yesterday, with Kayden. "Who?"

His hand dropped to his lap and curled into a fist. "Cyn's sister."

Kayden, Rabbit, Wolf, Bishop, Ricochet, Jinx; these names were familiar, all part of the PSY-IV team Tag served on under Delacourt. But Cyn? I hadn't heard that name before. From the way he said it, it meant something. "Cyn?" I couldn't quite quash my flare of jealousy.

"Cynthia Arden."

A flash of rare insight, and I got it. Love, but not that kind. "She was your teammate in MCIA, the one who survived."

He gave a jerky nod. "She ended up facing the inquiry board alone during Ellery's trial. I was in the hospital. Kayden and his team got reassigned because although Ellery was in custody, the information he was selling was in the air. By the time I got out, she had left the corps, returned stateside, and wasn't returning anyone's calls. Once we realized Ellery would be heading her way, we tried to reach her, but we didn't get to her in time."

From the self-directed anger in his voice, the guilt of that perceived failure was burying him. Me telling him it wasn't his fault wouldn't work. Tag and those he called friends were a different breed. Loyalty and protection went beyond bone deep, and once you managed to snag a piece of it, you'd be a fool to let it slip from your grasp. From the sound of things, whoever this Cyn person was, had been dealt a shitty hand and gone away to lick her wounds.

Not a surprise, it was something I would have done. But, it was clear that the death of Cyn's sister, someone Tag would consider an innocent bystander, had left deep wounds festering in guilt. That kind of failure broke most people. Good thing breaking wasn't an option for those like Tag and Kayden. Here's hoping Cyn was the same.

Needing to pull him back from the bleak edge he was standing on, I asked, "Is he just after Cyn and the remaining team members?"

Tag shook his head. "He's going back for the stolen information and getting ready to sell it to the highest bidder."

"So why are you here?" Because if all this was going down in Phoenix, no way would Delacourt send Tag to me unless she felt she had no choice.

He took a bite, chewed slowly, then swallowed. A deliberate action meant to give him time to pick his words. Which meant something, but I'd have to figure that out later, because he finally said, "Delacourt's admin assistant, Megan Rouser, left on a two-week vacation and we're now in week three. Delacourt's worried Ellery may have gotten to her. She asked me to come to you and find out if you could see anything."

Puzzled, because that seemed like something Delacourt could've just called me about, I said, "The Colonel sent you here to find her secretary?"

He shifted and dropped his legs to the floor, then leaned his arms on his thighs. "There are indicators someone in the know is sharing information with Ellery. Has been since the initial mission."

That explained why he was so quick to question my loyalty. He and his team were being hunted from the inside.

"There are three possible scenarios." He began ticking them off one at a time on his hand. "One, Ellery got his hands on Megan and made her talk. Two, Megan sold out Delacourt and the team and is now living it up in some Caribbean island. Or, three, we're facing something a lot bigger than Ellery. I'm hoping you can help narrow it down."

Okay, none of those sounded good. Especially the part about something bigger than Ellery, that one made me shiver. But I didn't ask for more detail, instead I needed to make sure he understood what he was asking for. "You know it doesn't work like that, right?"

Now it was his turn to be puzzled. "What doesn't work like that?"

As much as I wanted to help, he needed to understand how my ability worked and what it cost. Agitated, I rubbed my hands up and down my thighs. "I can't just pull out a crystal ball and decide what I want to see." If that was the case, I'd choose to not see a damn thing. "I'm not even sure if I can trigger a vision if I wanted to. Even if I did, I'm not sure how much of it you could trust. Visions are plural for a reason. It's not just one version of the future, it's all of them, all dependent on the decisions being made, the eventual impact, the players. The more what-ifs in play, the more answers are generated, which means more visions, which means trying to find my way back to here." I tapped the mattress with my fist.

When he continued to look at me, I reached for something he could understand. "It's as if I'm a broken mirror. Each player is an impact point. Each decision is a crack. Each outcome is a broken shard. And each piece carries a part of me with it, so I can stand witness, until I'm so fractured I can't pull the pieces together." I stared at him and gave him a small piece of me. "I break, Tag, over and over again. The visions don't let go."

His eyes held mine, his focus intent. "Cassandra Spiral."

I jerked at his softly uttered words and then gave a nod. "Yeah and asking me to initiate a vision is asking me to risk my sanity. I can't do that for a missing secretary." No matter how much I owed Delacourt, it was too big a risk. "Besides, I don't get a choice on what I see. The future comes, makes me her bitch, and only leaves when she feels like it."

He tilted his head to the side. "So, last night, you got no warning before walking into a murder?"

I shook my head. "I was uneasy, but that's a normal reaction when you're planning on breaking in and stealing information. When it comes to seeing things, I never see my future. Just the futures of those around me."

He frowned. "You never see your own future?"

I shook my head. "And I have no desire to see it." Because it wouldn't be all puppy dogs and roses, more like straight jackets and padded walls. I didn't need a vision to explain what my future held, I already knew what was coming. My brain shied away from poking at those shadows.

"And the visions in the SUV?" His question helped push the lurking nightmares back. Kind of.

I plucked at the bedspread and bit my lower lip. "Just you, dying, and all I could do was watch. The spiral started, and I was slipping." And feeling like my world was shattering apart.

"But you managed to come back."

"Because I could hear you, feel you." I looked away, gathering up the detritus of my dinner. "You gave me an anchor." One I hadn't wanted to let go of, so of course, as soon as I found my footing, I let go. No sense in getting used to someone who wouldn't stick around.

"How do you escape if no one's there to anchor you?"

"I don't." Unfolding my legs, I slid off the far side of the bed. The need to change the subject made my words sharp. I had no desired to share what that meant with him. "I'll call Delacourt and tell her I can't help with Megan. Then you can get back to Phoenix and help Kayden and Cyn." Which is where he'd rather be anyway.

"Risia."

I kept my back to him as I dumped the wrappers in the bathroom trash.

He waited until I turned back around. "If you think I'm leaving you alone with this mess, think again."

I folded my arms across my chest. Time to give him an out. When he wasn't sniping at me, I had a hard time remembering why I wanted to keep him at arm's length. And that could prove more dangerous than any Cassandra Spiral. "I'll be fine, Tag. I'll get the drive to Rabbit, Delacourt will help clear up the situation with the police, and things will be fine."

Maybe.

He stood and stalked around the bed.

As much as I wanted to back away, it would leave me cornered in the bathroom. So I pressed my spine against the doorjamb, holding still as he got close. Then he stood there, silent as I stared at his chest and refused to look up. A light brush of his fingers against my cheek as he tucked a curl behind my ear startled me.

Once he had my attention, he said, "I'm not leaving you. We'll go get the drive, get it to Rabbit, and we'll go see Delacourt. Together."

While part of me wanted to grab on to him and hold tight, another, bigger part, wondered why that sounded like a threat.

Chapter Seven

The moon hung high in the summer sky as Tag passed the same parking lot I ran through the night before. Just like then, nerves sent my stomach on a roller coaster ride. Even Tag's solid presence wasn't helping. "Did Rabbit say how fast he'd be able to access the information?" I asked, my jean-covered leg bouncing.

"He won't know until he gets his hands on it, but he's thinking it shouldn't take long."

But first, we had to get the drive.

Tag's hand went to my knee, stilling the jittery movement. "Why are you on edge? Did you see something?"

I shook my head, feeling curls bounce against my face. "Just worried."

"In and out, that's the plan, Risia."

Sighing, I turned to look out the window.

A couple of blocks past the garage, he turned into an apartment complex and parked in a spot along the far side. He shut off the engine and turned to me, his face nothing but shadows in the darkened cab. "You can always stay here."

"And let you have all the fun? No thanks. Besides, I know

which one is the drive." Disguised as a working pen, the flash drive was designed to hide in plain sight. Which was why we had to go back together, instead of Tag doing his British-spy routine solo.

"You sure you're up for this?" He reached over and opened the glove compartment and pulled out his gun.

"You have another one of those?" Not that I really wanted one, but it would give my hands something to do besides shake. I tried to corner my uneasiness and get some answers, but it wasn't working. Maybe because I wasn't anxious to revisit what haunted my very short nap. Granted, the three hours of sleep Tag gave me were great, but it was the shower, clean clothes, and food that really helped.

"Nope, so stay behind me." The snick of the slide and the sharp pop of the magazine rode under his answer as he handled the gun with practiced ease. He leaned forward and tucked it somewhere behind him.

"Tell me you're not shoving that down your pants." Visions of gory damage to unmentionables ran through my head.

He turned to me, and his lips curled up into what looked like an honest-to-god smile. "Back holster, easier to conceal." He adjusted his T-shirt, then grabbed something from the back seat. That something turned out to be a hoodie, which landed in my lap as a pile of material. "You're going to need this."

I held it up and raised my eyebrows. "Really? It's the middle of July, in Vegas."

"Take it."

Bossy man. Sighing, I tucked it over my arm.

He shrugged into his, then said, "Ready?"

Sucking in a bracing breath, I blew it out. "Ready."

We got out and began walking toward Aether's offices. Out on the sidewalk, I wasn't prepared when Tag grabbed my hand. I slid a glance at him. *What was he doing touching me? Was he fishing for something?*

He caught my look and grinned. "Relax, Duchess." Then he proceeded to pull me along.

Damn adrenaline junkie. "You're enjoying this." My comment came out like an accusation.

"Enjoying what?" he asked, even as he constantly scanned our surroundings.

"This." I waved my other hand, still holding the hoodie, around. "The secret-agent shtick."

His fingers tightened on mine. "So do you."

I nibbled on my lip. Yeah, maybe, when I wasn't getting the crap beaten out of me, or having to face the barrel of a gun. Things I normally didn't worry about. Unlike the missions he worked, mine involved cocktail parties, posh apartments, lavish dinners, and slipping into spots after hours to take what I needed, with no one being the wiser. Dodging bullets and stumbling over dead bodies wasn't so much exciting as it was terrifying.

Needing something less nerve-wracking to consider, I asked, "You got a plan to bypass their security?"

"Yep."

I waited, but nothing more followed. "One that doesn't include scaling the building?" I pushed.

He looked down at me. "Should we add heights to the spiders and bullets list?"

"Ha ha," I muttered, feeling heat crawl up my face.

He either didn't see it or decided to ignore it. "Rabbit found a weak spot in the camera setup, over by a service entrance from the garage. We're going to use it."

Oh, joy.

We stopped by a garbage dumpster outside the garage. With the structure looming ahead, my heart picked up its beat as memories spun their sticky threads. Tag didn't give me time to get tangled up. He pulled me behind the dumpster, keeping it between us and the garage. He crouched, using his hold on my hand to pull me down, and then he took the hoodie from my arm, shaking it out with a quick snap. "Put your jacket on, Duchess."

It took some maneuvering, but I got it on and even managed to wrangle all my curls inside the hood. He pulled his hood down until only the barest edge of his face was visible. I copied his movements and realized there was something different about the material. Small bumps ran along the edge of the hood. I rubbed my fingers against the line of bumps.

Tag tugged my hand down.

"What are those?" I asked.

"Infrared LEDs. They'll keep us from being ID'd if the cameras pick us up. Keep your head angled down and stick close." Then he pulled a pair of thin gloves from his front pocket and handed them to me. "Put these on."

He produced another pair, and once his gloves were in place, he palmed his gun, keeping it partially hidden by his leg. He waited until my hands were covered, then he was off, sticking to the shadows as he made his way to the garage. Left with no other choice, I followed, trying to stay in his footsteps.

He led us away from the entrance and headed to the side. There wasn't much light, just a lone, tall light post standing between the parking structure and the deserted parking lot surrounded by a chain-link fence. The concrete walls on the ground level of the garage rose to just above waist-level. Of course Tag and his long legs made quick work of it, while I managed a graceless scramble up to the top only to get stuck on the over.

Something in my ribs and shoulder protested, so my sharp inhale had him reaching over to help make sure I didn't fall to the ground headfirst. He waited until I was steady, then raised a brow in silent question. I answered with a small nod, and we were off. He kept to the shadowed areas close to the walls, and we worked our way down to the basement. We waited in a corner with a line of sight on the service entrance.

While I used the time to suck in quiet gulps of air, he leaned in, put his mouth right next to my ear, and whispered, "Wait here until I signal you."

Shivers worked their way down my neck and spine. He pulled back, waited for my nod, then took off. He made quick work of the lock with some kind of credit-card-looking thing. Only after sticking his head inside did he motion me forward.

I hustled over, trying to ignore the protest of my ribs. I stayed behind him as we climbed to the third floor, keeping my head angled down and concentrating on not jarring my aching body parts.

He stopped by the door on the third-floor landing and waited for me. When I stood next to him, he brushed a touch along the back of my neck. I looked up and caught his silent, *ready?* I nodded.

He slowly pushed the door open.

I followed him through the narrow opening into the dimly lit hall, careful to make sure the door closed silently behind us. The only lights in the hall came from the EXIT sign and the spaced security lights along the floor.

Since Tag didn't know which office was Curtis's, I stepped in front, prepared to lead the way. With the police already looking for me, the last thing I wanted was to be spotted on a security camera breaking into a crime scene. *Stick close to the walls, keep my head down*, I repeated the silent mantra.

Tag's arm came out, keeping me back. I snuck a look around him and caught the police tape crossing the second door on the right. Guess he didn't need me to lead the way after all. He crossed the remaining distance, and I stuck close. He tested the doorknob. It turned, and I held my breath as he pushed it open, slowly.

A beat.

Another.

Only when he gave me a bare nod, did I move around him to brace my palm against the doorjamb and did the step-duck combo over and under the police tape. Once on the other side, I went to take a step only to have his grip on my arm hold me in place. I turned back as he slowly let go and reached into his pocket, producing a small penlight.

Right, I needed to be able to see what I was doing. Taking it from him, I made my way to the desk, skirting the dark stains and scattered items on the floor.

As I got close to the desk, my stomach heaved as I tried to avoid the dried pool of blood still staining the top of the desk, but my gaze kept drifting to it. In my head, the whispers started, and my vision began to blur at the edges. I slammed my eyes closed and threw everything I had at what waited to suck me under, pushing it back with grim determination. Only when I was certain it would stay back did I open my eyes and force myself to look anywhere but the desktop.

I rounded the desk and dropped to a crouch so the drawers took up most of my field of vision. My hands shook as I pulled out the top drawer on the left. The penlight illuminated the distinctive gold, executive pen lying among the variety of others. Blowing out an unsteady breath, I grabbed it, closed the drawer, and skirted back around the gruesome desk, trying not to run.

Chills skated down my spine, and an uneasy sensation crawled through my veins. Another limbo session and then I was standing next to Tag, every sense keyed to hyper aware-ness. Giddy with relief, I opened my hand and showed him the pen, trying to ignore the fact it was shaking in my palm. Okay, so maybe he wasn't the only adrenaline junkie in the room.

He cupped my hand and forced my fingers to close around it, then let me go, a silent indication to keep it.

I tucked it into my back pocket. *Time to leave.*

We retraced our steps back down the hall and out the door, then down the stairwell and back into the garage. Even though chills still clung to my spine, I couldn't decide if I wanted to be relieved or disappointed that retrieving the drive had been so easy. Nor did I really have time to think about it, because Tag's long-legged pace was difficult to keep up with, especially since my heart was trying to beat its way out of my chest and rattling my aching ribs.

"Slow down," I hissed.

He ignored me.

Not a shocker. Solider boy could probably run a damn marathon with me on his back like a monkey. A little jog through a parking lot with sore ribs was a cakewalk.

Show-off.

We hit the sidewalk and only when he began to shrug out of his hoodie, did I take mine off. He wrapped his arm around my hip and pulled me in close, taking us away from the garage and strangely, the parking lot the SUV sat in.

"Tag, where are we going?"

He didn't slow, just kept a casual pace as he made his way down a poorly lit side street. A couple of cardboard homes sat along the grimy exteriors. He snagged my hoodie and bundled it with his. "Hang tight for a second."

He loped to a cardboard, blanket combination where a grocery cart stood guard. He crouched down and spoke to someone I couldn't see. His voice was a low, indistinct murmur, but a weathered, dirt encrusted hand came into view and snatched both hoodies from his grasp. He said something else, then stood and came back to me. "Let's go." He caught my arm and pulled me along.

Helpfully I pointed out, "We're going in the wrong direction."

His lips twitched. "It's the right direction, trust me." I didn't answer, too busy trying to keep pace. Another turn, then another, and he finally shared, "We're going to take the long way back to car."

One more turn and the quiet night filled with lights and activity. Looking around I realized we'd hit an upscale area lined with bars and restaurants, which translated to people. Lots of people. Lots of noise. The air was filled with the metallic music of slot machines, the occasional spike of drunken laughter, and clamor of street hawkers and taxi drivers trying their best to lure the tourists along. Still, an uneasy sensation stalked me. I twisted to look behind me, trying to pinpoint what was setting my nerves on edge.

Tag's arm curled around my hips, tucking me against a long, hard body. He leaned over, his mouth right by my ear. "Relax, Risia."

His unexpected move made me stumble, and a small hiss of pain escaped. His arm tightened and brought me around until we were face to face, our bodies pressed tight while the crowd surged around us. My nerves got shoved out of the way by a skin tingling awareness that had nothing to do with the possibility of danger, and everything to do with the man in front of me. Automatically my hands braced against his chest and I tilted my head back. "What now?" My breath stalled as waves of sensation buffeted my body. *Damn adrenaline rush.*

Instead of answering, he buried one of his hands in the curls at the back of my head and gave a gentle tug, tipping my head even further back.

I opened my mouth to say…something, and never got a chance.

His lips covered mine and that awareness turned into an inferno, burning away my self-preservation and leaving only the need to respond. Strong and sure, gentle and demanding, the combination destroyed me, even as I met each stroke of his tongue with mine. My fingers curled into his T-shirt, dragging him closer.

His hand tightened against my skull, controlling me while his mouth continued to explore and demand. Pressed so close I could feel him against me, and there was no mistaking my reaction as my body melted and perked up at the same time. Getting lost in the kiss, I let go of his T-shirt and wrapped my arms around his neck.

Our tongues tangled, then his mouth shifted, pulling back enough to pepper gentle nips along my lips, only to soothe the stings with a sweet sweep of his tongue. He pulled back and I could only blink at him. My mind was still caught up in the firestorm of need and the urge to keep going, common sense be damned.

He brushed his thumb over my bottom lip, and smiled, something I couldn't, wouldn't, understand lurking behind it. "Better?"

Finally, my voice made a comeback. "What was that?"

The smile turned into a full-fledged grin. "Do I really need to explain what a kiss is, Duchess?"

Confused and not liking it one bit, I unwrapped my arms and went to step back. Didn't get far, since he refused to let me go. "Why would you do that?"

His grin began to fade. "Seriously?"

Anger was coming up quick to take confusion's place, and I had no problem letting it reign. Folding my arms over my chest, I leaned back against his hold. "Yeah, seriously. You don't like me, Tag, so why are you kissing me?"

He shook his head. "Who said I didn't like you?"

"You."

Finally he let me go, only to run a hand through his hair. "Jesus, Risia, I was pissed when I said those things. I didn't mean it."

What the hell was I doing? I had made the decision to accept his apology, now here I was in full-on-bitch mode, throwing accusations like some wounded harpy. "Whatever."

I spun on my heel only to be pulled up short and brought back around.

He cradled my face with one hand, while he kept me captive with the other. "The problem is, I like you too fucking much to think straight."

His comment was so unexpected I could only stare, my mind completely blank. Unfortunately my mouth had no such issues, "You have a strange way of showing it, buddy."

Someone jostled me from behind sending fire across my ribs. I could feel my face pale and my hands landed on Tag's chest for balance. He shot a hard look above my head. "Watch it."

The two words came out in a growl, which vibrated in places I would rather Tag stayed away from. He turned back to me, his gaze roaming over my face with an inscrutable look. His arm loosened, and he stepped back. "Let's get back to the SUV."

He took my hand again and began weaving through the crowd.Since I was still reeling in shock over his unexpected declaration, I kept quiet and let him lead.

Where had that kiss come from? Better question, why? He always acted like a major stick was up his ass whenever I was around. The accusations he leveled at me earlier held the sharp edge of truth, or his truth at least.

But you showed him pieces of you, a little voice pointed out.

My heart sank. How much had he seen when I touched him? I was so angry when I grabbed him, was it enough to keep him blind to the damage his accusations caused?

The last thing I wanted was for him to know just how much power he had to hurt me.

Chapter Eight

Caught in the chaos of Tag's unexpected behavior, it took me a bit to realize we weren't heading back to the hotel. In fact, we passed the turn to the freeway a few minutes before. Maybe he got lost? Not that guys tended to do that, from my experience, but there was always a first time. "Um, where are you going?"

"We've got a tail." He delivered the unwelcome news with a disconcerting calm.

Since my ribs wouldn't let me twist around to check out his claim, I peered into the side mirror, which warned me objects were closer than they appeared. Which meant the bright, eye-searing headlights quickly taking up mirror real estate would be kissing our bumper pretty damn quick. My hands curled into the armrest and console. "Tag…"

"I see him." The SUV jerked forward. I tore my stunned gaze away from the mirror and caught the grim line of Tag's jaw as the headlights behind us raced to close the distance. He flicked his gaze between the road ahead and the threat behind us. "Damn it."

He yanked the wheel, zipping past a taxi with inches to spare, into the middle lane. As soon as he was clear, he hit the gas, leaving me digging my nails into the leather interior.

The lights behind us fell back. Unable to bear the suspense, I finally managed to shift in my seat so I could watch behind us. The lights weren't gone, but there was asphalt between the two of us. "He's dropping behind."

"Not for long. He's going to try to get alongside us."

And sure enough, as if waiting for Tag's prediction, the headlights switched over to the left lane, dodging traffic.

"He's coming," I pointed out, on the off-chance Tag missed the crazy driver racing up on his left.

"Turn around," he snapped, just as he jerked to the right and slipped past the brake lights of the van trundling along in front of us.

Since his abrupt movements yanked me around and set off a constant chorus of complaints from my ribs, I did as I was told, stifling the string of profanities trembling on my tongue. As my heart began to keep pace with the SUV, some inane part of my brain decided to chime in that perhaps it wasn't necessary to break a sweat to do my cardio. A car chase seemed to work well.

I wanted to ask Tag where he thought he was going, who the hell was behind us, and, more importantly, what the hell? Since he was busy playing a very lethal game of frogger at, I snuck a glance at the speedometer.

Seventy miles per hour and climbing.

I kept my mouth shut, unwilling to distract him. My grip shifted from the armrest and seat to the chicken handle above the door, as Tag took a corner on two wheels. My breath stopped as the SUV tipped precariously before rocking back to level. Closing my eyes might have helped, but then I wouldn't see the end coming. And some morbid fascination didn't like that idea. So open they stayed, bouncing from Tag, to the road in front of us, then to the headlights coming up quick behind us.

"Can you get any details on the bastard?" Tag kept his focus solely on maneuvering the SUV down an access road running parallel to the freeway.

As we raced under streetlights, I picked up what I could as we passed from one pool of light to the next. "Dark blue or black, four-door sedan."

"License plate?"

"Can't see one." My answer came out short since I was struggling not to snap at him about unreasonable requests, like trying to see a damn license plate at night while racing down a half-deserted street.

"Can you see how many are in there?" he pushed.

Sucking in a breath and bracing one hand against his backrest, I tried to see as we bumped along. One breath, two, then, "Just one, I think."

His hand came up and grabbed my wrist, pulling me back forward, then went back to the wheel. "Hang on."

It was the only warning I got. Tag jerked hard on the wheel. The SUV did a sickening spin, and the rear wheels scrambled for traction. I braced against the dashboard, while my stomach twisted with the spin.

Tag straightened the wheel and the SUV plowed over rough ground, bouncing violently. The jostling hurt, making me suck in a hard breath and close my eyes as a wave of pain echoed through me. Then the wheels found pavement, grabbed, and the SUV surged forward once more. I pried my eyes open and realized Tag now had us on a freeway on-ramp.

He cut across three lanes until he hit the carpool lane, then gunned it.

Here's hoping the police were busy elsewhere because I didn't think Tag would pullover for anyone. Using my trusty mirror, I tried to scan the road behind us. "Where is he?"

"Four cars back on the right."

A semi switched lanes and disturbingly familiar headlights glared into focus. My stomach clenched. Our tail was determined, really determined, and that could not mean anything good. "You think he's Hand Tooled?"

"Probably." Tag managed to get another truck between us and the sedan.

Prying my fingers off the dashboard, I fumbled at the glove compartment, drawing Tag's distracted attention.

"What are you doing?"

My fingers closed around the semi-automatic we'd tucked away earlier. Pulling it free, my hands shook as I flipped off the safety. "Taking precautions."

"You plan on shooting that, Duchess?" Humor danced along his question.

"If need be." My answer sounded stiff but hurtling down the highway of death would make any girl a little tense.

"Do you know how?"

"Yes." Just because I wasn't fond of guns, didn't mean I didn't know my way around one. "Could you please pay attention to the road?" I squeaked, as we practically crawled up the tailpipe of some low-slung sports car.

"Don't shoot unless we're not given a choice. Civilians."

"Got it." Since the freeway was about to take us to the desert and mountains lying outside of Vegas, I really didn't think civilians would be a worry for much longer. Sure enough, the traffic thinned, and the headlights began closing the distance between us. "We stay on this highway, he's going to hit us."

"We get off, he'll do the same," Tag gritted out.

"Yeah, but we have a better chance of ditching him on surface streets."

Tag grunted. "What's out here?"

Peering out the window, I spotted an upcoming exit sign.

"Industrial warehouses, older neighborhoods, and Nellis Air Force Base."

"That should work."

Work for what?

I didn't get a chance to ask, because he was cutting across the lanes and taking the exit. As we raced up the off-ramp, our headlights suddenly blinked off. Shadows settled around us. "Tag?" Panic suffused his name.

"Breathe, Duchess. There's enough light with the streetlights. This way, we're not as easy to follow." With that strangely calm explanation, he made a sharp left.

Uh-huh, until we hit the damn breaks, then our taillights would be demon-eyed beacons for our stalker.

The flash of light behind us meant our tail was still hanging on. Tag began making random turns in quick succession, until I'd need more than an electronic breadcrumb trail to find our way back. Of course, there were other things to worry about. Like not slamming my head into the window with each turn and keeping hold of the gun. I didn't even turn around to watch. Instead, I used the flashes of light dancing across our interior to gauge the pursuit.

It took a few heart-seizing minutes before the time between flashes began to lengthen. Only when we managed to weave our way deep into some industrial area without tell-a-tale lights on our ass, did I finally ask, "Did we lose him?"

"Maybe," Tag's answer was tight. "Or he turned his lights off as well."

"I vote for option one." I uncurled my death grip on the gun. "He had to be waiting for us to come out of the office."

"Probably," he answered absently, his head turning slightly back and forth.

Curious, I asked, "What are you looking for?"

"We need to ditch the SUV and get a new ride."

Peering out into the night-shrouded streets I wondered if

he expected this so-called new ride to magically appear. While some of the streetlights managed to spill pools of light along broken, weed-choked sidewalks, advantageously placed cars were not resting along curbs.

He took another turn, albeit much slower this time, driving by a building complete with concrete fence topped by coiled wire. A security light shone down on a weathered metal sign with CAMPOS TOWING in black lettering.

"We could try that," I pointed out, leaning forward to check out the shadowed hulks of cars sitting behind the fence.

"Nope, too hard to get in and out of," he dismissed as he took a left, away from the tow yard.

Obviously my criminal skills needed work. "Right." I settled back against the seat, my gaze nervously checking our mirrors.

He continued for a few more minutes, until a collection of older, blocky homes began to form off to the left. This time I didn't bother asking where he was going. I'd find out soon enough. Especially as he slowed and peered through the windshield. Finally, he said, "Perfect."

The SUV settled against a crumbling curb.

I looked around to see what was so great about where we were parked. A few feet in front of us, the streetlight was burnt out. The one behind flickered, as if deciding whether or not to keep shining on. Small homes lined the street, some windows dark, others lit from inside. Instead of garages, the homes had attached carports. Taking in the ones nearest us, two in front and one behind, I noted an older sedan, a mini-van, a Jeep with no doors or top, a small beat-up truck, a souped-up low-rider, and a jacked-up truck, which would require a ladder to get into.

Two options were a definite no-go. "Not the low-rider or the penis mobile."

"Penis mobile?" He leaned over, opened the glove box,

grabbed an envelope, and then closed it. He handed me the envelope, then twisted in his seat, reached behind and pulled up a black duffle bag. He dumped that in my lap as well, ignoring my grumpy growl.

I waved a hand at the ridiculous truck. "That."

He ducked his head to peer at it through my window. "Definitely not." Then he sat back up and ordered, "Out, Duchess."

"You sure about this?" I juggled the duffle bag, envelope, and gun, while the knots in my stomach tightened.

"We need a new ride. One he can't follow." He unzipped the bag, took the envelope from me, and dropped it inside. "Keep the gun out of sight."

Right, because we didn't need any more unwanted attention. Instead of rolling my eyes at the unneeded warning, I stuck to the important things. "Do you know what you're doing?"

He lifted the duffle's strap around my head and settled it across my chest. "Don't worry, I've got this." He grinned, then reached over me and pushed my door open. "Out."

"Why aren't you carrying this thing?" I pulled the strap away from my chest.

"Because I need my hands free." He didn't wait for a response but hopped out.

"Whatever." I got out, my disgruntled complaint turning into soft "Ow, ow, ow's" as the duffle bag's weight pulled the strap tight across my chest and settled heavily against my ribs. My free hand went to brace against the SUV until the ache subsided.

On the other side, Tag got out and rounded the hood, then slipped into the night.

Unwilling to lose sight of him, I followed, keeping one hand on the bag so it wouldn't bounce and the other by my side, hoping the gun wouldn't be readily visible. When I fell into step next to him, he wrapped an arm around my waist, and pulled me in close. If anyone looked out their window, they'd see a couple walking down the street. His pace was unhurried. All I wanted to do was run. How did he stay so damn calm? *Freakin' solider boy.*

We bypassed the house with the doorless Jeep and small truck. Wise considering not only was the porch light steady and bright, but the flickering light behind the curtains indicated late-night TV watching was alive and well. Tag skirted the driveway where the big truck and black low-rider with red pin-striping sat, side by side.

Memories of other shiny, decked-out Impalas and Continentals dragging their tailpipes as neighborhood thugs cruised the dirty streets crowded close. I gave my head a small shake, trying to knock the images back into the past where they belonged. Now was not the time for a trip down shitty-memory lane.

The arm around my waist tugged me over to the unlit house where the mini-van shared space with the sedan. I followed Tag between the two cars and up the drive. His barely audible "Damn," caught my attention. On the sedan's front passenger side blocks of wood stood where a tire should.

Silently I echoed his curse. With the sedan out, we were left with the mini-van. Before he could reach for the handle, I put my free hand on his arm. He stopped and looked at me. I mouthed, "Alarm?"

He leaned in to check, then gave a short shake of his head. I let him go, readjusting my sweaty grip on the gun. The way my luck was running, I'd drop it and shoot myself, or something equally stupid. He crouched for a second and when he stood back up, he had a thin blade in his hand.

I curled the fingers of my free hand around the strap across my chest. The man was a walking arsenal. He slipped the blade down between the door and window. The seemingly loud pop of the lock made me wince. He looked at me, then pulled open the door. He grinned, obviously enjoying his nighttime adventures.

Yep, the man was certifiable.

As he climbed into the driver's seat, I rounded the hood and took the passenger side, being careful to shut the door quietly. No use in standing around in the driveway. I settled the duffle bag in my lap, amazed to find my hand still wrapped around the gun.

Next to me, Tag was bent awkwardly, his hands under the steering wheel. While he hot-wired our latest ride, I scanned our surroundings. That uneasy itch between my shoulders was still there. Maybe because we were in the midst of committing a felony? Regardless, the street remained empty and no one was yelling at us to get out.

Seconds stretched into a minute, then the engine caught and turned over. Tag had the van backed out and heading down the street before he turned on the headlights and fastened his seatbelt. He glanced at me. "Buckle up."

My pulse dropped from frantic to anxious. Instead of following his order, I took in the van's interior. It was an older model, with the trappings of small humans. A small package of, I picked it up to see it better, fruit snacks, sat in one cup holder. The other held a Styrofoam cup with a straw. In-between the driver and passenger seat sat a large console.

Popping the top, I carefully laid the gun on top of a box of Kleenex and DVD cases decorated in bright colors. With the gun safely stashed, I unwrapped the strap from my chest, and set the duffle at my feet. Only then did I buckle up. A pair of women's sunglasses clung to the driver's visor and the dash's lights glinted off the tinted side windows. "We're screwed if we get in a chase, you know that, right?"

He shrugged. "Probably, but our tail is looking for a black SUV, not a soccer mom." As he spoke, headlights headed our way. "Get down." His order was quiet, but the hand on my head pressed firmly.

Undoing the belt I just fastened, I slouched down, knees bending, ribs protesting as I huddled behind the dash.

"Shallow breaths, Duchess," the gentle reminder accompanied a slight ease in the pressure of his palm against my head. Instead of disappearing altogether, his fingers slipped through my curls, as if petting me.

The gesture was strangely intimate, but I didn't dare move. Using that touch, I concentrated on keeping my breathing light. The lights flashed over the interior. Only when they faded, did I lift my head. "Was it him?"

Tag looked down and something very male filled his face as he studied me. His hand drifted from my hair to my jaw, cupping it. Caught in that heated gaze, I could feel my breath deepening, my body waking up. The damn attraction rose, paying no heed to what my mind wanted, even as my body cheered it along.

I reached up and curled my fingers around his hand. "Tag?" I choked out, needing one of us to think.

He blinked and that curious connection broke. He pulled free of my hold, even as he brushed his fingers over the side of my face. Then he turned back to the road. "Yeah." His voice was a rough rasp. He flicked a glance at the rear-view mirror. "He's trolling, so we need someplace safe."

Carefully pushing upright, I settled onto my side of the seat. "Got some place in mind?"

"Short of making a road trip to San Diego or Phoenix, nope."

Sighing, I ran through my options. My condo was out for obvious reasons. The no-motel was a bust as well. No telling if Hand Tooled knew about it. Plus, if we checked into a new place, we'd be hopping hotel rooms until Rabbit showed up.

If Hand Tooled could get to Curtis, finding out my connection to Aether wouldn't be all that hard. Of course, he'd still think he was dealing with a DOD consultant, but I didn't think that would keep him away. Who knew who Hand Tooled worked for, or how determined they were to get ahold of whatever was on that flash drive that cost Curtis his life. That kind of price tag meant big, bad people would do big, bad things to get it. They already proved they had no compunction about risking public attention to do so.

I was beginning to feel like a scrambling mouse caught in a trap I couldn't understand. Staring out at the black pavement, whatever kept me going for the last couple of hours disappeared, leaving behind the urge to crawl into some bed where no one could find me, pull the covers over my head, and sleep.

"You got any friends we can bunk with until Rabbit shows up?"

Friends? Like people I could call up and ask for help? That would be a big fat no. In my line of work, relationships tended to be superficial. Add in the fact I tended not to get close to anyone because seeing their future never boded well, friends were a rare commodity. I would have turned to the team, if things were desperate, but as Tag pointed out, they were busy in Phoenix. Which left us with what? A place where we would be one of the many. "What about hotels on the Strip?"

He shook his head. "Too easy to track either one of us to those. And I'm limited on identities right now. Besides we need to keep a low profile."

Right, then. Low profile meant hiding out. And Vegas was anything but low keyed. Unless you went out of your way to stay hidden. While most of those I came in contact with were all about being seen, there was one person I knew who was all about hiding. But landing on their doorstep may not be the best solution.

We needed someplace safe and quiet to hole up. Somewhere we could review what was on that flash drive so we'd know what we were up against. Someplace no one would look for me. A place with no known ties to me or any part of my life. While logic dictated my decision was the right one, worry plagued me.

Not for me or Tag, but for what I was about to bring to one of the few people I knew who wouldn't betray me.

Chapter Nine

I directed Tag through a sprawling development tucked into one of Vegas's many neighborhoods. The houses all looked the same, the only variation was the paint colors. Even now, at close to eleven at night, the streets were quiet, a contrast to the raging lights and crawling crowds populating the strip. Here was the Vegas most visitors never saw. The normal city.

I made sure to take him through the nice, new neighborhoods, because on the other side was what these neighborhoods would be in fifteen, maybe twenty, years. A little less refined, and more paranoid. Last thing we needed was a neighborhood-watch intervention.

As we drove further away from the highway and closer to the mountains looming along the outskirts of Vegas, the homes spun through uniform new builds, then established subdivisions, and finally into a unique gathering of one-of-a-kind, custom homes on wide lots.

Tag let out a low whistle as we passed an impressive wrought iron gate complete with an authentic-looking ranch logo. "If your friend has a setup like this, we should be golden."

"She doesn't, and we're still a bit out."

I could feel the weight of his gaze as he turned to me. "You want to call whoever we're going to see and give them a heads up?"

"I'd rather not."

"Why?"

Because I didn't want to give her the chance to tell me no. And with the trouble nipping at my heels, that no would be justified. "Not my story to tell, Tag."

He didn't like that answer. "Can we trust her?"

"Without a doubt." I turned away, hoping he'd take the hint and stop pushing. "No one would think to look for me here."

"Why?" He rolled right over my non-verbal hint.

Why? Well, my lips twitched, because the answer would be obvious when we arrived. "You'll see."

"Not sure I like this mysterious shit, Duchess."

"Not sure I care," I shot back, because really, I didn't. He asked for a place to hole up and my options were limited to one. "Look, Tag, the last thing Melisande wants is to be found, which makes her place the best option we have."

That earned me a frown and a quick glance. "She's hiding? Is she like you?"

Understanding the unspoken question of psychic abilities, I answered, "Nope, Meli's straight-up normal."

"So how come she doesn't want to be found?" he pushed.

I folded my arms across my chest. "Again, Tag, not my place to tell you. You asked if I had a friend I trusted, Meli's it. You be nice to her."

"Fine," he grunted.

"I mean it." Because if he upset Meli, I'd beat the crap out of him myself. "And no touching her."

A wicked grin lit his face with something breathtaking, and

heat burned my face as I realized how that sounded. "Jealous, Duchess?"

"No, oh sir jackass," I grumped. "Meli's secrets have no bearing on our situation, so don't go peeking."

The wicked grin disappeared. "That's not how it works." He didn't wait for me to respond. "As long as she doesn't plan on killing or betraying us, she'll have nothing to worry about."

Something in his voice hinted that maybe I was being unfair, but Meli had earned my loyalty and protection. And Tag… well, it was one thing to forgive his accusations, forgetting them was a whole other deal. "Just because you're a cynical bastard, doesn't mean everyone is out to betray you, nor does it give you the right to go poking around in people's heads."

A muscle in his jaw flexed, and he jerked the wheel to the right, bringing the van to a sudden stop. He turned in his seat, one arm braced against the back, the other on the steering wheel, while anger lent his face a dark cast. "I don't go poking around in anyone's head, Risia."

Oh boy, seemed I hit an unintentional nerve.

Those gold shot green eyes fairly glowed with fury. "You may call me a cynical bastard, but I've learned, over and fucking over again, that what someone says to your face and what they intend are two very different things. You might have the luxury of trusting what someone tells you, but I don't."

His lips twisted into a sneer. "I don't read fucking minds, I read their damn demons. The ones that drive a mother to strap a bomb to her child and walk her down a dirt road toward an enemy, without flinching. The ones that whisper it's okay to take what isn't yours, and even if she's screaming no, it's fine because you know she wants it. Or the ones that say you deserve more and set a price on the lives of those who trust you to have their backs and would never expect you sink a knife deep. The same demons that make people hurt those closest to them, to destroy something precious because they just can't stand the beauty and then lie to cover their asses."

Under his fury boiled a searing pain, one I wasn't sure he even knew he felt. It escaped in heavy self-condemnation and slammed through every emotional wall I erected to keep him out. My heart ached with the pressure, and hot tears pressed against my eyes, begging to escape. But I couldn't cry for him. It wasn't my place, no matter how much I wished it was. Still, I couldn't keep quiet. "What about your demons? Who fights those?"

"Me."

My throat was tight, but I didn't stop. "They're winning, baby." The endearment slipped out without permission.

The anger disappeared under agony and for a moment, I caught sight of Tag without his protective shell. "Not yet, but they will."

His response broke my heart. Uncaring of what it revealed, I leaned forward and cupped his face in my hands, ignoring his flinch. "You can't let them win, Tag." I gently pulled him toward me as I leaned forward until our foreheads touched. My thumbs brushed his cheekbones, feeling the scrape of his scruff just beginning to shadow his face. "You can't save everyone, but you can save yourself. And, I promise, that's enough."

I caught the flash of denial in his eyes and pressed my lips against his before he could speak. It was meant to stop what I knew would come out of his mouth, instead it changed into an offer of comfort, of solace. I traced the edges of his tight lips with soft, gentle strokes, offering him what I could. I didn't rush, I didn't press, but kept my touch delicate, trying to show him there was more than dark, ugly demons in this world.

When his lips remained rigid under mine, it was enough to free the tears behind my eyes. Maybe the darkness was too deep, because I didn't think I was getting through. As one hot tear escaped, my breath hitched. At that sound, whatever held him back shattered.

His hands came to my face as his mouth opened under mine. He took the kiss over, his hands tunneling through my curls to hold me tight while he plundered my mouth. He angled his head, leaving me to follow.

I did, without complaint.

His tongue dueled with mine, igniting the fire under my skin into an inferno. It burned through all my bullshit and flimsy denials of what I wanted. What I wanted was this, this need, this aching desire to soothe away everything, every hurt, every question, and leave no doubt that what burned between us could become a dangerous addiction.

The fury of his kiss changed, the rough edges smoothing into tenderness. His lips left mine and trailed a hot path down the side of my neck. His fingers gently pulled my head back exposing more skin to his lips. The brush of touch on such a sensitive area had me arching closer, needing more. The move pressed my aching breasts against his chest and gave him more access to my neck. My low moan escaped, then the hand against my face disappeared, and his lips lifted from my neck.

Dazed and overwhelmed, I could only draw in ragged breaths while I took in the harsh lines desire carved into his face. Savage masculine beauty stared back at me, my need reflected back in his burning gaze. Then my spine bowed as his hand cupped my breast, my eyes closing as he brushed his thumb across a sensitive nipple, sending whips of fire along my nerve endings.

"Tag," his name came out on a breath. One he stole, when his mouth found mine.

His talented fingers teased and tormented, while his lips and tongue continued to stoke the need higher. At some point, my hands went to his shoulders, my nails digging in deep.

When lights burned through the interior, the reality of

where we were intruded. Not just for me, but him as well. The sound of the passing car faded as he pulled back, his gaze glittering as he watched me.

Our ragged breaths echoed heavily in the heated air. I shivered as his hand left my breast, only to cup my face, his thumb gliding over my bottom lip. Without thought, I licked my lower lip, tasting us both.

His eyes darkened as he followed the small movement. "God, you're dangerous," his voice was a curious combination of rough and gentle.

Staring into his face, my body wailing for more, my heart unguarded, I whispered, "So are you."

In that golden-green gaze a new light emerged, and he smiled. He leaned forward and pressed a quick kiss against my lips, then set me gently back in the seat.

My hand shook as he helped me straighten my shirt and get my seatbelt buckled. For the moment, my mind was curiously blank. Since I wasn't sure what just happened or what it meant, I was good with that. I was unable to miss the obvious evidence of his arousal as he settled in behind the wheel with a wince and adjusted carefully. For some reason, that distinctly male move made me smile.

He caught it as he fastened his seatbelt. "Dangerous," he muttered before putting the van in gear and pulling back on to the road.

I let the quiet linger between us. I didn't want to break this moment, it wouldn't last. Just because we wanted each other didn't erase everything else. We still had to find out what was on the flash drive, avoid a loan-shark killer, and figure out who was betraying Tag and the rest of the team. Plus, I was about to land unannounced on my friend's doorstep until we could complete my recently acquired to-do list.

Once we had everything Tag needed, he'd be gone. Back to San Diego, leaving me here. And I would have to pick up the pieces of my life and my heart, of which there would be many. If that wasn't enough to bank the need rushing through me, I still hadn't figured out how to avoid Lawrence Rawlings's unwanted attention without him following through on his threat. Ice settled in my veins.

One thing at a time, girl. First deal with the immediate threat of the person chasing us, then worry about a broken heart and dreams later.

The van pulled to a stop, bringing me out of my head. The road ended, leaving only left or right. Realizing where we were, I said, "Take a right, and in about five miles you'll see a wood signpost. Turn right."

Instead of following my directions, he covered my left hand, which was nervously plucking at my jeans. "You okay?"

I buried my earlier worries deep, took a big breath, and gave him a small smile. "Fine, just worried about our reception."

He studied me. "I promise to play nice so long as she doesn't turn on us."

"Good." Because betraying me wasn't something Meli would ever do. I knew that without a doubt. Just like I knew I'd do the same for her.

His gaze didn't waver, and his steady regard made me want to squirm.

"What?"

"Layers."

I frowned at his nonsensical answer. "What?"

He shook his head. "Never mind." His hand left mine and he turned the van to the right. "Wood signpost?"

I let him change subjects. "Vientos Salvajes."

"Wild winds?"

Not surprised by his grasp of Spanish, I answered, "It's a cluster of holiday villas. Meli runs them while the owners travel." Neither of us spoke until the headlights illuminated a sign down the road. "Right here."

The van slowed, then turned onto the rough road snaking between straggling trees. He followed the pitted path, which was more gravel than pavement, until the lights washed over a house. The porch stretched along the front, guarded by a wooden railing. Huge terra cotta pots were spaced outside the railing. White stucco walls fairly glowed in the night, while the windows and door provided darker accents. The pueblo-style home fit in well with the desert scenery, cradled in the shadow of the mountain looming in the background.

The door opened, and a slender figure stepped out on to the porch.

Tag pulled to a stop. I put a hand on his arm before he shut the engine off. "Let me talk to Meli. Then you can park around back."

"I'll come with you."

I looked beyond him to the woman standing so still on the porch, then back to him. "No, let me talk to her first."

He searched my face and then gave me a short nod.

Not giving him a chance to change his mind, I undid my belt and scrambled stiffly out of the van to bring my troubles to my friend's doorstep.

Chapter Ten

TAG

I left Risia sleeping. As much as I wanted to finish what we started in the cramped space of the van, exhaustion had given her skin a gray cast. She'd been too tired to argue about our sleeping arrangements. Not that I would have listened. No couch was made for a male.

Instead of taking my time sating the need clawing through me, I got her into bed, then lay awake for the rest of the night, making contingency plans. It didn't help that sleep kept its distance.

I tried to list what needed to be done now that I managed to get the drive from Risia without an argument. First up was getting the damn thing into a secured location. Not difficult, but it required a trip into town. Which gave me a chance to ditch the van.

Next to me, she shifted in her sleep, and her warm scent wrapped teasing fingers around my cock, derailing my thoughts. I stifled a frustrated groan. Rationality took a hike, leaving my mind to whirl in vicious circles as I listened to her breathe beside me, unaware of the turmoil she created.

In the van she unearthed damages I thought long gone.

Hell, most of the time, I could ignore the gaping holes memories carved out of my soul. No use in acknowledging what couldn't be fixed. I wasn't the only soldier who'd seen some pretty horrific shit.

No one walked away from a war without scars, something my dad told me the day I informed him I was entering the navy. At eighteen, arrogant and stupid, I brushed his words off. Only to learn the hard way he nailed it. When you returned, if you returned, you were never the same.

Tonight, when Risia was so adamant that her friend would never betray her, her naive belief pissed me off. The only thing you could bank on was that every human possessed a core of self-preservation. If someone found the right pressure point, offered the right thing, her friend would fold like tissue paper. And if that ignorance wasn't enough, then Risia made the same damn accusation Cyn had about me poking around in people's heads.

As if I wanted to know shit about people. I'd be perfectly happy seeing only the masks they wore and nothing more. I didn't need more nightmares, I carried enough of my own to last lifetimes. But somewhere in explaining that shit to one irritatingly beautiful woman, I showed her the real me. Not all, but enough for her to recognize it.

I pressed an arm over my eyes. *Stupid, fucking stupid.* I knew better than to show anyone a weak spot. They'd figure out a way to use it. Risia's job was all about exploiting weaknesses. Why would she consider me any different?

An arm snaked around my waist and a warm weight settled against my chest, pressing along my side, all silk and heat. Lifting my arm, I looked down. The moonlight seeping around the edges of the blinds above the bed cast just enough illumination to study the woman curled next to me, her hair spreading like a curtain over my chest. While my dick perked up at the visual, my heart thumped hard. A warmth began seeping under my dark thoughts.

So damn beautiful.

I dropped my arm and wrapped it around her, holding her close, remembering her pained, *'They're winning, baby'*. The emotions behind her statement had been pure, no hidden motivation, just a hand in the dark. *'You can't let them win.'*

But they were. I'd been fighting for so long, and I was tired. Done. Even here in the middle of the night with the one woman I couldn't forget wrapped around me, I could feel them dragging me down.

I asked Delacourt once how much a touch empath could take before walking away. She didn't have an answer. Mainly because the other two empaths who came close to my level had killed themselves before they were forty. Their version of walking away, I guess. My twenty-ninth birthday was three months away and I'd already considered following in their footsteps.

More than once.

The first time, I stepped back because I'd been approached to be part of PSY-IV teams. The lure of getting some answers while protecting others like me kept me going. Then Ellery ambushed the teams, and my hope was washed away in blood. What use was being psychic if you couldn't stop the monsters?

Kayden dragged my ass back the second time. He offered me a chance to hunt Ellery and I took it, letting revenge take hope's spot in my soul. Who would stop me next time? Because there would be a next time.

Against my chest, Risia stirred. "Tag?" Soft and sleepy, her voice seeped in, chasing away the chilling numbness creeping through me.

"Shh, Duchess. Sleep." Unable to fight the urge, I pressed my lips to the top of her head, the soft strands of her hair clinging to my lips. God, I loved those damn curls. Like silk ribbons.

"You okay?"

No. My throat tightened, but I choked out, "Yeah, baby."

The curls drifted over my skin like delicate fingers as she lifted her head. Sleep still clung to her long-lashed, crystal blue eyes even as her gaze roamed my face. "No you're not. The shadows are back."

Somehow, the dark room made it easier to be honest with her. It was already too late to hide behind my walls. She bulldozed her way through once and I hadn't had a chance to rebuild them. Hell, at this point, maybe it would be best to leave them down, since something taunted that I'd constantly be trying to rebuild them around her.

"How about this? I'll be okay." She continued to stare at me, unconvinced, so I leaned down and brushed a kiss across her forehead. "Sleep, Risia. You need it. I'll be fine."

"You better be," she mumbled before dropping her head back to my chest. The butterfly brush of her lashes felt like electric currents against my chest.

Closing my eyes, I acknowledge, if only to myself, what I held. Hope, forgiveness, a chance to crawl out of hell. This would be the reason why I wouldn't take the easy way out. She believed I could win.

For the first time, I was beginning to think maybe I could too.

⸻ ••◆ ◆•• ⸻

I managed an hour or two of catnaps, but when sunlight replaced moonlight, I untangled myself from her. I was going to take her at her word and believe she would be safe here in the outskirts of Vegas with her friend. I left her a note and let her sleep.

Meanwhile, I had things to do. First, ditch the van. Second, stash the drive. Third, find out who was dogging Risia's heels. If that all went well, then maybe I could figure out what Rawlings was holding over her head.

I hadn't forgotten the quick glimpse of guilt and shame she tried to hide when we talked about Rawlings yesterday at the hotel. That kind of reaction meant secrets, and secrets in our world were bargaining chips. Whether Rawlings was part of Falcon or not, the idea of him having some hold over Risia wasn't working for me. Since I'd bet good money she wouldn't share, maybe I'd see what I could find out on my own. Of course, that all depended on how it went with tracking Hand Tooled. Risia's name stuck and worked as well as Fucking Bastard.

Caught up in my head, I wasn't paying attention as I crossed the gravel path and made my way toward the van parked behind the main building. Which meant I didn't see Risia's friend until I almost ran over her. Our unintentional impact sent her stumbling back and instinct had me reaching out to steady her so she wouldn't fall.

My hands wrapped around her arms, bare under the oversized T-shirt paired with faded jeans. Bone crushing fear swamped me. A feral need to escape so intense my fingers tightened before I thought better of it. Then as if a light switch had been thrown, it was gone. The sudden absence of emotion left me blinking.

"Sor…sorry." The stuttered word came out shaky, even as she tried to pull away, a pile of towels clutched to her chest.

I shook my head, trying to clear the clinging webs of remembered fear, my curiosity rising. "My fault, wasn't watching where I was going." I eased my hold, not letting go completely because I was worried she'd yank back and hurt herself. "You steady?"

She nodded, her ponytail bouncing with the movement even as she put distance between us. "Tag, right?"

I nodded.

"You're up early." She managed to meet my gaze for about three seconds before hers shifted to somewhere past my shoulder, her arms tightening around the towels.

"I have to go back to town."

Her gaze went to the villa where I left Risia, then came back to me. "Is Risia up?"

I shook my head. "I'm letting her sleep. She's had a hell of a couple of days and could use the rest."

This time she had no problem meeting my gaze. "What trouble did you get her into?" Accusation colored her question.

I refused to free my grin as I watched her get all fired up at some perceived injustice to her friend. It was cute, in the way a small dog bristles in the presence of a bigger one. "It's more like what she got me into, actually."

Heat washed under her pale skin. Brunette may be the color she was currently sporting, but I was guessing with her pale complexion and vivid green eyes, there was a hell of lot more red in those strands than she was showing. "You look as if you could handle trouble just fine," she muttered.

There was no fighting the grin now, not after that. "Well, ma'am, I'm trying."

Her brow furrowed as she studied me. At some point she decided I wasn't going to bite, because she offered, "Well, then maybe I should be wishing you luck. Knowing Risia, you're going to need it." The tension riding her dropped a notch, and she offered a shy smile. "You clean up pretty well for a cowboy."

Since I was dressed in what I considered business casual, tan cargos and a shirt with a collar, I wasn't sure what made me a cowboy. Still, I couldn't resist tipping an imaginary hat and played it up, "Much obliged."

It was enough to get a surprised laugh out of her. It was a good look for her, one I was pretty sure she hadn't much practice with. Whoever dampened that spirit deserved an ass kicking. She brushed a loose strand of hair behind her ear. "If she asks, when do you expect to be back?"

"Hopefully later this afternoon."

We said good-bye and I watched her walk away and make her way to one of the villas.

How in the world had Risia and Meli hooked up? You couldn't find two more opposite women if you tried. Shaking my head at the vagaries of the female species, I got in the van and headed back to Vegas.

After a minor detour to secure the drive, and dumping the van in a mall parking lot at the north end of the strip, I began the long haul to the airport to hit up a car rental even though taxis zipped by every two minutes. I weaved through the early risers strolling along. At just after eight in the morning, the amount of people roaming the sidewalks was mind-boggling. Guess Vegas really was the city that never slept.

As if to confirm my assumption, a bleary-eyed man stumbled out of one of the casinos. I sidestepped him, shaking my head, while he was busy blinking owlishly in the bright morning light. Roughly thirty minutes later, I hit the rental counter at McCarran Airport, flashed my alternate ID confirming my status with the NCIS, and made my way back to Risia's high-rise condo.

I found a coffee shop conveniently situated next door with a great view of the condo's main entry, and grabbed a parking spot down the block. I ordered my preferred caffeine fix, and then made myself comfortable at a table where someone left the scattered remains of a local paper. I found a write-up on

Curtis Trammel's death on page two. Seemed Trammel was up to his eyeballs in debts accrued at various casinos. While no one was currently identified, various leads were being followed. No mention of Risia, but that didn't mean anything. Especially since the police had been knocking on her door yesterday.

Normally I'd reach out to Rabbit and Delacourt, have them work their magic and get me access to the case. But since they were sniffing out Ellery's trail in Phoenix, I'd try going it alone first. See how far I'd get before tapping that line.

While PSY-IV Team wouldn't mean jack shit to anyone outside the military, my ID with NCIS was still intact and active with a small caveat. Anyone calling in to check my credentials got transferred to Delacourt's domain. That and the fact Risia's cover put her as an employee of the DOD, might work in my favor with the locals. Since walking into the LVPD without knowing who the lead detective was, would be a clear indicator I might not be on the up and up, I'd play the odds.

When in Vegas, right?

No doubt the detective would be back today, keen on making contact with Risia. It shouldn't be too hard to run into him at her place and see if I couldn't get him to share some information. Not the best plan, but doable. And if the police didn't show, at least I'd get a chance to see who did.

Patience played a huge part of any investigation and today proved no different. Two hours ticked by, filled with three coffees and a half-completed crossword puzzle before my hunch panned out. While most people would dismiss the detective as another business man out and about on the Vegas strip, when he shifted to miss a trio of laughing college kids, his shirt pulled tight for just a moment, revealing the slight bump of his service weapon. Medium height, stocky, Hispanic, dark hair, black sunglasses, blue shirt, and khakis.

I stretched and casually began cleaning up my empties,

even going so far as to refold the paper for the next patron. A handful of minutes later I stepped out on to Risia's floor, serious government face in place.

The detective stood in front of Risia's door down toward the end of the hall, his fist raised. His head turned toward me, and I caught his eye, giving him a short nod. His hand dropped, and he waited for me to approach, his face blank, his gaze cautious.

A few feet out, I took a chance he was the same man I used Risia's balcony to avoid yesterday. "Detective Ochoa?"

He dipped his chin in acknowledgement.

"Thomas Gunderson, NCIS, I was asked to liaison with you in regards to a DOD employee, Risia Lacoste." I held out my hand and thinned my mental walls.

He took it, his grip solid. Suspicion, determination, and frustration hit first, then under it, a solid core of dogged determination which meant this was one detective who'd ensure every question was answered before he closed his case. Before I could get sucked any deeper, I let go.

His dark eyes took on a speculative gleam. "Is liaison a fancy-ass way to claim jurisdiction?"

I grinned, understanding the dance. Local law enforcement didn't like government types mucking up their cases. "No sir, I'm actually here to see if we can share information."

He folded his arms across his chest. "Such as the whereabouts of Ms. Lacoste?"

I hooked my thumbs in the corner of my front pockets, and rocked back a bit on my heels. "Now that tidbit is above my pay grade. What I can tell you is I received a call from my commanding officer asking me to stop by and offer my assistance to the local authorities."

"Uh-huh."

Knowing this cat and mouse game could go on a damn long while, I ran a hand through my hair, letting impatience twist my lips in a grimace. "Look, I was in town, trying to enjoy the weekend. Colonel Delacourt called, told me to go and offer my help to the local police with a situation involving a DOD employee vetting a civilian contract. Between you and me, Lacoste is either currently answering to her bosses, or if she's MIA, I'm supposed to find out if it's tied to her assignment. Either way, I'd be happy to relay whatever you want to the colonel. I'm sure it'll get to the right people."

He studied me, his skepticism clear. "Right." I endured his hard perusal, and let him draw his own conclusions. Finally, he blew out a long breath. "I'm not sure either one of us will be much help to the other. The only reason I'm looking for her is because Rawlings called in a favor with the chief."

Well, well, well. "Rawlings?" I frowned as if trying to place the name. "Isn't that the civilian contractor being vetted?"

A man of few words, Ochoa gave me another nod.

"Why is he calling your chief about a DOD employee?"

"Because two nights ago one of his employees was killed, and Ms. Lacoste failed to show at the office yesterday." His rather dry tone indicated he thought doing a favor for a friend of the chief was a waste of time.

Capitalizing on that, I murmured, "Maybe he called in favors with the colonel then, too."

Some of Ochoa's suspicion faded.

I hid my satisfaction with a frown. "Does Rawlings think Lacoste has something to do with the murder?"

"Rawlings told the chief he became concerned when she didn't show up yesterday morning. Especially as she was known to meet with the victim after hours, running through contracts. He's worried she's either dead or injured somewhere."

That last part sounded like he was repeating someone else. Clearly Ochoa thought differently. "Any sign she was with your victim at the time of the murder?"

Ochoa shifted, then motioned his arm back down the hall. "Since we're obviously going to share, let's go do it someplace besides a hallway." He led the way and I followed. "Hungry, Gunderson?"

"I could eat."

He grunted. "There's a little mom and pop pancake shop just down the street."

"Sounds good."

We waited for the elevator to arrive. "Do you have any ideas?"

Not quite following Ochoa's question, I said, "Pardon?"

"On where Ms. Lacoste is currently," he clarified. "Missing or currently answering to her boss?"

Without blinking, I lied through my pearly whites. "I'm hoping she's busy answering questions, but my money's on missing."

Ochoa's face went grim. "Mine too."

The elevator chimed.

Chapter Eleven

TAG

Tucked away from the typical tourist areas, Delia's Diner wasn't much to look at, but the food was damn good. Even the coffee. Enjoying the first sip of current cup number three, I gazed over Ochoa's shoulder as the little bell on the door gave its perky jangle.

An older couple came in, exchanged greetings with both waitresses and then made their way to a booth. Must be regulars. They barely got settled before one of the waitresses set two cups of coffee, a bowl of creamers, and offerings of pink, blue, and white packets in front of them. Definitely regulars.

Ochoa sat back, wiped his mouth with a paper napkin, then picked up his own cup of joe. "Do you know Ms. Lacoste?"

"Not personally. Why?"

He took a sip, then set his cup on the table, his gaze shuttered. "Yesterday, when interviewing Mr. Trammel's friends and family, her name came up a few times."

"Trammel being your victim?"

He nodded.

Curious as to where he was going with this, I rested my arm along the back of the booth, the picture of casual interest.

"You said she worked with him a great deal, so that's not unusual."

"Some speculations weren't limited to her professional capacity." He paused, his gaze sharpening. "Have you seen her picture?"

"Part of the sparse information I was given. Beautiful woman." Wondering if I underestimated Ochoa's intelligence, I offered a puzzled frown. "You think they were involved and she what? Knocked him off?" I hooked a finger in my cup and lifted it.

For the first time a real smile broke over his features. "If only it was that easy." The smile began to fade. "No, the victim was in debt to some serious heavy hitters, and considering the state of his body..." He trailed off, shaking his head. "The speculation is probably no more than sour grapes. Unfortunately, it's one of those things I have to check out."

The coiled tension locked around my muscles unwound a notch. "So, you're ruling Lacoste out as your suspect."

Those dark eyes met mine. "Would be happy to, if I could find her to ask a few questions."

I raised my cup in acknowledgement. "Understood, sir. I'll make sure to pass along your request."

"Appreciate it."

His grumpy tone had me smiling into my cup as I took a sip. Setting it down, I decided to start my own line of questions. "This Rawlings, he's a major player in town?"

Ochoa scratched his temple. "One of many, but he's got fingers in quite a few places. Not that anyone in Vegas seems to mind, since he pours enough money into various charities and under-funded humanitarian projects."

Considering his sarcastic edge on the last part of his explanation, I bet Ochoa wasn't one of Rawlings many fans. "Money can blind quite a few."

"Yeah." His eyes darkened with worry for a moment,

before clearing. "Unfortunately, the chief considers him a professional friend of the department."

Which meant Ochoa was under pressure to close this case. Something that could work in Risia's favor. "Any idea which heavy hitter took out your guy?"

He rubbed a hand through his short hair, blowing out a breath. "Thankfully the list is pretty short, so hopefully I'll actually make it home before midnight tonight, which will please my wife."

From the warmth in those two words, it'd please him too. "Happy wife…"

"Happy life," he finished with a small smile as the waitress left a tab on our table with a grin and "have a nice day". He waited for her to move away before he continued, "For now, my day's packed with interviews of those I missed yesterday." He pulled out his phone, thumbing through screens. "And it seems I'm up at the city's beloved Mr. Rawlings's office in thirty minutes."

Not wanting to miss the opportunity, I asked, "Want some company? I was planning on stopping by his place this morning." Snagging the tab, I dug in to my pocket and pulled out enough cash to cover and laid it on the table.

He gave me a short nod. "I'll get the tip." Ochoa lifted his cup, and took one last drink. Setting it down, he shifted and dug out some bills, adding them to the pile. "Want to ride along or follow?"

"I'll ride along."

"Good enough." He pushed out of the booth, collected our bill, and I followed. He reached the register and handed the money and bill to the waitress, then turned to ask, "You any good at the political game?"

"I've survived ten years in the military."

"Good enough," he grunted. "Let's go play with the big boys."

Ochoa parked in the same garage Risia and I snuck through the night before. This time, there was no unwatched emergency exit. Instead, I followed the detective as he waltzed through the expansive lobby doors. Straight to a security-slash-reception desk where a young, dressed-to-impress man greeted us with one of those empty, professional smiles. "Good afternoon, gentlemen. May I help you?"

Ochoa flashed his badge, taking care to be discreet. "Detective Pete Ochoa, LVPD and Agent Thomas Gunderson, NCIS. We have an appointment with Mr. Rawlings, Aether Industries."

The desk boy tapped away on a keyboard. "Yes, sir, I have you here. If you'd be so kind as to take elevator two, it will take you to the fifth floor." He handed Ochoa a security badge, and then held one my way. "Sir?"

"Thanks." I took it, clipped it on my front belt loop, and then walked with Ochoa to the second set of elevators. It quietly slid open and we stepped inside.

Ochoa went to hit a button and then stopped. "Seriously?" he muttered under his breath. "A four-floor building and you need a second set of elevators for the top dog?"

I shared a look and a knowing grin. Rawlings really thought he was the shit.

We were quickly deposited on the rarified fourth floor and greeted with another empty, professional smile. This time attached to an attractive blonde decked out in a modest black skirt, pencil thin heels that would look better on Risia, and a silk blouse that rode the edge of professional. "Gentlemen, this way."

She didn't wait for an answer, but led us down a short hall, past a plush waiting area, and to a solid door. Two short knocks, then she twisted the handle and pushed it open. "Mr. Rawlings, Detective Ochoa and Agent Gunderson."

So pretty boy's tapping was a direct line to Ms. Shark, because God forbid Rawlings should be taken by surprise. In front of me, Ochoa's shoulders rose and fell slightly, indicating a silent sigh. Poor guy must really hate dealing with politicos. Still, he led the way into Rawlings's office, and I followed along like the grateful sidekick.

"Gentlemen." Behind an austere desk, Lawrence Rawlings set aside papers, removed a pair of wire-frame reading glasses, and then rose to his feet.

Absently I wondered if he needed them, or were they, like the two guard dogs, affectations of a man determined to portray a benevolent, yet powerful businessman?

Trim frame, dressed in pressed black slacks, a pearly gray collared shirt with a jewel-tone tie, and a mane of white hair, Rawlings more than looked the part. "Thank you, Ms. Flynn."

"Of course." She paused with her hand on the door. "By the way, another confirmation came in a few minutes ago, so we're only waiting on a few more responses."

"Wonderful."

A professional flash of teeth and then she disappeared, pulling the door shut with a subtle, but resounding click.

Rawlings walked around the desk. "Thank you for making the time to come see me, Detective." He held his out his hand.

Ochoa took it, no sign of his earlier opinions in sight. "Not a problem, Mr. Rawlings." He let go, then turned to introduce us. "This is Agent Gunderson with NCIS, he's here at the request of his colonel."

Rawlings turned to me, hand out, his gaze sharp.

Yep, glasses were just another prop.

"Your colonel?"

"Colonel Charlene Delacourt," I offered, taking his hand. As soon as our palms touched, cold calculation edged in contempt seeped through me. Oh yeah, Rawlings was a stone-cold fucker, who viewed everyone as mere pawns in his brilliant game. I checked my urge to curl my lip in response. "I'm here to help Detective Ochoa understand what happened to Ms. Lacoste."

At her name, the sexual predator Rawlings tried to bury raised its head.

I dropped his hand before the urge to deck the bastard won out.

"Yes, I'm quite worried about Risia." He waved us to the chairs angled in front of his desk. "Please, have a seat." We sat, as he leaned back against his desk, folding his arms across his chest. "Have you found her?"

He directed his question to both of us, but it was Ochoa who answered. "Nothing yet, but I stopped by her place this morning."

In no rush to join whatever game Rawlings thought he was playing, I kept my mouth shut.

He turned to me, and I found satisfaction in catching the flash of irritation he couldn't hide when I failed to add to the conversation. "Agent Gunderson, do your people have any idea where Ms. Lacoste may be?"

"As I explained to Detective Ochoa earlier, that information is above my pay-grade, sir." I sat back, resting one ankle on my knee, a nonchalant pose guaranteed to piss him off. Sure enough, his lips tightened a fraction. I hid my satisfaction and continued, "She could be cloistered with her bosses, or she could legitimately be missing. Regardless, at this time, I'm here gathering information."

"And will that change?" A subtle challenge peeked out under the urbane sophisticate.

I shrugged, unwilling to step outside of my "I'm-a-lowly-peon" role. "Only if my orders do."

My answer seemed to make him happy, because his shoulders slumped, even as he created a concerned frown. "I truly hope she's okay." His hesitant doubt was just enough to invite questions. He even braced his hands on the desk's edge next to his hips, dropping his gaze to the floor, completing the image of the worried man.

"What makes you think she's not?" Ochoa broke in, snapping up Rawlings's bait.

He heaved a sigh and lifted his head, his body bracing. "My Chief Information Security Officer ran across a concerning breach in Mr. Trammel's computer history."

This did not make Ochoa happy. He leaned forward. "I thought you were turning over his computer to our lab."

Rawlings's gaze shifted for a moment before returning to Ochoa. "Unfortunately, due to the highly confidential nature of my business, my lawyers had to intervene. We will gladly give your techs access, but the computer must stay within Aether's walls."

Tension sang through Ochoa, and he opened his mouth to respond, but before he could, Rawlings raised a hand. "I understand your frustration, Detective. However, please understand I owe my clients the discretion they've come to expect from me. I'm happy to help as much as I can, but I must take steps to ensure my non-disclosure agreements are kept."

As much as I didn't want to admit it, the cagey bastard was working the system brilliantly. A businessman caught between the government and local police, otherwise known as a rock and hard place.

Ochoa swallowed it with obvious difficulty as his hands curled, then uncurled against the armrests of his chair. "What did you find on his computer," he growled.

A heavy sigh preceded Rawlings answer. "Files of a highly sensitive nature were encrypted on his computer. Files he shouldn't have access to." He turned to me. "You are aware of why Risia was vetting my company, Agent?"

I gave him a short nod, even as my blood ran cold as the suspicions Delacourt shared with me earlier gained weight. How much would Rawlings reveal?

He kept going, "That project and what is in those files are connected."

Not enough to hang his ass out to dry, but definitely enough to set up a dead scapegoat. "That will be an issue." An understatement of the century.

His grimace would've been convincing if I hadn't had a peek at the conscienceless monster living under his skin. "I'm quite aware of that fact. At this point, it seems that Mr. Trammel's intent was to sell that information to eliminate his debt, but if that was the case, it wasn't followed through."

"But you can't be a hundred percent certain," I pointed out. No one could. Just because a file remained on a computer didn't mean it hadn't been copied. Especially since a copy of said files was currently hiding out in a location known only to me.

"No, I can't, but my people are damn good at what they do, we only hire the best. If these files have been compromised, I should know in another day or so."

"What's in the files?" Ochoa picked up the tense vibe underlying our exchange.

Rawlings turned his attention to Ochoa. "Highly classified information on a contracted project. As I stated, we will verify they haven't been compromised."

"You realize this situation does not help your contract possibilities with the DOD," I pushed, unwilling to let him slither out of this mess just yet. "They won't accept assurances from your people. They will bring in their own to ensure their information and your project can't be used against us."

Which meant, if Rawlings was considering brokering the information on the black market, he needed to move fast, because the government would be crawling all over his ass in a matter of days.

Irritation crossed those aristocratic features. "Yes, Agent Gunderson, I'm highly aware what this means. However, I have faith my pending contract will survive this."

Stunned, I could only stare at him. *Was he fucking crazy?* No government intelligence agency would trust him after this fiasco. Maybe if Trammel hadn't been killed, Rawlings could have hidden the compromised files, but Trammel's death meant Rawlings's plans hit a major hiccup. Now Rawlings was scrambling to pin any future leaks on a dead man, because he knew a fall-out was coming.

How in the hell did he think he was going to keep the contract? The government could take his prototype and leave him with nothing.

Unless, a little voice well trained in how insidious evil could be offered, *he had someone fairly high up helping to cover his ass?* Add in the possibility of Rawlings working with a Falcon contact, and the possibility of said contact being one and the same skyrocketed. The concept made my stomach curl, but it had merit.

Shit, I needed to talk to Delacourt ASAP. Careful to keep my racing thoughts hidden, I murmured, "There's always a first time, I guess."

He dismissed my response and went back to his own agenda, turning to Ochoa. "Are you any closer to identifying the person who killed Mr. Trammel?"

Professional blankness coated Ochoa's face. "We are still pursuing leads, and processing evidence."

"If you are in need of more resources, mine are available to your department. I've already cleared it with Chief Lewelyn."

For a supposedly smart man, Rawlings was fucking idiot.

My opinion was echoed as Ochoa's jaw tightened. "I appreciate the offer, but my department is more than capable of handling a murder investigation, Mr. Rawlings." And the detective sure as hell didn't like Rawlings's implication otherwise.

Chagrin washed over Rawlings's face as he leaned forward. "No offense to you or your department, I have complete faith in your abilities to solve this."

The urge to cough "bullshit" nudged me. It took effort, but I ignored it. This guy was a piece of work.

Rawlings kept going, rubbing Ochoa's nose in Rawlings's relationship with the chief of police, "Rob mentioned the recent budget cuts during a dinner a few weeks back. I only intended my offer to help."

"Appreciate it," Ochoa bit out, not so graciously snubbing the insincere apology. "Were you able to get a list together of Trammel's travel and meetings for the last two months? We'd like to be able to eliminate them from our records of his movements."

"Of course," Rawlings said. "My assistant has that ready for you, as promised." He rose to his feet, effectively ending the meeting he orchestrated to ensure Trammel would be seen as a desperate gambler who'd sell out his country to cover his own ass.

It was so well played, I almost wanted to applaud, except the urge to deck his smug ass was bigger.

"Please, let me know if I can be of further help."

Ochoa and I both got to our feet. We followed Rawlings to the door and waited until he opened it. He turned to Ochoa, hand extended. "Thank you again for stopping by."

Ochoa shook it. Then it was my turn. I took his hand knowing it wouldn't be pleasant.

This time, Rawlings let his inner predator peek out. "I hope you find Ms. Lacoste soon, Agent. I'm worried about her." Warning bells clamored as that cold, evil presence shoved forward. This time it was tainted with a sexual hunger focused solely on Risia. Behind it a whisper of gloating satisfaction. He had something on Risia all right, something big. And he had every intention of collecting his due.

Worry slid under my surge of sick fury and I could only manage a nod as the need to bring this bastard down while keeping Risia safe set itself in stone.

————•◦●◦●◦•————

Stepping outside the glass doors of Aether's offices, the shift from air-conditioned interior to hot afternoon didn't even put a hitch in my step as I followed Ochoa through the garage. He slammed his sunglasses in place. "That son of a bitch has balls."

"Big, shiny brass ones," I agreed. "A disease that tends to impact over-confident dicks with money." Maybe I should've tempered my response, but my blood was still boiling, and the need to wipe the floor with Rawlings hadn't subsided. In fact, if the itch between my shoulder blades was any indicator, I wouldn't be surprised if he was watching us right now.

I slipped on my own sunglasses, even though we were still in the shaded areas of the parking garage. Once they were in place, I scanned the ceilings, pinpointing the cameras discreetly tucked in the corners. If I flipped off a camera, would we make it out of the garage before his trumped-up security guards made it down here? Better question, was it worth the hassle?

Ochoa reached his car and stared at me over the roof, his face tight with fury. "If I find out he had anything to do with this shit, I will enjoy taking his ass down." He didn't give me a chance to answer, but yanked his door open and got behind the wheel.

I shifted my shoulders as the itch between my shoulder blades got worse, and opened my door. I dropped into the passenger seat, and did another scan in an attempt to figure out what was bothering me. It couldn't just be Rawlings. Nothing seemed out of place. I closed my door. "I'd be happy to help."

"Care to share what's so damn important about that contract?" Ochoa turned the key and the engine grumbled to life. He backed out of the parking space and headed to the exit.

Sincere regret echoed in my answer. "Wish I could, man, but can't. He wasn't shitting about the highly classified nature of the contract. The rest of his story…" I shrugged my shoulders. "That I can't vouch for."

"Yeah, convenient find his tech made." Ochoa made a right out of the garage, and turned in the same direction as Risia's condo. His fingers drummed against the steering wheel. "Let me ask you something."

"Shoot."

"You're a company with multiple connections to government entities. Wouldn't your employees, especially those closest to you, have to undergo an extensive background check?"

Nice to know the detective hadn't been snowed by Rawlings's performance. "In my experience, yes."

"Wouldn't a gambling habit raise a few flags?" he pressed as we merged with traffic heading toward the Strip.

"It would, unless he was smart enough to hide it." And someone like Trammel, used to moving in big social circles, would know what his secret could cost him. No doubt he would've buried it in the darkest pit he could find.

An eyebrow rose above Ochoa's sunglasses. "You think Rawlings's hired best would've missed that? When they managed to uncover encrypted files on Trammel's computer."

Something in his voice made me look at him. "You think Rawlings knew Trammel had a problem."

His lips tightened. "What I think and what I can prove are two very different things, Agent."

Therein lay the problem. As tempting as Rawlings was to target, even Ochoa knew it would be career suicide to do so without solid proof of Rawlings's involvement. Thankfully, I didn't have to worry about shit like that.

I opened my mouth to respond, only to stop when my phone vibrated against my hip. I pulled it out of my pocket and checked the screen. Unknown local number. Since I was betting it was Risia and talking to her right now wasn't advisable, I sent it to voicemail.

Ochoa didn't miss much. "Avoiding calls, Gunderson?"

I shifted to my hip and tucked my phone back in my pocket. "It's just a friend I had plans to hook up with tonight. I'll call them back later."

"Female or male?"

"Male." Turning, I caught the tail end of Ochoa's smile, even as my phone began vibrating again.

Just beyond his window, sunlight glinted off fast approaching metal and caught my attention. "Ochoa! Wa—" The rest of my warning was cut short as a familiar dark sedan slammed into the driver's side door. I tried to brace but couldn't stop my head from slamming into the window. Metal screamed and glass shattered under the impact.

My last conscious thought was maybe I should've answered Risia's call.

Chapter Twelve

"Risia! Sweetie, talk to me."

Meli's frantic voice cut through my panic as I struggled to pull back from the visions splintering around me. Each one showed the same horrible outcome, Tag caught in a tangle of metal and glass, bloodied and unconscious. A figure in the rear-view mirror approached. Hand tooled leather shoes stepped over broken glass. A gun rose. The harsh bark of a shot followed. The trashed remains of the car coated in blood.

I couldn't catch my breath as the scene broke, and then reformed, this time Tag was awake but unable to move, pinned in place while Hand Tooled aimed and fired. Then it broke again, and reformed.

Unable to move, my frantic urgency escaped in a frustrated scream. The echo of Tag's name was followed by a sharp sting against my cheekbone. The visions shuddered but didn't break. I sucked in harsh breath.

"Dammit, Risia!" The half-choked sob managed to finish what the unexpected slap against my face started.

The visions drew back, and reality began to seep back in.

Hard fingers dug into my arms, and someone was shaking

me. The hold hurt a little, but not enough to keep me from raising my hands blindly and locking them on whoever held me. I blinked and Meli's pale, pinched face wavered into focus. "Meli." Her name came out in a weak whisper.

"Risia?" Slow tears tracked down her face, her eyes held haunted shadows.

My grip changed from punishing to clutching. I didn't want to let go and slide back into the sucking morass of possible futures lurking on the edges of my mind. "I need a phone."

She didn't bother with pointless questions, but reached up to the table beside us, and brought back her cell. My hands shook as I took it from her and punched in the number I memorized when I found Tag's note this morning. I pressed the phone against my ear as it rang, useless prayers echoing in my head. "Dammit, Tag, pick up the fucking phone."

As if my desperate plea could reach further than an electronic signal. It went to voice mail. Caught between the urge to scream or rage, I did neither. Just raised my gaze to Meli's worried face. "He won't answer."

She took the phone from my numb grip and swiped the screen. She held it to her ear, her attention never veering from me. Fear and worry created a familiar mask on her delicate face. She grimaced. "Tag, it's Meli. I need you to call me immediately." She hung up and stared at me. "We can try again in a minute."

I shook my head and reached for the phone, frantic. "Tag doesn't have a minute." Hell, I was probably too fucking late as it was. Fear crowded close. "We have to go find him." I redialed, this time putting it on speaker. It rang. And rang. I hung up. Redialed.

"Stop." Meli's voice was gentle, even as she pried the phone out of my hand. "This isn't going to help, Risia."

My hands curled into fists as I watched her set it up on the table above us. Only then did I realize we were sitting on the floor next to the kitchen table. "We have to go and find him." I had to know if I was too late. *Please don't let me be too late.*

She shook her head. "No, Risia, you're in no shape to be out looking for Tag. Besides, you just finished telling me how you have cops and some psycho after you." She wrapped an arm around my back, and helped me stand. "I'll go."

My legs felt like rubber and didn't seem to be responding, but I got up. Meli guided me to a chair and I collapsed. I knew she was right. Even if I could avoid the cops and Hand Tooled, I was in no shape to go and look for Tag. It wouldn't do him any good if I got in an accident as well.

"He's near my condo on the Strip." I tried to ignore the lurking threat hovering on the edges of my mind and focused on what I saw. "Two…no, three blocks south, near that antique shop you like. If not there, check the nearest hospital."

She sank into the chair next to me. "Hospital?"

"Tag's going to be in one." It hurt to admit, but I kept talking, "Or he might already be there. Check for a victim of a car accident. Maybe a hit and run. He was with another man, dark, Hispanic." I studied one of the few people I called friend. "Meli, you have to find him."

She frowned. "He means something to you, doesn't he?"

I gave her the only answer I had. "I don't know. Maybe."

She bit her lip, a recognizable sign she wanted to say something, but thought better of it. She grabbed the phone and stood. "The nearest hospital to your place is St. Angel's, right?"

Unable to squeeze any words out around the growing pressure on my chest, I nodded.

"Okay." She straightened her shoulders. "I'll go in and tell them I'm his girlfriend." She looked over my shoulder. "We still have a land line, so I'll call you on that as soon as I find out anything, okay?"

I grabbed her hand. "Thank you." It wasn't what I wanted, but it would work.

She tightened her grip and leaned forward to press a soft kiss against the top of my head. "He'll be okay, Risia."

I squeezed my eyes tight, unable to muster the same level of confidence. "I hope so." I let her go. "Take your gun." I hated to say it, but I couldn't let her walk out into a potential shitstorm unprotected.

Her eyes met mine, and I watched old fears crowd close, only to be chained back by an indomitable will. She gave me a short nod, turned and headed to her room. She was back in a few minutes, her T-shirt untucked and hanging to mid-thigh. "Are you going to be okay?"

No. "Yes. Be careful."

"I will. I'll call as soon as I can."

I gave her a nod and watched her leave. The door shut behind her. Silence filled the empty kitchen, and a few minutes later I heard her car make its way down the drive. I stared blindly at my hands pressed against the table. *Useless. I was so fucking useless.*

Rage rose, fueled by fear. Why hadn't he answered his damn phone? How could I keep him safe if he avoided me? What if I was too late? Worse, what if sending Meli was a mistake? What if…and the thin barrier holding the cascading futures back broke, and dragged me under, screaming.

⸺⸺ •◆◆•• ⸺⸺

The ringing of the phone penetrated my awareness first. The shrill summons demanding an answer. I jerked awake, and then stumbled toward the phone as darkness pressed close. My palm slapped against a wall, hitting a light switch. I squinted against the sudden brightness, and continued to feel along the wall until I hit the phone. I yanked the receiver out of the cradle and leaned against the wall. "Hello?"

"Risia?" Meli sounded tired.

"Did you find him?" Panic tried to rise but didn't get far. My brain felt curiously numb. I rubbed at the stickiness under my nose. Drawing my fingers back, I took in the partially dried blood coating them. Psychic overload. "Meli?"

"He's going to be okay."

"Where are you?"

"St. Angel's. They wanted to keep him for observation. He hit his head pretty hard on the window. Hang on."

There were muffled sounds, then, "Duchess."

"Tag." I couldn't stop the ragged relief in my voice, and slid down the wall, holding the phone tight. "You're okay?"

"I've got a thick skull." Steady and sure, his voice carried a bit of humor.

I closed my eyes, and pressed my lips together, trying to keep my jagged breathing quiet.

"I'm okay."

"He shot you." It came out like an accusation.

"Probably planned to, but he didn't."

"Why?" And why did it matter? Tag was okay.

"I don't know. The crash stunned me, but didn't knock me out. Maybe there were too many witnesses? Maybe he injured himself? Regardless, I'm okay."

The gentleness in his voice snapped the leash holding back my tears. "I couldn't see…I couldn't…" I tried to explain but couldn't get the words out around the sobs.

"Shh, baby, I promise I'm fine. Meli's bringing me back. We'll be there in just under an hour. I just need to…" He paused.

I rubbed my free hand over my face, as I listened to the muffled sound of his voice as he spoke to someone else.

Then he was back. "Hey, you still there?"

"Yeah."

"You going to be okay until we get back?"

That careful note was back in his voice and I realized I needed to suck it up. Tag was fine. Not dead or bleeding out on the pavement. I drew in a steadying breath. "Yeah, I'll be fine. You two be careful on your way back."

"Roger that, Duchess." Then he hung up.

I cradled the phone to my chest and leaned my head against the wall. I didn't bother fighting the tears, just let them fall. Here, where I was alone, and no one could see, it was safe to be weak. Minutes ticked by. When the hot tracks finally cooled, then stopped, leaving me curiously numb, I pushed to my feet and hung up the phone.

I made my way to the kitchen sink, and splashed cool water on my face, hoping to erase the signs of my crying jag before they got back. Instead of being alone in my head, I needed to focus on something else.

I looked around, and caught sight of the clock. It was closing in on eight, which meant I'd been fighting my way out of the future for over six hours. That kind of fight required tremendous psychic energy, and no human brain was made to handle that much energy. Which explained my nosebleed. Psychic overloads caused nose and ear bleeds. I touched my ears, checking for traces of blood and found it.

Great.

Turning the faucet back on, I dampened a paper towel and wiped away the evidence. At least my eyes hadn't bled, a gruesome, but effective warning system. It did, however, explain why I felt so hollowed out. The future had come in, made me her bitch, and then left me curled into a mindless ball. *Damn her.*

I tossed the used towels in the trash, and then washed my hands. I turned to survey Meli's kitchen, determined to do something that didn't require much thought. I doubted either

Meli or Tag took time to eat, so I'd make something. Plan in place, I started making dinner.

I'd just pulled the garlic bread out of the oven next to where a pot of spaghetti and meatballs simmered, when head-lights flashed over the living room. I set the bread aside, wiped my hands, and braced. No way would Tag walk in and find me a hot mess.

"Risia?" Meli's voice called. "We're home."

"In the kitchen." I kept my back to the entryway as I pulled out plates. "I thought you two might want something to eat."

"Smells good." Tag's warm baritone curled around me.

I closed my eyes and gripped the counter so I wouldn't throw myself into his arms. That would be beyond stupid. "Hope you're up for spaghetti and meatballs."

"Thanks, sweetie, but I'm not that hungry."

I spun around at Meli's subdued response, and snapped, "Melisande you are going to sit down and eat." No way was she leaving me and Tag alone. Plus, the girl rarely took the time to take care of herself. She'd lost more weight since I saw her last.

She held up her hands in surrender. "Fine, I'll have a small plate. Geez, Risia."

"Geez yourself." I turned back to dish up her plate. That it gave me an excuse to avoid Tag was a bonus.

A warm hand settled against the small of my back. "You going to dish me up a plate, too?" Tag wasn't going to let me ignore him.

Not given a choice, I looked back over my shoulder, Meli's plate forgotten. There was a white bandage on his forehead. His normally wild hair defied logic and was even wilder. I couldn't resist and raised my free hand to gently trace the edge of his face.

His gaze sharpened, deepened.

I dropped my hand, turned back to the stove, and finished

filling Meli's plate. I handed it to him, forcing him to give me room. "Could you hand this to Meli, please?" Not giving him a chance to answer, I snagged the next plate and filled it. When he came back, I handed it him. "If you want more, you're welcome to it."

His lips twitched. "This is good." Then, before I turned away, he leaned in and kissed my forehead. "Thank you."

I stared at his back until he settled at the table. I raised my eyes to meet Meli's wink. Blushing, I turned back to the damn stove and dished up my own plate. Finally, I settled across from Tag, keeping Meli between us. For a few moments the only sounds were utensils against plates. Now that there was food in front of me, my stomach decided to pitch and roll.

Picking bread as the safest option, I tore it to pieces. "What happened, Tag?" I popped a piece in my mouth and finally looked up.

"I met up with Detective Ochoa at your place this morning."

"Does that mean Risia's a suspect?" Meli's brow was furrowed.

Tag went to shake his head, only to stop with a pained grimace. "No, they were checking on her because Lawrence Rawlings told the chief of police, he was worried about her."

Good thing I hadn't eaten anything, because right about then it would've all come back up. "Shit." Because, really, there wasn't any other response.

Tag leaned back in his chair, and studied me. "Oh, it gets better, Duchess."

I'm sure it did. I gritted my teeth and played with my spaghetti.

Tag continued, "Ochoa and I went to Rawlings's office."

My head snapped up. "Why?"

"Because he wanted to share with Ochoa that Trammel had

encrypted files on his computer. Files he shouldn't have access to."

"The same files as our drive." Which meant we were racing against a clock.

"Yep."

"We need Rabbit up here, like yesterday." Because whatever was on those files was the reason Tag's lifeless body kept haunting me.

"Delacourt mentioned they're closing in on their current case. Rabbit will be here as soon as he can."

"You need to tell Delacourt what happened today."

"Can't. My phone got trashed in the crash."

"You can use mine," Meli offered.

Tag gave her a gentle smile. "Appreciate it, but it's an unsecured line. I'd rather not put you at risk."

"Monday," I murmured, then blinked.

"What?" Tag looked at me.

"They'll be here Monday." When he continued to stare at me, I gave an awkward shrug. "Some things just come out of nowhere."

"Handy."

"Not really, annoying is a better word choice." If it was handy, I would've been able to keep Tag here this morning, instead of letting him waltz out to tango with death. My hand tightened on my fork as I stabbed viscously at the innocent noodles lying before me.

"Risia." The serious tone in his voice brought my eyes to his. "Stop it. No matter what, I was going in today. If he hadn't tried today, he would've come here to try."

"How do you know?"

"Because it's what I would've done."

And there is was. The dark world where Tag lived. You had two choices—hunter or prey. I just didn't want Tag to be prey.

Needing to get back on course, I asked, "The detective. Was he the one with you in the car?"

Tag nodded.

"Is he okay?"

"Dislocated shoulder, concussion, cuts, bruises, but breathing. They were keeping him overnight."

"How did Hand Tooled find you?" Suspicions wiggled their way in and refused to leave. "Did Rawlings call him in?"

Tag raised an eyebrow and crossed his arms across his chest. "Why do you think he's working with Rawlings?"

I set my fork down. "You said Rawlings was setting Curtis up to take the fall for stealing government secrets. Who's to say he isn't trying to finish what he started? What if he's behind this upcoming sale you told me about?"

At his skeptical look, I took him through my logic. "Delacourt wanted me to get dirt on Rawlings. I can tell you the man is brilliant in an evil-genius sort of way. Using people and their weaknesses is his standard operating procedure." Something flashed too fast to catch in his face, but I wasn't done. "Who's to say he didn't use Curtis to set him up? Get him in debt to the wrong people. Make it so he can't dump the information Rawlings lets him have."

Because there was no doubt in my mind, if Curtis had those files it was because Rawlings wanted him to have them. I held Tag's gaze with mine. "Then, when they come after Curtis to collect, and he can't pay, they kill him, leaving Rawlings with the perfect patsy in place. All that's left to do is sell off the information, and it all looks as if it's Curtis's fault."

Tag didn't look away, clearly thinking it over.

"That makes a twisted sort of sense," Meli agreed. She knew what was happening since I had shared the whole story with her. "Which means when Hand Tooled found you in Curtis's office, you threw a monkey wrench in their plans. But it doesn't explain why he went after the detective and Tag today."

Tag's mouth twisted and the cold, hardened warrior emerged. "Because neither one of us believed Rawlings's shit."

Homing in on his comment, I asked, "What do you mean?"

"Rawlings thought he snowed us, but he overstepped," he explained. "First, he went around Ochoa and kept Trammel's computers at the offices where his people could comb through them. Then, he offered his resources to the poor, budget-strapped police."

Meli grimaced. "Bet that didn't go over well with the detective."

"It didn't," Tag said. "But I'd say Ochoa's radar went off the charts when Rawlings's admitted to analyzing the computers in-house."

Meli paused with her fork halfway to her mouth. "He compromised their evidence." Tag shot her a considering look, and she blinked, then began to look uncomfortable under his regard.

"Or planted what they wanted found," I added, needing Tag's attention off Meli even as a new worry emerged. The sense that my life was being taken away, piece by carefully constructed piece, settled around me. "What if he planted something about me?"

Meli shook her head. "If he doesn't know the real reason you were there, why would he?"

Why? Because Rawlings wanted me. Not solely because of the contract, but the way someone collected shiny things. He wanted to own me.

"Because the dick has a hard on for Risia." Cutting and brutal, Tag laid it out. "Isn't that right, Duchess?"

I refused to flinch, although deep inside I cringed, even as I held his gaze. "Yes, he wants me."

"Risia?" Shock ran under Meli's question.

Without looking away from Tag, I reached out, and covered her hand with mine. "I'm safe, Meli."

"I don't think you are," Tag snapped.

"Really?" I threw back, uncaring of the fire I was unleashing. The whole damn day crashed around me. "I'm not the one out there poking at the monster just to get a damn rise out of him."

He leaned over the table. "I didn't have to poke very far. Especially since he was the one bringing up your name. Why is that, Risia? You said it yourself, he finds people's weaknesses to get what he wants. He wants you. What the hell does he have on you?"

Frustration and fear whipped through me, searing away every sense of self-preservation. I shoved back from the table, and shot to my feet. "For the last goddamn time, Tag, I am not the one selling out the team." I threw my hands up, the faint protest of my ribs a distant ache. "God, you make me crazy!"

Across the table, he mimicked me. "He's got something on you!"

His fury hit me like a shockwave. "No he doesn't!" The defensive lie shot out before I could stop it.

He slapped his hands on the table and leaned forward. "I shook hands with the bastard, Risia."

I could feel the blood rushing from my head and the room took a sickening spin. "What?" A small panicked voice screamed a warning.

"He thought of you." And going by the black look on Tag's face, whatever those thoughts were, they weren't good. "He thought of you, and he considered you his because he held the power. So, I'm only going to ask you one last time. What does the fucker have on you?"

Chapter Thirteen

"Tell him." Solid steel wrapped in gentle warning, Meli's voice cut through the strained silence. "You can't do this on your own, Risia."

Shocked, I turned to look at her. "No."

"Then I will." Her delicate looks hid a will of iron, but never had it been directed against me.

Unwarranted betrayal rose, closing brutal fingers around my throat. "Don't you dare, Melisande." *Please, don't.*

She flinched under the pained plea, but didn't look away as she ripped me open in front of Tag. "He threatened her son."

Everything in me stilled, like the quiet before the storm. "Damn you," I choked out, unable to move for fear of unleashing the fury swirling tighter and tighter inside me.

Her shoulders stiffened, but she continued burying me to Tag. "She didn't agree to anything."

"But she didn't disagree." Tag's harsh response brought Meli's attention to him.

I closed my eyes, trying to find my footing in a world gone fucking mad.

"She's buying time," Meli snapped. "Until she can ensure Rawlings can't touch him."

I couldn't stand here and listen while Meli continued to shatter our bonds of friendship, even as she unknowingly destroyed whatever fragile truce existed between Tag and I.

"Where's your son now?"

The calculation behind his question snapped the invisible chains holding me in place. No one, not Rawlings, not Delacourt, not Tag, not even me, would threaten the innocent world in which my child existed. The one I ripped my heart out to ensure he got twelve years ago.

I tucked away my hurt and froze it over with frigid fury. "If I wouldn't give that information to Rawlings, why do you think I'd share with you?"

Whatever emotion Tag felt was hidden behind the familiar mask of the PSY-IV operative I was familiar with. "Because if Rawlings knows you have a kid, he already knows where he is. You know that. If you're trying to keep him safe, the team can do a better job."

"And what will it cost, Thomas?" I sneered. "Because no one does shit for free." I narrowed my eyes, all of the ugly things haunting me spilling out in cutting accusations I threw at the unbending man in front of me. "Everyone's looking for an angle, right? It's how this world we crawl through works. I wanted my child protected. Delacourt wanted to keep her precious operations safe. She found someone who could serve as an early warning system. I found someone to bury my son so deep no one should be able to touch him. Our deal's been in place for ten years. Do you know what my price was?"

His jaw twitched, but he didn't say a word.

"Come on, I'm sure you'd love to know. Because everyone has a price, right?" I didn't give him a chance to answer. "All she has to do is ensure that when, in the next however many years before my mind breaks for that final fucking time, I get a nice, private, all-expense-paid room in an exclusive government-run sanitarium. One where no one will ever find me, or what remains of me, because broken tools can still cause damage."

Ignoring the paling undertones of skin, I continued, "And she is to make sure the child I was forced to give up twelve years ago never fucking finds out his biological mother was insane. She promised he and his family would never, ever be a target of anyone I screwed over. The problem is, as you so aptly stated, everyone has a price and right now someone is selling out the team."

Even thought I knew I should stop talking, I couldn't. I was done with his judgement, done with his contempt, I was just done. He wanted my secrets, he could choke on them. "Rawlings knows I have a child, a child he shouldn't know about. You may want to know who's selling out the team, but I need to make sure my child isn't collateral damage. Which means I need Rabbit to get his ass up here, break the encryption, and figure out how to bury Rawlings so deep he'll never see the light of day. It's the only option I have to keep the one good thing I've ever done safe from the shit that is my life."

"Risia." Next to me, Meli reached out to touch me.

Flinching, I jerked back. "Don't. You've done enough." My voice was hollow and empty.

"Tag's not the enemy." Try as she might, Meli couldn't hide the pain of my rejection. "Neither am I."

I didn't have an answer for her, because everything was tangled up. Worry, fear, anger, and strangely, a sense of loss snaking so deep the pain of it created cracks in things buried long ago.

"Did Rawlings specifically threaten your son?" Tag's unexpected question made no sense.

"What?"

"Answer the question." Something fierce burned in those

hazel eyes and a strange intensity lay under his words. "Tell me what happened before you went to Trammel's office."

I wrapped my arms around my waist, and forced the emotional upheaval back so I could bring back every detail from that night.

Walking into my condo, kicking off the Jimmy Choos, and tossing my keys and purse on the counter. Flipping on a light.

"Good evening, Ms. Lacoste." Suave, cultured tones formed ice in my veins.

Trying to figure out where I'd slipped up, was my cover compromised? Years of training kicked in, and I feigned being startled as I turned to find Rawlings and his bodyguard in my living room. "Mr. Rawlings, I was unaware we had a meeting scheduled."

"I apologize for showing up unannounced. You left the offices before I could catch you. Since I was in the area, I thought I'd just swing by and wait for you." Cunning intelligence studied me from behind wire-frame glasses. "Drink?"

Playing for time, for an opening, I kept it together. "Booker Noe, neat."

A creepy, knowing smile as he told his sidekick to make it two.

Taking a seat on the sofa as he watched, I deliberately crossed my legs, forcing the edge of my skirt to mid-thigh, hoping to keep him distracted enough not to notice my nerves. His eyes darkened with male appreciation. "Why are you here, Mr. Rawlings?"

The feel of his gaze shifting up my body left a nasty trail of distaste behind. "You strike me as a very intelligent young woman, Risia." A shark-like smile. "One who understands the value of connections."

The bodyguard handed me a glass filled with smoky amber and ice. I took it, and instead of gulping it down, managed a fortifying sip. "I understand you very much want to get in bed with the Department of Defense. Whether that turns out to be a flirtation or a long-lasting commitment is entirely up to my findings on your project."

"I've never been one for passing pleasures, and certain commitments can be very beneficial." Unvoiced avarice lightened his eyes confirming it wasn't just the contract with the DOD he wanted. "After the last few weeks, what's your opinion on Aether?"

"The company or the man behind it?" It was dangerous to play to his ego, but I needed to uncover his agenda. Setting my glass of bourbon on the small table beside the couch, I used the small avoidance to let him think he was getting to me.

"Touché." The purr of satisfaction under his response confirmed I'd asked the right question. "One should be the reflection of the other."

"You're a devil with the details, something that sets you and your company apart from others. The Boyau project outpaced expectations and its potential could be far reaching. You've uncovered unrealized issues and offered solutions."

His smile changed, gaining a superior edge. "Just my way of showing your employers how beneficial a relationship with me would be."

Beneficial wasn't what I was calling it. "Perhaps, but it does speak to a uniquely far-seeing perspective the agencies under the DOD would find strategically optimal."

"Then should I advise my board of a pending contract with DOD?"

Contempt rose at his unabashed arrogance, but I hid it with a delicate twist of my lips. "So sure of yourself?"

"Sure of you."

Those three words set my pulse into a hard rhythm.

He leaned forward and set his half-finished glass on the low-slung table in front of him. "It's all in the details, Risia." He remained in that position, his arms resting on his knees, his gaze pinning me in place. "Did you think I wouldn't have you investigated before I allowed you inside Aether's walls? The DOD isn't the only corporation with a paranoia fix."

With no safe answer to his unspoken threat, I stayed silent, while fear began to seep through my composure.

"Your tastes are quite elegant." The weight of his perusal was almost physical as he skimmed over my designer blouse, trim skirt, and tasteful pieces of jewelry.

It left me cold and slightly nauseous.

"Quite expensive."

It was a carefully laid trap, but I couldn't see a way out of it. "What do you want?"

"You think I want to bribe you to approve my contract."

"Don't you?"

"Oh, I'll get the contract." Lust deepened his voice and chilled my blood, "and you."

Furious at his self-assurance, I unsheathed my claws. "You can't afford me."

"Perhaps not, but I'm not offering you money." He sat back, that damn smile growing bigger and more confident as my creeping fear grew. "How would you like to find your son, Risia?"

Years of training crumpled under swelling panic. "Excuse me?"

"He said that?" Tag's voice brought me out of the memory and back into Meli's dining room. At some point Tag had rounded the table and come to stand by me.

I stumbled back, but he grabbed my arms, holding me in place.

"Are you sure he said that?"

Still tangled in the remnants of my confrontation with Rawlings, I couldn't follow what he was asking. "Said what?"

"'How would you like to find your son?'" he repeated.

I nodded.

"He's playing you, Risia."

I jerked against Tag's hold, but he wouldn't let go.

Instead he gave me a short shake. "Listen to me. The colonel is many things, calculating, methodical, and ruthless, but she's not a liar. If she buried your son, he's buried."

"Then how did Rawlings find out about him?"

"Public records," Meli offered. I looked over Tag's shoulder to see her watching us, her face pale but resolute. "He said he had you investigated. A good investigator would uncover public records showing a live birth, of a boy."

"But that's all they'd find," Tag added. "Knowing Delacourt, the trail ended there."

"You don't know that." My voice shook as I tried not to let the desperate hope grow.

"Yes, I can," he said. "He asked how'd you like to find your son, as if you didn't know where he was. But you do, don't you?"

I nodded.

"You said it yourself. He's brilliant in an evil genius sort of way. He finds a weakness and exploits it. It wouldn't take much for him to put the pieces together and form the picture of a woman who'd search for the baby she gave up as a teenager now that she had the money and the lifestyle to support him." His hazel-eyed gaze roamed over my face. "Only you're not looking for him, you're trying to protect him. So his offer became a threat, and your fear fueled it."

Tag's reasoning sank in and my knees folded. Only his grip on my arms kept me from falling at his feet. Sickening knowledge slammed through me, and my stomach churned in protest. "If I had gone after him, I would've led Rawlings to him." And I would've. Because once I handed over the flash drive, my next move was to ensure my child was okay. "Oh my God. How could I be so stupid?"

"You've been running on fear and adrenaline for two days. When have you had a chance to actually stop and think?"

His simplistic explanation hit with the clarity of a wrecking ball. Fury, clean and bright rose in a crushing wave, burning through the fears haunting every move since Rawlings invaded my home. "That son of a bitch!" I was going to take his arrogant, smug, lying ass out if it was the last thing I did.

"You're going to have to wait in line."

Only then did I realize Tag was reading every emotion flying through me. "Not fair."

"I never claimed to fight fair." A real smile tipped his lips. "Besides this seems to be the only way I can figure you out."

"What happens now?" Meli broke in.

I turned and caught her carefully blank mask. Pulling free from Tag's hold, I went and stopped in front of her. The flinching around her eyes hurt my heart, even worse was knowing it was my words, my actions that caused it. But I didn't know where to start.

"I'm not sorry," she said in a soft voice. "I couldn't stand by and watch."

Because she knew me and was one of the few who could stop me. "Wouldn't expect you to, Meli. Friends don't stand by, ever."

Tears welled, and some of the stiffness drained from her shoulders. I wrapped my arms around her and held on, wondering what I had ever done to deserve a friend like her. "I'm not sorry," she murmured.

Knowing what she risked to keep me safe, I held on tighter, feeling the hot fall of tears against my shoulder. "I'm not walking away." I repeated a promise I made over a year ago when our friendship really began. "I'll always be right here."

"Me too," she whispered. A shaking breath and then she pulled back, and drew herself together. "What do we do now?"

"*We* don't do anything," Tag cut into our little bonding session. "Meli, as much as I appreciate you coming to get me, I don't want you involved in this. We're going to wait until Rabbit gets here."

The bruising around his bandage seemed darker than before. Now that I was paying attention, I could see lines of strain and exhaustion around his mouth. Time to get someone off his feet. I gave Meli one last hug. "Lock up behind us. Time for me to take our super hero and tuck him into bed."

A wicked light appeared in her green eyes.

"Don't go there," I hissed under my breath knowing exactly what she was about to say.

She didn't, instead she giggled while I mock-glared at her.

Huffing out an aggravated breath, I went back to Tag. "Let's go."

"Super hero?" His gaze danced, taking away some of the strain on his face.

Rolling my eyes, I led him to the door and called over my shoulder, "Lock up, Meli. See you in the morning."

Chapter Fourteen

The companionable silence lasted until we reached our shared villa. Once the door was closed, Tag went to the bed and collapsed with a groan. "My damn head hurts."

"Did they give you anything stronger than aspirin?" I hadn't spotted a prescription bag, but then again, I hadn't been paying much attention.

"No, just the normal advice to get up every couple of hours."

Lovely. A yawn threatened to dislocate my jaw, while lead replaced my bones and added to the heavy weight of exhaustion. I was in for a long night. Not that I minded. Much. "Okay, then let's get you settled because if you pass out, I won't be able to move you."

He pushed upright, grabbed the edge of his shirt, and lifted, revealing a well-defined chest, marred by the lightest line of hair arrowing where other more intriguing body parts lay. I tried not to stare as he stripped. My head was still a mess, even if my body was focused on the temptation in front of me.

A muffled curse snapped me out of my hormone-induced

daze. He stopped with his arms up, shirt around his head, and I hurried to help maneuver the cloth around his bandage. I took his shirt and folded it, setting it on the dresser, while the faint sounds of his belt coming undone filled the room. With my back to him, heat hit my face, and need settled low as tantalizing images played through my head.

"We need to talk."

Wasn't that supposed to be my line? Sighing at the serious tone of Tag's voice, I ushered my illicit imagination into the corner. Might as well get it over with. At least he waited until we were alone. I turned and leaned against the dresser, keeping space between us. "Where do you want to start?"

He propped himself against the headboard, the pillows piled behind him. The top button on his slacks was undone, his belt carelessly tossed on the floor.

I tucked my hands behind me so I wouldn't do something stupid, like touch. Instead, I held his gaze and waited. It didn't take long.

"A son?"

I studied him, looking for signs of condemnation or judgment, but found none. Finally, I gave a small nod.

"When?"

Behind me, I gripped the edge of the low dresser. "Sixteen."

"The father?"

"As soon as he found out a baby was on the way, he was out of the picture."

"Shitty move."

I shrugged. "Not his fault. I was a mess and looking for solutions in the wrong place. Mistook youthful hormones for love. It happens."

His gaze sharpened. "Still a shitty move."

Looking back through the lens of experience, I agreed, but sixteen did not an adult make.

"Your parents pressure you to give him up?"

Memories crawled in, an old ache surfacing. I straightened, rubbed my arms, then made my way to the overstuffed chair in the corner, positioned to face the bed. I kicked off my shoes and curled into it. "No, my decision. It was just my mother and me. We had a hard enough time keeping food on the table for the two of us, much less trying to take care of a newborn." No sense in sharing the arguments and threats that replaced my relationship with my mom. That story was long gone and done.

"Hell of a decision for a child to make."

I held his gaze. "The minute that test came back positive, it wasn't about me." It couldn't be because the minute I realized I harbored a sweet, innocent new life, the future made sure I saw what was in store. Forget the crap my mom threw at me, Fate's film reel topped it all by a damn mile. Destroying every fragile hope and dream I held, until the only option left was letting my child go.

"What happened, Risia?" Tag's question meant something must have shown on my face.

Shit, I must be more tired than I thought. "It took me three months to make the decision." Three months of trying to desperately hold on to the only beautiful thing I knew.

When I fell silent, he pushed. "Why?"

I dropped my gaze and plucked at my jeans. "I got to see what would happen to him if I kept him." And God, it had hurt and ripped pieces from my soul because my decision would create such havoc and chaos for him. I was scared to sleep but determined to protect what was mine. Finally, exhausted, scared out of my mind, and hanging on by a thread, I let my stupid dreams go and did what was necessary to keep my child safe. Without me. It broke something in me. "He deserved happiness and joy. The only way I could guarantee that was to give him up."

"And the family he's with now?" The question was gentle, soft. "How did you find them?"

"That wasn't me, that was Delacourt." I laid my head back against the chair, closing my eyes. Against the memories, not tears, those had been shed long ago. "I had a vision about a school shooting and made the mistake of calling it in to the police."

"They thought you were involved."

Hearing the thin cynicism behind his words made my lips twitch. "Normal reaction, but they couldn't prove it. Guess Delacourt had been monitoring unusual events, because a couple of weeks later, there was a knock at my door. She made me an offer, and I took it. Sixteen and pregnant, my options were rather limited."

"Sounds as if you did the best you could."

I'd done the only thing I could. Couldn't say I regretted it exactly, but as I told Tag, my options were limited. My mother hadn't even batted an eyelash when I told her I was leaving. Even now, I swore she'd been relieved. Having a pregnant daughter who saw horrific things didn't make for a calm home life. Especially since she feared my ability. I was about six when I realized the reason she wouldn't touch me was because I'd tell her what I saw. Things no child should see.

"Come here, Duchess."

Lifting my head, I watched him from under my lashes, wondering if I could resist what being that close would tempt. "Nope, think it's safer if I stay here." I patted the chair, enjoying the small smile my response invoked.

"If I promise to behave, will you come here?"

Problem was, I didn't want him to behave. Still, today had been a roller coaster ride. Part of me would love to just throw my hands up and enjoy the ride. Unfortunately, a bigger part knew better. That way lay disaster of epic proportions.

"I promise to be good," he cajoled.

Good lord he was dangerous when he teased. Unable to resist, I heaved a put-upon sigh and made my way to the bed. Careful not to jostle the bed, I climbed up. He raised his arm and I slipped under it to rest my head against his chest, palm against his skin. It was a position I discovered I liked last night. It felt comfortable. Safe. An illusion, but tonight I needed it.

I listened to his heart beat steadily under my ear. Little by little the knots in my shoulders began to unravel and the sickening pitch of my stomach calmed. He was here. Warm. Alive. A little banged up, but here. Not dead. My heart clenched, and the fragile hold on my emotions broke. Tears leaked, falling silently to his chest. He didn't say anything, simply tightened his hold. Silent minutes passed before the tears stopped.

His hand stroked my hair, and I traced absent lines over his chest, basking in this moment out of time. Emotionally drained, I let my thoughts drift. They fluttered like moths, alighting for a moment on the past, then drifted to the future.

Home wasn't something I understood. I tried to recreate it with my condo. But my carefully collected things were gone. Yet, lying here surrounded by the solid strength of Tag, I wondered if this quiet well of comfort was what I'd been searching for. Was this what people meant when they said they found home with someone? Safe, protected, as if what existed outside the door couldn't touch me so long as I was here. A long-closed door creaked opened, and a fragile dream peeked out. Before it could fully form, I stepped back, too scared to watch it come to life.

"Will you really go insane?" The careful question landed in the room like a bomb and blew that emotional door shut with a resounding slam.

I closed my eyes for a moment, while a vise squeezed hard on my heart. "Probably." My voice was equally soft.

"How do you know?"

Because every time a vision hit, I could feel myself splintering, and when I put the pieces back together the cracks never closed. But he didn't need to know that. Instead I gave him what I could. "There aren't many seers out there. I asked Delacourt to look when I joined. I had questions and no one to ask. She could only find two. One was in his late thirties, the other her early forties. Both were locked up in psychiatric wards, heavily sedated."

I remembered the wild shadows rippling behind their eyes. The younger one managed to grab my hand in a bloodless grip, begging me to make it stop. That scream, hidden in a whisper, sent me stumbling from the room to be violently sick. Three words cemented the knowledge that even caught in the drug-induced haze a seer couldn't escape the visions. It was a hellish foreshadowing of what waited for me.

"Doesn't mean it's your future." He paused, his chest stilling under me. "Unless you've seen that."

"Told you, I don't see my future."

The breath he held escaped. "Then why are you certain?"

I raised my head and rested my chin on his chest, tracing small circles on the expanse of exposed skin. "Because every psychic ability comes with drawbacks. Nobody is meant to see the future, not even me. It hurts to see every possibility."

He coiled one of my curls around his finger, bringing my gaze to his. "You're stronger than anyone I know." The depth of conviction in his voice didn't allow for an argument. "I don't think you'll end up in a straitjacket any time soon."

From your lips to God's ear, the small prayer rose before I could stop it. I ducked my head and resettled my cheek against his chest, before he caught how deep his words hit. "Go to sleep. I'll wake you up in a couple of hours."

He reached over and clicked the light on the nightstand off. Darkness fell over the room. I lifted enough so he could lie down, then resumed my previous position. It took awhile, but he finally fell asleep. The arm around my shoulders loosened, and his breathing deepened.

Only then did I dare to press a soft kiss to his chest and whisper, "I wish you were right, Tag."

Chapter Fifteen

Warmth trailed over my spine, pushing back the weight of sleep. I spent most of the night waking Tag up every couple of hours. After the second time I woke him, I removed my jeans and bra. They weren't comfortable for sleeping, but the oversized T-shirt worked just fine for a sleep shirt. Finally, around three, I felt confident enough to let him sleep without interruption. I curled up next to him, and dropped off into a surprisingly dreamless sleep.

The warmth that woke me traveled down my side, then slid over the bare skin of my thigh. Now that same shirt was inching up. A warm hand glided over my hip, teasing and light. Anticipation heated my blood, while an ache bloomed. I sucked in a breath as the warmth slipped to my waist, only to stop.

"Tag?" His name came out on a soft exhale. Lips nuzzled my neck, just behind my ear, sending a trail of goose bumps over my skin. My heart picked up speed and the ache intensified.

"Morning, Duchess." Spoken in a husky voice, his pet name sounded like an endearment, creeping past my broken walls.

The hand at my hip glided over to my stomach, his fingers spreading, touching as much skin as possible.

Every muscle melted, curving closer, wanting more. I lifted my lids to a darkness that proved morning was still a way off. "Not morning," I mumbled. Unable to resist, I covered his hand with mine, unsure if I wanted to stop him or encourage him.

"Mmmm, technically it is." His tongue traced a delicate path down my neck.

I sucked in a breath, arching for more. Desire rose, hot and bright, blurring the edges of rational thought. "Okay." Closing my eyes, I rode the need, letting it take over. My breath came in short pants.

The weight behind me shifted slightly and I turned to follow, only to find my mouth taken with heated ferocity. My hand rose, careful of his bandage, and sank into all that wild hair as I opened wide, letting him take what he wanted. Still, I took advantage of his offering, exploring, tasting.

Our tongues glided and teased with wicked licks and gentle nips. Each sip driving the craving for his taste deeper. His hands began moving with utter gentleness over my ribs, careful of the sore spots, but relentlessly dragging the T-shirt up and off.

I broke our kiss long enough to get rid of the shirt, then dove right back in, pushing him to his back so I could take my time discovering him. He let me. His hands doing their own exploring as I ran my palms over his chest, tracing the map of muscles that so fascinated me, my tongue committing their lines to memory as they flexed under my touch. Taking time to taste here and there. Seeing his reaction, hell, feeling his reaction, knowing I wasn't the only one affected, gave me a sense of power in this dance.

I drifted back up, dropping a soft kiss at the hollow of his throat. When his palms cupped my breasts with a careful, but firm touch, it woke an ache between my legs. He brushed his thumbs across my nipples, setting nerve endings on fire, deepening my want, and eliciting a groan. I lifted my head, gasping for much needed air.

He took advantage and reared up to kiss his way down my neck. The double assault seared my mind. I cradled his head, reveling in his touch and the mindless desire it created. His hands lifted my aching flesh, guiding me until his lips wrapped around one tight nipple, drawing it in.

I whimpered as the sensation spiraled. God, it felt so good, better than good as his tongue played with the sensitive skin. I lost myself in the heat, letting the need arise. My hand drifted down, until my fingers could curl into his shoulders.

He drew my breast deeper into his mouth, his tongue laving fiery lashes, and my spine bowed, giving him more access. His wicked fingers played with one nipple, while his teeth raked fine lines of exquisite pain over the other, stoking the fire higher, hotter. Then he switched, his mouth tormenting one while his fingers played with the other.

The tugs of his fingers and mouth echoed between my legs, my need growing, cresting. "Tag, oh God!"

It had been so long since anyone had touched me like this. So long since I wanted anyone to touch me. The fact that it was Tag, the man I fantasized about for months made it that much more surreal. Not wanting to wake up and find it all some cruel dream, I closed my eyes and surrendered.

He rolled me to my back, his mouth abandoning his play. "Look at me."

It took effort, but I managed to lift my lids and meet his burning gaze, watching the need and want wage the same battle being fought under my skin. His face darkened with male satisfaction. "So fuckin' beautiful."

He held my gaze and kissed his way down my stomach, inching downward, his hands gliding ahead of his mouth. The combined sensations twisted me higher. His fingers found the lace of my panties and traced the edge over my hip and down along the sensitive skin. A finger dipped under the lace in a sensual tease.

My body arched, and I couldn't hold back the small sob of need. "Please."

Mesmerized by the sight of him between my legs where I wanted him so badly, staring at me, etched itself in mind in brilliant detail. Reaching out with shaking hands, I sank my fingers into his hair and tugged. He lifted his head and shifted up until I could cradle his face and trace his lips with my thumb. He caught the pad with his teeth and drew it into the hot cavern of his mouth.

My lips parted as I fought for air, need rising harsh and fast. A heated swipe, then he let me go and turned his head to press a kiss against my palm. "Let me in."

Even sinking under the wave of desire, I knew he meant more than what would happen between us in this bed. But fear rose. "It's just sex," I gasped. It had to be. Because if I let him in, he could damage me.

Too late. God, I hated that voice, especially when it was right.

"Liar," he growled and nipped the palm he just kissed.

"Damn you," I whispered, knowing what was rising between us was more than anything I'd felt before. Hotter, deeper, needier. This man, full of shadows and light, watching me so carefully, tempted me.

"Please, Risia." Determination and desire burned in those hazel eyes, as he watched me.

Skin to skin, there was no way to hide the emotions twisting through me. "Why?" It had to be asked.

"You keep the demons back." He slid lower, never breaking eye contact and pressed a kiss against the inside of one thigh. "This," he dragged his hands over my hips, down the outside of my thighs and then up the inside, "doesn't scare you."

He meant his touch. I shook my head, trying to clear the sensual haze, and took another step toward the inevitable.

"God, Duchess. Take a chance on me." The harsh, almost broken groan before he pressed another soft kiss against my skin, curled around my heart. "I need you."

As if his words were the trigger, I tumbled forward. Dragging in a shaky breath, I gave a small nod. I didn't want to miss this. Didn't want to miss him. The devastating sense of loss following yesterday's vision was a stark reminder why I didn't want to chance missing out. Maybe we could figure our way to more, maybe not, but life was brutally short.

I let him go, and rested my fisted hands on the bed next to me, giving up and giving in. His smile was fierce, desire adding a wicked edge to his mouth. Still holding my gaze, he laid his mouth on me over the silk of my panties. The dance of his tongue had me falling back, my hips rising for more. Desire, need, and want twined into an inescapable storm. His mouth continued its wicked assault.

My eyes fluttered closed as he brought me higher and higher, until all I could do was beg. "Please, Tag."

He stopped.

My eyes flew open, my hands reaching out to tangle in his hair in protest. "Don't!"

His husky chuckled filled the air as he rose above me, forcing my hands to let go. His hands hooked under the lace and drew them down my legs. He took his time, drawing it out. Tossing them aside, he wrapped his fingers around one ankle and lifted my leg. "God, I love your legs."

He bent his head and laid his mouth against my overheated skin, following the path of his hands. He moved down the inside of my thigh, hands and lips creating devastation and havoc, until my muscles quivered. His tongue traced a path only he knew. His fingers followed, leaving fire behind. Gently he placed my foot on the bed, bent my knee, and left me open.

My fingers curled into the sheets under me as I fought not to shield myself from him.

As if sensing my struggle, he lifted his head and his hands began long, gentle stokes, as if trying to calm me. "So fucking beautiful like this, Risia."

The depth of truth behind those uttered words chased away my rising insecurities. The tension that started to rise drifted away. I offered him a smile. "Do I get to play too?"

He grinned and sat up on his knees. With a dramatic flourish, he held his arms open wide. "See something you want?"

Enjoying the sense of fun, I scrambled up and crawled to him, relishing the way his eyes darkened. Taking my time, I stayed on all fours and pressed my first kiss just above his belly button. When his erection visibly jerked against his zipper, just inches away from my lips, I gave a low laugh. Wanting to tease, to torment, I continued my slow path upward until I caught his mouth with mine, savoring my exploration until both of us were struggling to breathe.

He widened his knees, letting me settle between them so mere inches separated us.

My breasts brushed against his chest, adding another teasing layer of touch. Using my nails, I drew them gently over his chest until they hit the waistband of his pants. "You're overdressed."

Sliding him a look from under my lashes, I dipped a finger under the loosened waistband until I found what lay underneath. Tracing the silken tip, I spread the heated dampness. This time it was his turn to clench his fists, his lashes coming down into a slumberous half-mast.

Slowly I removed my finger, brought it to my mouth, and licked it clean while he watched. His low groan made me smile. Then, leaning forward, I traced his lips with my tongue before slipping inside to taste and tease. When his hands curled over my hips, I drew back, laying small kisses along his jaw and down his neck. Something mischievous rose, and I sucked hard against the tender skin, leaving a lasting impression.

His breathing deepened, and his fingers dug in for a moment.

Feminine power was a heady aphrodisiac. More small kisses retraced my path until I could tease the edge of his ear with my tongue. Pressed against him, his chest vibrated with another near-silent groan and the sensation rippled through me.

"Strip," I whispered, then drew back to sit on my heels and watch.

He rolled off the bed until he was standing at the edge. No strip tease for me. He wasn't wasting time. Instead he pushed his pants and underwear down in one economical move.

I leaned forward and indulged in the view. *Nice.*

He bent down, fumbled with his pants, then straightened, a small square package in his hand. Only then did he come to stand next to the bed.

I rose until I was kneeling in front of him, my head almost level with his. Impatient, I took his lips as I wrapped my hand around the hot, solid length of him. My fingers played and teased as my tongue delved deep.

He got the condom out and together we rolled it over his length. Then he wrapped a hand in my curls, holding my head still as he ravaged my mouth. Unable to let him go, I kept stroking him; the feel of him in my hand and in my mouth stoked the fire into inferno territory.

It wasn't long before he had me under him, his hand wreaking havoc, his mouth setting me ablaze. Limbs tangled and the need to feel him deep inside had me begging, "Now, Tag! Please!"

He wrapped my hair in his hand, the slight pain only making the ache deeper. His lips moved down my neck. His other hand slipped to the base of my spine, lifting me and then he was there, filling me, inch by careful inch.

My nails dug into his shoulders. He slid deeper, then pulled back. "No!" I curled closer, my hand slipping to his ass, trying to take over.

His deep chuckle fell over me. "Like this, Duchess?" Desire deepened his voice into a husky growl. He slid forward a little more.

"Tease," I hissed, trying to move as he held me still.

"Isn't that my line?" He drew back.

"Tag." Feeling hollow and empty, I whimpered. "Please!"

"Always, Duchess." He surged forward, and a keening wail escaped as he took me over. His hips began to move, creating a wild ride.

Lost in a haze of cresting hunger, I held tight, thrilling to every surge and withdrawal. Need and want morphed into something more, sinking deep into the hollow spaces in my heart. Then his hands were there, adding to the sweet torment. A beautiful, bright wave rose, taking me higher than I'd ever been.

"Come with me, Risia," he whispered against my lips.

Unable to do anything but obey, I did.

Chapter Sixteen

I was hiding in the damn shower. Stupid, maybe, but necessary considering my heart wanted to go back out there and spend some quality nookie time with the man who just rocked my world. The lame expression made me wince, but dammit, it fit.

The only thing holding me up was the tiled wall. Heated water rained down my spine as I buried my head against my arm, trying to figure out what I'd just done. Water swirled around my feet, and I curled my toes remembering the feel of Tag's hand wrapped around my ankle. Which led to reliving the feel of his lips against my skin. The sated embers flickered and reignited as my body began to wake up.

"Stop it," I hissed, even as I fought a losing battle.

With a groan, I turned to face the spray, water sluicing over my face and making its way through my dense curls. If I could wash away my need, this would be so much easier. It would also mean this was nothing but the scratching of an itch.

Unfortunately, Tag wasn't an itch. He was a soul-deep scar. One I'd carry beyond my last breath. Because, fool that I was, I was falling for him. Easy thing to admit in the privacy of my head. Sharing that tidbit with him? Not so much.

Not that you haven't already.

Stupid voice wasn't only back, but it was distressingly right. No way he missed how deep he managed to sneak in while running those capable, scary hands all over my body. Hiding your emotional vulnerability from a touch empath became an impossibility when you were sharing naked time.

And, of course, realizing that freaked me out.

Grabbing the little bar of gardenia-scented soap, I put it to use so I wouldn't tear out my own hair. Maybe, if I could get a peek inside his head, I wouldn't feel so exposed. A chance to reassure myself what was happening here was shared.

You could ask.

Right, because Tag wasn't closed up tighter than a steel drum.

He'll let you in.

You don't know that.

Won't know until you try.

Say he does let me in, what if I can't handle his demons?

You've survived worse.

But his might take us both down. Admitting that sent cold dread deep, chasing away the warmth of the shower.

So could yours.

Swallowing hard, I shoved damning tears back. Damn, why couldn't I ever win an argument with myself?

Focused on my internal counseling session, I didn't realize Tag was in the bathroom until he pulled back the shower curtain in all his nude glory. "You okay in there, Duchess?"

Those sleepy embers perked right up and made themselves known, but all I could do was grip my soap tighter and nod.

His hazel eyes narrowed. "You're doing the woman thing, aren't you?" He pulled the curtain back further and stepped over the edge of the tub.

"Woman thing?" It came out a squeak as I shuffled back, giving him room.

"Over analyzing things," he explained, even as he reached out and curled an arm around my waist, drawing me close.

I dropped the soap, and my hands grabbing his shoulders for balance. "Thinking, not over analyzing."

"Po-tae-toe, Po-tot-to." He dipped his head to take my mouth in a gentle kiss, backing me up until water fell over both of us.

My spine hit the wall, a hard contrast to the warm muscled male chest deliciously crushing my breasts. Desire lit along my veins, burning through my tumbling thoughts. Letting go of his shoulders, I tunneled my fingers through his hair, holding him close. Pressed together I could feel him hot and hard against my lower stomach. Not breaking our tangle of tongues, I rose on tiptoe trying to get him in the right spot.

His dark chuckle joined the steam curling around us, but he dipped his knees and we both groaned as he found his place. Rolling my hips, I danced with him, savoring the enticing glide of him against me. His lips left mine and made their way down my neck. I gasped, trying to get something cooler than burning air in my lungs.

At the small sound, he lifted his head, desire igniting the gold in his eyes. "We're not doing this in here."

My fingers curled against his scalp, and I pressed closer. "Looks like we are."

Laughter and something gentle lit his face, as he traced a finger along my jaw. "You like playing with danger, baby?"

My heart caught at the telling gesture. Dropping my hands back to his shoulder, I caught his finger in a light nip, before whispering, "I like playing with you."

He rubbed his finger over my lips, his laughter slowly fading. "I like playing with you too, Risia."

My insecurities escaped. "For how long?"

A strange mix of startled gentleness rode over something darker, deeper. "However long you'll let me."

My pulse sped, and I tightened my grip as everything seemed to shift under me. "I don't bore easily." I skated closer to the edge. "If ever."

There was no mistaking the heart-stopping mix of possession and satisfaction my answer sparked. "Works for me." He leaned to the side and flicked off the shower before wrapping one arm under my ass and the other behind my shoulders. "Lift those sexy legs, Duchess."

Not given much choice, I did, locking my ankles in the small of his back.

He turned, got us both out of the tub, and took me back to bed.

The sun was well and truly up as we lay in a tumble of sheets and skin. With my T-shirt back in place, my back against the headboard, and Tag's head in my lap as he curled into me, I was currently indulging in what was fast becoming my new favorite pastime, playing with his hair. "So, what's our next step?"

"I need to pick up my rental car." He uncurled and settled next to me on his back. "We should probably stop by and see Detective Ochoa."

"You think that's wise?"

He folded his hands on his stomach. "Necessary. We have enough people on our ass, let's try removing Las Vegas's PD, shall we?"

"Think my showing up might look a little suspicious?"

He grinned at my sarcastic tone. "Nah, I told him chances were high you were busy answering to your superiors. Now that you're done, you're back and willing to help in any way."

"Uh-huh." I worried my lower lip with my teeth. Considering the sensitive nature of Rawlings's contract, it might work. "And when they realize my prints are all over Curtis's office?"

He managed a shrug even as he remained in a prone position. "You're known for spending time in his office going over contracts. No surprise there."

Since he had an answer for everything, I blew out a small breath. "Fine, we'll go see the detective, but," I stared down at him. "I need to swing by my condo."

His shoulders tensed. "No."

I plucked at the T-shirt. "Tag, I need clothes."

"We'll hit a store, get you new stuff."

"That's ridiculous. I need my things."

"You place is trashed."

The sense of loss hit unexpectedly, and my chest ached. "There has to be something to salvage." Even I couldn't miss the plea in my voice.

Tag shifted until he could brace an arm beside my hip and sit up facing me, one leg braced on the floor, the sheet tangled at his waist. His free hand rose and cupped my face as he studied me. "I'll go in and see if I can't get some stuff for you."

Lifting my chin, I met him gaze for gaze. "I'm going with you."

His hand dropped to my bare thigh and he frowned. "Why are you being so stubborn about this? You have to know how dangerous it is for you to go back. It's probably being watched."

Hard to argue with that, especially since I agreed with him, but, "I want to see how bad it is."

"Why?" he pushed.

Because my life was in those four walls. A life I'd built piece by precious piece. Seeing it trashed would be hard as hell, but if I could find just a couple of things still intact, it would mean I hadn't lost everything. Instead of explaining all that, I said, "I have to."

Tense quiet fell between us as I held his searching gaze. Finally, he dropped his chin. "Fine, but we go in when I say."

I leaned forward and gave him a soft kiss. "Thank you."

"Don't thank me yet. Wait until we get out of there without being shot at."

His grumpy tone made my lips twitch. "A whole day without being shot at, chased, or crashed into. What are the odds?"

"Since we're three for three, I'd say we're due a break."

I blinked. "Has it only been three days?"

He resettled next to me, shifting until he could lie alongside me. He propped his head on one arm and tugged my hand back to his hair in a silent command. "Yeah, time flies when you're being hunted."

His sarcastic quip sent a rush of unwelcome goose bumps over my skin, while something faint and illusive brushed against my mind. Giving the hair curled around my fingers a tug, I frowned. "Don't joke."

He pulled my hand down, pressed a kiss against the palm, then trapped it against his bare chest. "I'm not, Duchess. Right now, the rest of the team is in Phoenix trying to trap one hunter. Delacourt's worried the info on your drive will paint even bigger targets on our backs. No way to deny that the PSY-IV team is being hunted."

"I'm not one of the team," I pointed out.

He gave me an incredulous look. "Are you shitting me, Risia?"

Heat rose under my cheeks as I suddenly found his hair immensely fascinating. "I'm not like all of you. Never served a day in my life. I don't scale buildings in a single bound, disarm bombs with seconds to spare, or fend off entire teams single handedly."

He snorted. "No, instead you waltz alone into the middle of high-power arenas where everyone's out for blood, armed with nothing but fuck-me heels, silk, and lies. If your targets ever discover how dangerous you are to their secrets, they'd bury you so fast and so deep no one would find you."

He reached up, slipped his hand under my hair, and wrapped his warm palm against my neck, bringing me down to him, even as he met me halfway. Male ire darkened his face. "Rawlings wants you. Hand Tooled has a hard-on for you. No telling who else is out there circling."

His dire tone and even more intimidating words scared me. Nerves rose, and I swiped my tongue over my dry lips. His eyes flicked to the movement, then came back.

My voice came out husky, "Rawlings wants the contract with DOD. Hand Tooled wants to shut me up. I think that's enough to keep any girl on her toes. You don't have to make up more boogeymen."

Frustration and desire etched their way across his face. He closed the distance between us and took my lips with an unexpected gentleness. He drew back, keeping his hand curled over the back of my neck. "You're not just any girl, Risia. What worries me is, if that drive turns out to hold the information Delacourt fears and it's about to hit the black market, then the target on your back is just as bright, if not brighter, than the rest of ours. Not only that, but the number of interested parties will only increase until this sale goes live."

The faint uneasy sensation from earlier made a comeback and gained strength. I shook my head, and pulled back against his hold, needing space as the walls seemed to close in. Unfortunately, the stubborn male in front of me wouldn't move. I pushed against his chest. "I can't outrun everyone, Tag." My breath was coming faster, and my pulse picked up speed. "Dodging verbal daggers, I can do. Bullets? Not so much."

Something nudged at my mind, but I shoved it back. *This was not the time for another damn vision.*

He let my neck go and ran his hand over my shoulder down to my wrist, then tangled our fingers together until he was holding my hand. "Maybe we make it so they'd think twice about pulling the trigger?"

My laugh sounded as panicked as I felt. "And how are you going to do that?"

His face was carefully blank, and his fingers tightened for a moment before relaxing. "We convince whoever's watching that taking you out of the equation takes out the information."

"How do we do that?" Not that I really wanted him to answer that, because something told me I wouldn't like it.

His jaw flexed. "You have to team up with Rawlings."

Team up with Rawlings? What the hell? Stunned, I stared at him, trying to wrap my brain around what he just said. "And that's going to keep the vultures from dive bombing my ass, how?" I snapped.

"It makes you a player worth negotiating with."

It was more than that, and my stomach churned as his logic began to make sense. "Because if I'll turn traitor for Rawlings, what's my price for turning on him?"

Grim but determined, Tag watched me. "They won't be able to stay away from you."

He was absolutely right. They would see a beautiful woman who could be bought. It was a role I'd played before, but this time the higher stakes made my nerves skitter. "Like damn bees to honey."

"Not only will it keep you relatively safe, it will help us identify who's involved in this sale."

My mind was stuck on "relatively safe". Instead of focusing on that, I asked, "Like who Hand Tooled is working with?"

Tag nodded. "He's either an independent or Falcon. Either

way, he doesn't want to wait for the sale. He made sure to find Rawlings's weak point and exploit it."

"Curtis." I bit my lip, thinking. "Hand Tooled might be Falcon, but I don't think Rawlings is."

Tag tilted his head. "How do you figure?"

"If he was working for Falcon, why send in Hand Tooled?"

"To ensure Rawlings would turn over the information."

"No," I shook my head. "That doesn't feel right. I never found any ties between the two." And I had dug deep.

He studied me. "That doesn't mean much. They could've had a deal and Rawlings's decided to back out when he realized the importance of what he had. If it's what we fear, he can set the price. Someone will pay for it. He's arrogant enough to think he can play all sides against one another without getting caught."

Tag's assessment was spot on. That same arrogance lay behind why Rawlings had no problem threatening me. To him, I was nothing more than a pretty tool, one he could use and one he didn't want anyone else to have.

Unless there was something more behind his threat?

That paranoid little voice drove me nuts. If that disk held PSY-IV profiles, mine would be there. If Rawlings could find out about my son, who was to say he hadn't figured out my other weakness—being able to predict the future. Which meant he'd consider me not just a tool, but a bargaining chip.

The feel of Tag's fingers against my chin had me blinking eyes I hadn't realized I'd closed. "What are you thinking, Duchess?" He studied me, watching every nuance even as I tried to tuck it all behind a blank mask. "Too late," he said. "What is it?"

Unable to avoid his demand, I tried to lick my lips. "What if Rawlings accessed the files? He'd know who I am and what I can do."

Tag was shaking his head even as my breath caught and my stomach pitched with possibilities.

Standing next to Rawlings put me within Falcon's reach. A dangerous move on so many levels. The minute they realized who I was and for whom I worked, it would be like waving raw meat in front of a starving wolf. If Falcon got their hands on me, they'd get a damn magic eight ball. Didn't matter if white jackets with buckles wasn't my style, they'd do whatever it took to get what they wanted from me.

Tag mouth firmed. "I don't think he knows exactly what he has yet."

"Why?"

"Because he had no idea who I was when I walked into his office. If he had, he'd never touch me."

"Okay." I tried to regain control of my breathing. "So maybe we won't have to worry about him selling me out to Falcon." Maybe. "But there's nothing stopping him from killing me himself. Kill me and he doesn't have to worry about my loyalties."

Strange how steady and clear my voice sounded, considering the gut rending fear coursing through me.

Tag let go of my chin to wrap his hand around my wrists. His grip tightened as he watched me, a fierce determination wiping away the boy-next-door mask and revealing the dangerous soldier underneath. "I won't let you be killed."

Don't make promises you can't keep. How I wanted to believe him, but reality was, that particular outcome wasn't in his hands.

Not that my previous jobs had been without risk, but I never had to play witness to the final plays. Get in, get the info, turn it over, and on to the next job. This time was different, and the potential fallout could be disastrous. So when weighing the loss of one agent against the lives of dozens, it made my role... expendable.

His face darkened, and he pressed in so quickly I jerked back. I didn't get far as my spine sank into the pillow behind me. Still, he didn't stop until mere inches separated us, one hand braced on the bed near my hip, the other locking my other hand against the bed. As his body held me caged, my false calm disappeared under a wicked combination of fear and nerves, shortening my breath into small pants.

"Dammit, you are not expendable, Risia," he growled.

My gaze dropped to where he still shackled my wrist. *Stupid touch empath.*

Twisting my wrist, I pulled sharply and broke his grip. "If that drive contains the identities of the PSY-IV team and other covert operatives, then in the big scheme of things I am." Cold and harsh, but true nonetheless. A muscle in his jaw flexed, and I stopped him before he could speak. "Don't Tag. I've known the risks since I took Delacourt up on her offer years ago." I offered him a shaky smile. "This is just the first time it's really hitting home."

"I won't—"

Covering his mouth with free hand, I shook my head. "Not your decision to make." I held his furious gaze, needing him to see that despite the crippling fear, I understood exactly what I was getting into. If playing a Mata Hari role would keep Tag and the others safe, so be it.

The thunderclouds on his face didn't disappear, but he finally gave me the tiniest of nods.

I took a deep breath and dropped my hand. "Okay, so what's your plan? How do we convince Rawlings to keep me around?"

He pulled back and ran a hand through his hair. Then he lifted the sheet and left the bed. The man was completely comfortable in his naked skin. "We're going to let him come to you."

Even with the seriousness of our conversation, I couldn't

tear my gaze off his ass as he bent over and grabbed his jeans off the floor. "Uh-huh." Watching him slide commando style into half-buttoned jeans made formulating more succinct words difficult.

"I'm pretty sure he'll know you're back in town by the time we leave Ochoa's office. Once he calls you, you make arrangements to meet him." He sat on the edge of the bed.

The surety in his voice was enough to break through my fascination with him. "What makes you so certain he'll call me first?"

"Because he made sure the police believe he's worried about you. He hasn't offered you up as suspect or victim. He's waiting to see where you land before he makes his next move." Harsh certainty made his words clipped. "Tell him you have the information Curtis stole. You're willing to give it back, for a price."

"Information on my son." I pulled back the sheet and got up, needing to move. As much as I hated to admit it, this plan was our best chance at figuring out what the hell was going on. Risky as hell, but I hadn't given up my son only to put him in the line of fire now. Whatever happened to me, that was my choice. But no one and nothing would touch him. Cold resolution seeped under my fear. "Before I do this, we need to call Delacourt. I want to make sure he's safe." And that he and his family stayed that way.

"We'll use Meli's phone to call her," Tag agreed.

I kept my back to him and tugged on my jeans. "Once I know he's safe, we'll head in." And start luring the predators out of the shadows. A shiver ran down my spine, that uneasy feeling from earlier rising again with a vengeance.

"Risia." He waited until I turned to face him. "If there was another way—"

I cut him off. "There isn't." It was time to get my head in

the game. I tucked the debilitating fears and doubt into a dark corner where they couldn't mess with mind. "I need some fuck-me heels and silk."

Chapter Seventeen

I waved as Meli drove off in her sedan after dropping Tag and me a few blocks from my condo where his rental, the second of the trip, sat undisturbed. She was picking up a few things since tomorrow night, as Rabbit, Jinx, and Wolf were flying in from Phoenix.

At least that was the plan according to Colonel Delacourt, one she shared after assuring me that my son and his family would soon depart for a surprise, all-expense-paid vacation that took them out of Rawlings's reach, and kept them under the watchful eye of a handpicked security detail. While it didn't calm all my worries, it was the best I could do.

Tag, on the other hand, remained fairly quiet after our conversation. Probably due to the noticeable strain in Delacourt's voice. One that prompted him to ask what was happening in Phoenix. It hadn't escaped my notice that she dodged his question, slipping around it with a "It's under control" even I could translate as "shit is hitting the fan".

Tag didn't push, but he did shut down. Part of me wanted to reach out and offer comfort, but with no idea how without making it a big deal, I kept silent and gave him space. Only as the familiar sights of the Strip came into view, did he seem to shake himself free of whatever forbidding thoughts huddled in his head. He asked Meli to make a quick stop to pick up a burner phone, until the more secure one Delacourt was sending arrived.

Now, dressed in jeans and T-shirts, complete with sunglasses, Tag and I stood in the scant shade offered by the cloth overhang in front of a storefront plastered with touristy T-shirts and hats. Despite the mid-afternoon summer heat, crowds still milled along the sidewalk, Vegas had no use for a day of rest.

Tag wrapped an arm around my waist and pulled me into the stream of people. He kept us in the middle of the group as we made our way toward my condo. Even though I couldn't see it, I could feel him scanning our surroundings. Not sure how he could tell if we were being followed in the shifting crowd.

After the umpteenth time of being bumped by someone not watching where they were going, I snaked my arm around Tag's waist, using his tall frame for an anchor. The press of his gun tucked against the small of his back was a solid presence under my arm. Tucked together, there was no missing the fine tension vibrating through him.

We stopped at the corner and waited for the light to change. Taking advantage of our momentary stop, I tilted my head up. "Tag?"

He looked at me, but all I could see was my reflection in his lenses. "We're good, Duchess. Let's make this quick, yeah?"

"Yeah," I agreed.

The light changed, and we crossed with the crowd, peeling off as we wove through the sidewalks to the condo's entrance. Instead of going through the main doors where you could choose to go to the condo elevators or head to the attached casino, I turned us toward the smaller, locked entrance tucked off to the side. This one was used by those of us who chose to call this building home.

We stopped in front of the ornate, wrought-iron gate and its security panel. Tag dropped his arm and used his hand on my hip to guide me in front of him until I could enter in the security code. The protective move curled around my heart. I tapped out the five-digit code and listened to the subtle buzz and click as the door unlocked.

We stepped into the lobby and the wave of cool air hit the thin layer of sweat from the heat, leaving chills in its wake. Only when the door closed behind us, shutting away the street sounds, did I let out a long sigh. I didn't waste time, but headed directly for the elevators on the left, Tag on my heels. We stepped inside and rode in silence to the tenth floor. The doors drew back, and I went to step out, only to be brought up short.

"Hang on, Duchess." He stepped around me and led the way down the hall to my door. He stopped at the door and held out his hand. "Key?"

For a moment I blinked at him, and my mind stumbled to a halt. "Shit," I muttered. I lost my key in my mad dash from Curtis's office. "I'll go down and see if I can get the manager." I turned on my heel, only to come to a stop when Tag caught my wrist.

"Come here." He pulled me back until I was standing between him and the hall. "Don't move," he said softly.

I caught the telling direction of his gaze as he flicked a glance just beyond my shoulder.

Right, the security camera down the hall.

I leaned my shoulder against the doorjamb, and kept my body solidly between him and the camera. To give my hands something to do, I shoved my sunglasses up and pulled my curls back. It took him under thirty seconds to get through my lock. First Rawlings, now Tag. "Secured, my ass," I grumbled.

Swear to God, once this crap was done, I was looking at getting a new place, with better locks.

He pushed the door open. The smell hit me, making me gag. I went to step through only to come up against his arm as it barred my way. "Wait here."

Turning to look at him, I raised an eyebrow in challenge. "Seriously? Isn't that a little too late?"

He frowned down at me. "Just wait here."

"Whatever." Ungracious as hell, but I was edgy knowing I was walking into a disaster zone. I just wanted to see it, maybe it wouldn't be as bad as I was imagining.

Tag shoved his sunglasses to the top of his head and stepped inside. With him taking up most of the space in the narrow entry hall, I couldn't see a damn thing. As soon as he disappeared around the corner, I counted to five and followed, unable to hang back any longer. I made it to the end of the entryway and froze in stunned disbelief.

Obviously, I needed to work on my imagination.

My once-immaculate living room was trashed. The heavy curtains on the floor-to-ceiling windows leading out to the balcony hung in drunken disarray. One panel shredded, one gamely trying to hold on by a single hook. Sunlight poured through the drapes' ragged edges and glinted off the shattered glass mixed with the splintered remains of my side tables. The couch looked as if rabid cats decided to use it as a scratching post. Stuffing spilled out like fluffy innards.

My collection of decorative hourglasses was reduced to shattered pieces of glass and sand. Something, probably the leg of the coffee table, had been used against the electronics with an undisguised fury. The pictures on my wall were nothing but wooden kindling, shredded paper, and glass shards.

"Dammit, Risia." The low curse turned my attention to Tag, who stood in the doorway to my bedroom. "I told you to wait."

Ignoring him, I completed my turn to stare at the war zone of my kitchen. The door of the fridge hung open, and the tile floor was strewn with food. The cabinets were ransacked, and the dishes smashed, nothing left untouched. The smell of rotting food wound around me and I choked. The sound came out suspiciously close to a sob.

Something snapped underfoot.

I turned just as Tag reached me. His arms gathered me close, and I buried my face against his chest, gripping the back of his shirt in my fist. My mind spun. Sick fury, frustrated tears, and an aching sense of loss collided in my chest, pressing down. Tears burned against the back of my eyes, but this time I wouldn't let them fall. No, anger was quickly wiping everything else away.

"Why?" My question came out harsh.

A hand in my hair, cradling my head against his chest, his voice vibrating under my ear. "Chances are they were looking for something."

I pulled back until he let me go. I went to suck in a deep breath, then thought better of it when the nauseating odor of my kitchen intruded. I stepped around Tag, watching where I put my feet. Picking my way through my living room, I made my way to my bedroom, bracing for what waited inside.

Tag turned but didn't stop me.

I stood in the doorway and took in the scene. The mattress was shredded, and the bedding was strewn across the floor. Gouges, deep and unmistakable, scarred my dresser.

Again, nothing had been spared.

Lamps shattered, pictures destroyed, clothes and shoes tangled with the overwhelming odor of broken perfume bottles, ratcheting the sick roiling of my stomach higher. Swallowing the urge to gag, I forced emotions away. I needed to figure out what, if anything, was salvageable.

I moved through the room, every step adding fuel to the

cold furious flame of my anger. Stopping at the entryway to my closet, my lip curled in a silent snarl. My clothes had been torn off the hangers and now lay in a brutalized pile on the floor. Using the toe of my canvas sneaker to nudge some of the material away, I uncovered what was left of my shoe collection. "Bastards," I hissed, taking in the deliberately snapped-off heels.

The oddity of that made me re-examine the closet with narrow eyes. Little things snapped into focus. The hangers were still on the rods. A few on the floor. The desecrated shoes weren't mixed in with the clothes but buried under the pile. I crouched and began to separate the pieces. After the initial layer of material, which now resembled rags, the remainder of my clothes were curiously intact.

Shoving part of the pile back, I found that not all my shoes were destroyed. In fact, the boxes tucked neatly in the corner remained untouched. Frowning, I rose to my feet, turned, and went to look at my bedroom. Stepping into the mess, I took in the trashed dresser and bedding, the smashed lamps, and half-opened drawers. I could feel Tag come up behind me as I studied the room. "It's deliberate, not rage fueled." My voice came out flat, as locked down as my emotions.

The destruction was too staged, the top layer being the worst, nothing being left untouched. A deliberate, malicious statement.

"A threat."

"An intimidation tactic," I corrected. "A statement that you're not safe in your own home. We can get to you anywhere."

"Which is why I didn't want you to come back here."

I waved his growled comment away. "If it's Rawlings, he's trying to make it so I have no choice but to take him up on his offer."

Tag shook his head. "I don't think this is him. He's

counting on his blackmail being all he needs to get you where he wants you. My money's on Hand Tooled, especially since we know he's been watching for you."

The vision hit with no warning, and no time to brace for impact.

Tag emerging from my condo. A rush of shadows. A grunt. Blood blooming low and dark on his side. Tag falling to the ground. Me, unable to scream, falling to my knees, eyes held captive by that spreading pool of darkness.

A sickening shift as the world spun, then snapped into place.

Tag behind a wheel. The click of an ignition turning. A breathless second filled with numbing dread. Then a world-shattering explosion throwing me back. Lifting my head while the squeal of tires against pavement screamed in my ears. Scrambling to my knees and raising a useless hand in protest as a car slammed into Tag with singular brutality.

My scream of denial blending into a chorus of screams, punctuated by harsh coughs of gunshots. Around me, people fell like dominos. Panic pushed me to my feet, only to stumble as a body fell against me. Automatically, I reached out and caught the person, only to look down into Tag's face.

"Risia!" His lips shaped my name as my legs crumpled under our combined weight.

I tried to hold on to him as we dropped, but the blood coating my hands made my grip slippery. I tore my gaze away from his face, what little air was in my lungs escaping in a gasp as I took in the rest of his body. Crimson stains created a horrific Rorschach painting.

Even as I tried to staunch the worst of them, I knew there were too many. Staring down into his pale face, I could barely breathe through the heavy weight pressing on my chest. *This couldn't be happening.*

"It's not, Risia." Blood bubbled up as he spoke. His hand

rose, blood-smeared and shaky, but he laid it against my face. His touch searingly hot. "See me."

See him? I was watching him die in my arms.

The hand against my face slid to the back of my neck and yanked me down. I gasped at the unexpected move, and my mind spun. He dragged me to him, his grip inescapable. On a half sob, I closed my eyes, unable to watch the spreading stain. His lips met mine. Instead of the coppery tang of blood, his familiar taste exploded over my tongue. The unexpected demand, wrapped in heated spice, snapped my eyes open.

Fiercely burning hazel stared back, even as he lifted his lips from mine. Heart racing and breaths coming in short gasps, I desperately held the very-alive gaze with mine. "Tag?" His name came out half sob, half plea.

The hands cradling my face tightened for a moment, before gentling. "Right here, Duchess. I'm right fucking here."

Still not sure what was real, I dropped my gaze. Under my palms, his chest rose and fell. My hands scrambled, pulling up his T-shirt until tanned skin and heat met my touch. Needing the reassurance, I ran my hands over his chest, finding only old scars and smooth, unbroken skin. Relief sang through me, leaving me shaky. "You're okay."

He caught my hands, stilling their nervous touch. "I'm okay." He lifted my chin, holding me still. "What happened?"

"They were watching us." The words started shaky. I sucked in some air and tried to regain my balance. I licked dry lips. "I'm sorry, we shouldn't have come here." I tugged my hands free, and his T-shirt fell back into place. I wrapped my arms around my stomach.

His somber gaze roamed my face. "We knew it was a possibility. Tell me what you saw."

Blood drained from my head, leaving me light-headed, as memories rushed back in. "You on the sidewalk outside the entrance, stabbed. Car bomb on your rental. Getting hit by a car. A drive-by as we're coming out of the condo."

He let go of my chin and enfolded my trembling body in a tight hug.

I burrowed against his chest, needing a moment to pull my shit together. "So basically, we're screwed trying to get out of here."

One of his hands stroked down my spine. "We could always use the balcony again," he teased.

"Nope, not even for you," I said, grateful for his humor. "Hate heights, Tag. Even if I managed to get on the other side of the railing, I'd be so freaked, I'd end up killing us both." Drawing in one more big breath, I drew back. "We can't stay here."

"We aren't." Furrows creased his brow. "What you see, does it all always come true?"

"You mean can you change what's going to happen?"

He dipped his head.

"Maybe, but it's a crap shoot."

"Have you tried it?"

"Yes, but the results were disastrous. The thing is, the future isn't determined by a single decision, but by a progression of decisions. Each one building on another, until you're left with the end result."

"Okay, so we have to think outside our comfort zone, then."

I gave a hesitant nod. "But I can't guarantee it will change anything."

"Fair enough." He looked around. "Can you find enough in this to pack an overnight bag?"

Puzzled, I gave him a nod. "Probably. Why?"

"Do it and make it quick. I'm going to call the police."

"The police?"

He gave me a deadly grin. "Since we're probably dealing

with Hand Tooled, he's trying to isolate you so he can get the drive. Make it so you can't go to the police or anyone else. He's probably banking on the fact that he can get to you before you get to the authorities. Especially since you didn't head to the police straight from Curtis's office. Which means you're either working with Curtis or working for someone else you don't want anyone to know about. He's trying to corner you by taking away your home, any possible allies, until you're left alone, then he'll close in. He's already tried to get rid of me." He waved his hand at the destruction surrounding us. "This is enough to get most people so freaked they'll try to burrow in and hide, not dart out in the open."

It made a convoluted sort of sense. Calling in the police meant I'd be stuck at the station for hours answering questions. "What's to stop him from coming after us, even with the police here? Having Ochoa with you didn't stop him from crashing into your car."

"But the crowd of witnesses did stop him from pulling the trigger you kept seeing. We go in with a police escort and even he's not stupid enough to try and take you against those odds."

But going to the police opened a whole other can of worms. I laid my forehead against his chest, closing my eyes. "You know if we go to the station, Rawlings will show up."

"I'm counting on it." He tucked a curl behind my ear. "Let's see which role he decides to play, the concerned employer or the suspicious one."

"It's my freedom you're playing with here, Gunderson," I muttered, turning until my cheek rested against the heated wall of his chest. The reassuring beat of his heart doing more to steady my nerves than anything else.

His chuckled vibrated under me. "I promise to break you out if they decide to lock you up."

"You better." I fell quiet, stealing time while he ran a comforting hand down my spine.

After a moment he added, "This buys us time, Duchess."

"I know."

"We've got backup coming in tomorrow. Spending the afternoon at the station is better than trying to outrun anything Hand Tooled has planned."

"It also gives the other players time to join this damn party."

"True, but we can't do anything until we know what's on the drive and confirm Rawlings is heading up the sale, or we get lucky and figure out who the hell Hand Tooled is."

My mind clicked through various scenarios as we worked through the story I needed to have in place when I sat down across from the police to answer their questions. "Maybe I can take Hand Tooled out of the equation."

His hand paused and rested in the middle of my back, a warm weight. "What are you thinking?"

I gave his chest a light pat and stepped back.

He let me go, and watched me.

"If I give the police Hand Tooled's description, he's going to be a little busy ducking them to bug us."

Tag thought it over, then finally agreed. "Not to mention we might be able to get an ID on him."

Looking around, I took another deep breath. "Go call the police and I'll pack a bag."

Chapter Eighteen

The hours crawled by as the police ran me through the wringer. The lingering headache turned into a full-blown migraine by the time Ochoa's replacement, Detective Williamson released me into Tag's custody. Years of swimming in the pool of half-truths and slight of word served me well.

As far as the Las Vegas Police Department was concerned, I was sent back to them after a two-day de-brief by my superiors at DOD to find Agent Gunderson waiting to take me home before bringing me to the local authorities. Unfortunately, the plans were derailed when someone broke into my home and trashed it.

The barrage of questions was relentless and tap dancing around them required every verbal skill I had acquired over the years. The questions started out easy.

Did I know Curtis Trammel?

Yes, we worked together on contract negotiations for Aether.

Were you aware of his gambling debts?

Sorry, no, I only knew him in a professional manner.

Yet you were known to spend time beyond normal business hours in his office.

Yes, some aspects of the proposed contract could be very complex and far-reaching, requiring more-detailed analysis before finalizing.

Were you aware he stole information from Aether?

Not until I walked in on his murder.

Then the questions began in earnest.

Did you see his killer?

Yes.

And he just let you go?

No, he's the reason behind the shiner I currently sported, along with the lovely set of cracked ribs.

Can you describe him?

Gladly.

Why were you at Curtis's office after hours?

I found a disturbing discrepancy in my files and before I presented it to Lawrence Rawlings or the DOD, I went to Curtis's office for answers.

What discrepancy?

As a DOD employee and government consultant for Aether, I was bound by two very airtight non-disclosure agreements. However, they were more than welcome to ask that same question to my superiors.

Why didn't you go to the police?

I work for the DOD, I've got a killer chasing my ass, I'm sorry, but I'm going to the DOD for protection. Especially considering what my work revolves around.

And you couldn't inform Mr. Rawlings or anyone else that you were safe?

For the last two days, I've been answering my superiors' questions. They're not going to give me a courtesy phone call until they're ready.

Why would anyone break into your home?

Maybe because I walked into to find Curtis Trammel murdered in his office?

Did I know what they were looking for?

No.

Could it be connected to my work?

Since I worked for a company that excelled in secrets, yes, it could very well be connected to my work.

Do you know what was on the files Curtis stole?

No.

Round and round we went, until finally they conceded that I answered all I could or would. Their abrupt "Don't leave town", coupled with their obvious frustration at my stonewalling, meant the LVPD and I didn't part on the best of terms.

I walked out of the interrogation room to find Tag waiting in the hall.

"Ms. Lacoste," Detective Williamson called.

Stopping outside the door, I turned to face the older of the two detectives standing in the room behind me. "Yes?"

"The composite artist will be here in about twenty. Would you mind waiting?" Behind him, his partner picked up the files they brought with them.

Since it wasn't really a request, I dipped my head in a nod. "Any chance I could get some coffee?" I didn't dare ask for aspirin, but maybe the caffeine would help chase back the pounding in my head.

"I'll have someone bring it," he answered as he stepped into the hall. "You and Agent Gunderson can wait in the conference room."

Tag and I followed him through the maze of hallways until he ushered us into a bland room with a large oval table and chairs. "Have a seat. I'll have your coffee delivered." He looked at Tag as I took one of the chairs. "Agent, anything?"

"Water, please."

A short nod, and the detective left, closing the door behind him.

Tag settled into a chair next to me. "You okay?"

I grimaced and rubbed my temple. "Other than a headache, I'm fine."

"Another ten minutes and I would've called in a lawyer."

"I'd have been grateful."

Both of us were keeping our voices low, conscious of where we were and who could be listening. Knowing neither one of could talk freely, we fell silent. The minutes ticked by before a quick knock preceded the door opening.

"Risia."

At the sound of Lawrence Rawlings's voice, I half turned to the door and quickly schooled my expression. Tag didn't visibly react, but I couldn't miss the sudden tension coiling through him. It raised the hairs along my arms. Refusing to rub the anxious feeling away, I curled my hands into the chair's armrest. "Lawrence?" I made sure to inject surprise into my voice as I began to rise from my chair, taking in the well-dressed man standing in the door.

He waved me back. "Sit, you look like you could use this." He handed me a Styrofoam cup, steam curling from the top.

"Thank you." I sank back down and cradled the cup between my hands. Someone had been chatting with the detectives.

"Two sugars and cream, right?" He dug out four little packets from his pocket, knocking his ID badge from its clipped position on his belt.

I rescued his badge and gave him a small smile before collecting the packets. Then I began doctoring my coffee. Not that much would probably help what was being passed off as coffee in my cup.

"Agent Gunderson," Rawlings finally acknowledged Tag as he pulled out the empty chair on my other side. He pushed a bottle of water across the table. "They said you asked for this."

"Thanks." Tag reached over and grabbed the sweating bottle.

Rawlings settled in his chair, turning it so he could face me. "Are you okay, Risia?"

I managed a shaky smile, playing up the image of a nerve-wracked mess. Not that it was much of a stretch. "I've had better days." I took a small sip of coffee and controlled the urge to wince at the still-bitter taste. "I'm sorry about Curtis."

He shook his head, light glinting off the lenses of his wire-frame glasses, obscuring his eyes. "I'm still trying to figure out what happened." He leaned forward and wrapped his hand around my arm. "I was worried about you."

It took everything I had not to yank away, and it didn't help that I could feel the weight of Tag's stare boring between my shoulders. Instead, I gently pulled my arm free and ran my hand through my curls. "I'm sorry, that wasn't my intention. Considering what I walked in on…" I let my voice hitch, then swallowed and rested my fist on the table. "I felt safer calling my boss for a pickup."

Rawlings covered my clenched hand with his. "I wish you had called to let me know you were okay."

I finally looked at him, his concerned expression almost nailing it, if you discounted the edge of calculation lurking just under his skin. "A little banged up, but I'm fine." Now, if he'd just stop touching me, I'd be able to get through this farce.

Obviously, I didn't hide my distaste of his touch fast enough, because something maliciously gleeful peeked out before slipping away. His hand tightened for a second, before he lifted it and sat back in his chair. "Did I hear right? Was your condo broken into?"

Taking advantage of having my hands free, I wrapped both around the Styrofoam cup. As a barrier, it wasn't much, but it'd do for now. "Yes, and someone had a grand time trashing everything."

"Do the police have any clue who it is?"

Twisting my lips into a mirthless smile, I met his gaze. "I think it's safe to say Curtis's killer wasn't thrilled with my unexpected visit."

He drummed his fingers against the table. "That's worrisome. Do you have some place to stay?"

"She'll be staying at a safe house," Tag broke in, diverting Rawlings's attention. Which gave me a second's respite.

Rawlings frowned, looking between Tag and me. "Safe house?"

Tag answered, "So long as Trammel's killer is loose, she'll be staying in protective custody." The slight emphasis he put on "protective custody" made it clear custody was the operative word.

I turned away from Tag and took another sip of my coffee, hiding my twitching lips. Guess I knew what image we were going to go for now.

Rawlings didn't miss the hint and flicked a questioning glance at me.

I added to Tag's impression with a delicate shrug and a flash of an irritated grimace, a silent indicator of my displeasure. To further the picture that having Tag dog my every move irritated me to no end, I snapped, "I already told you, Agent, I have friends I can stay with. If you'd let me call them."

"And as you were told, ma'am," his slight sneer was a nice touch. "Until this situation is rectified, I will be ensuring your safety. Until my orders change, you're stuck with me."

"Joy," I muttered, glaring at him.

Watching our byplay, Rawlings cleared his throat. "Agent, do you think Ms. Lacoste and I can have a minute alone? I'd like to discuss some business with her."

Tag switched his glare from me to Rawlings. "I have security clearance."

"Not enough," Rawlings replied pleasantly.

"Go away, Agent." I upped my snotty quotient, playing the society princess to the hilt. "I'm perfectly safe with Mr. Rawlings."

Tag got to his feet, his posture military straight with restrained anger. I watched him leave and wished I could go with him, but I had a part to play. A sigh escaped as the door closed behind him. "Finally," I said under my breath as I rubbed my temples.

A small smile played over Rawlings's mouth. "I take it you're not happy with your latest attachment?"

"Not even close," I answered, shifting in my seat until I could cross my legs. "What the hell is going on Lawrence?"

"That's what I'd like to ask you, Risia." Gone was the faux concern and in its place was the ruthless businessman. "Why were you at Curtis's office?"

I drummed my nails against the tabletop, studying him, making sure all he saw was cool calculation. "Did you really not know?"

"Know what?" His voice was low, controlled.

"Don't play coy, it's not you," I admonished.

His lips tightened and with whip-like quickness, he captured my wrist. His grip was tight enough to leave bruises. "Know what?" he bit out.

Twisting my wrist, I yanked it free, narrowing my eyes. "Curtis was selling information. Information you stole from various agencies when you were discovering," I used air quotes, "the weakness that exists in the government's communication lines."

His smile was cold and predatory. "Careful, Risia. Slander like that can cost you more than you're willing to pay."

I gave him an equally cold smile. "It's not slander when I

have proof." White lines appeared around his mouth. The tiny signs of his rising temper indicated I was on the right track. Problem was, it wouldn't take much to derail the psycho train. Time to pull it back. "Proof I haven't shared with my bosses. Yet."

"And what proof do you think you have?"

"A flash drive, one I found in Curtis's office hours before he was killed. Until you showed up at my condo with your… offer, I was planning on turning it over to my boss." I held his gaze. "After you left, I realized I needed my own bargaining chip."

"Don't play games you can't win." His soft comment didn't detract from his spine-chilling implication.

"I'm not looking to zero in on your prize." I kept my expression blank. "I just want to make sure I'm still breathing after whatever this is, is done."

"And what exactly do you think this is?"

Heeding my gut, I decided to take a dangerous bluff. "Information various agencies wouldn't want made public, but others would pay a pretty penny for."

His lips twisted with smug arrogance tinged with fury.

My stomach sank. Damn, Delacourt's suspicions were right.

He watched me with the flat, deadly gaze of a cobra. "If information such as that existed, then that would be Curtis's doing, not mine. Even if I dared to syphon such delicate information, I'd never be so foolish as to leave it unencrypted."

"Really? That's your defense?" I kept my voice level and cool. "You do realize you're not the only communication company I've worked with? You'd be surprised at how sophisticated decryption programs are now."

He didn't even blink but kept staring at me.

My muscles tensed, and a little voice screamed at me to get the hell out of the room. Instead, I kept my shoulders relaxed and gave him a knowing smile. "Of course, I'll be happy to hand you what I have, as soon as you give me what I want."

The silence stretched between us as we engaged in a stare down. I didn't dare blink, afraid he'd kill me in that mere second of inattention. Perhaps I pressed my luck just a teensy bit too much. Finally, he sat back, and templed his fingers over his mouth, his elbows resting on the chair arms. "And what is it you think I can give you?"

Lifting my chin, I swallowed. Adding a slight edge of nervousness to my voice wasn't difficult. "Proof you have what you offered earlier and protection."

Sitting so close, there was no missing the flare of triumph before he tucked it away. "One I can guarantee." He gave a shrug. "The other, well, we'll see."

Before I could respond, there was a sharp knock on the door. Both of us turned as it opened and Tag stood framed in the doorway, his gaze sharp. "The composite artist is here."

He stepped back, allowing an older woman who looked as if she should be baking cookies somewhere with a white apron into the room. She juggled an artist's sketchpad and graphite pencils as she freed up a hand to offer. "Ms. Lacoste, I'm Wanda Evans." She looked between Rawlings and me. "Am I interrupting?"

I pushed to my feet, strength slowly returning to my shaky knees, and took her hand. "No, please come in. Mr. Rawlings and I were just finishing up."

Rawlings rose and greeted Wanda, flashing a charming smile, the cold, calculating predator nowhere in sight. "Lovely to meet you, Ms. Evans." He turned to me, his smile firmly in place. "Risia, you don't mind if I stay, do you? I'd like to see the final sketch. Perhaps I might be able to help identify him."

As if I could refuse such a request. With a polite, "Of course not," we all settled into various chairs. Much to my relief, Wanda took over Rawlings's previous chair, leaving him to take a chair behind her. Tag settled in behind me. With two more people in the room, I managed to block out Rawlings's unsettling presence.

The clock ticked the minutes away while Wanda patiently took me through the description of Hand Tooled. When she finally added the last bit to the sketch and turned it to me for confirmation, an hour had come and gone.

"That's him." My voice was husky, and I rubbed at a spot in the middle of my forehead trying to dissipate my raging headache.

Wanda set her pencil and pad down on the table, then reached over and touched my arm. "You did good. Why don't I ask the detectives to get you some aspirin?"

I mustered a small smile and even smaller nod. She smiled in return. Behind her, Rawlings pulled the sketchpad over, his face blank as he studied the sketch.

"Recognize him?" Tag asked from behind me.

Rawlings pushed the pad back over to Wanda. "Unfortunately, no."

"Well," Wanda gathered her things and rose. "I'll pass this over to the detectives."

"I'd like to show this to my security team. Could you ask them for a copy?" Rawlings asked.

"Make that two," Tag added.

"I'll do that," Wanda said, then left the room, leaving the door open behind her.

Rawlings rose, tugged on his cuff, and said, "Risia, we'll need to finish our conversation." He looked up and pinned me in place. "Tomorrow, lunch? Say twelve thirty at The Attic?"

The rather posh, yet private restaurant was situated in the heart of The Spires hotel and casino. "I'll be there."

"Until then," he said, then looked beyond me. "Agent."

"Rawlings."

I watched as Rawlings strode out of the room, and

suddenly the heavy atmosphere lightened. My shoulders slumped, and I wanted to collapse in my chair.

"Head's up," Tag murmured softly.

Yanking my protesting head up, I winced.

"Ms. Lacoste." Detective Williamson stood in the doorway. "Wanda mentioned you needed some aspirin?"

I pushed to my feet, took the little white pills.

Tag held out his water bottle. "Here."

I gave him a small smile of thanks, took it, and downed the pills praying they'd kick in sooner rather than later.

When I finished, the detective said, "You're free to go." He shifted his attention to Tag and held out a piece of a paper. "Agent, you requested a copy?"

Tag stepped around me and took the copy of the sketch. "Thanks."

Williamson's lips thinned for a moment before he resumed his bland expression. "Ochoa said you offered to help on this?"

Tag nodded.

"How soon do you think you can get your people to run that?"

"Hopefully tomorrow, maybe Tuesday at the latest? If we get a hit, I'll let you know."

"Appreciate it." Williamson turned to me, gave me a polite nod. "Have a good evening, Ms. Lacoste."

"You as well, Detective." But he was already walking away.

I stepped in front of Tag and felt his hand in the small of my back as we made our way out of the station. Neither of us said anything, and once we were through the entrance doors and out in the evening's heat, I sucked in a deep breath, then blew it out.

"You okay?" Tag dropped his hand and scanned our surroundings.

"No, but I will be." Because, really, there wasn't any other choice.

The fading sunlight caught on the mirrored surfaces of the buildings around us, and the dance of light joined my headache. Narrowing my eyes, I tried to keep the pain at bay. God, my head hurt and that uneasy feeling that followed me to the police station was back. Not caring what it revealed, I grabbed Tag's hand.

His fingers tightened on mine as he left the sidewalk and headed to a nearby concrete ledge. Since my vision was down to blurry shadows, I didn't balk. He pulled his hand free and then they were on my shoulders, pressing down. "Sit before you pass out."

I sank down and felt heated stone hit my butt. Warm, but not uncomfortably so. The press of light against my closed lids lessened and without opening my eyes, I knew he was standing in front of me. The protective move was more settling than irritating, and I leaned forward the scant inches to rest my forehead against his hard stomach.

His hand gently slipped under my hair and began a slow, soothing rub at the base of my neck. Minutes ticked by, but he didn't move, didn't fidget, giving me time. As the tension ebbed, my uneasiness began to follow suit and I slipped into that in-between place as the sounds around me blurred into white noise and my focus centered on Tag's rhythmic strokes.

Like seeping water, the vision trickled in before I could recognize what was happening.

A half-formed room.

Meli's pale face, streaked with dirt and tears.

Her eyes wide with desperation and dread.

A male hand swinging out with viciousness, whipping Meli's head to the side.

"Meli!" I gasped, jerking to my feet, only to weave as the world tilted around me.

The vision snapped into nothing.

"What the—"

"Phone, we need a phone!" *Oh God, was Meli okay?*

My hands raced over Tag, fumbling over his pockets before he managed to halt them. "Risia, take a breath and look at me."

Unable to escape his grip, I met his gaze. "You have to call Meli. Right now!"

He transferred his hold to one hand and reached into his pocket with another. "Number?"

I rattled it off and watched him. As close as I was, I could hear the phone ringing down the line. Once. Twice. Three times.

"Hello?" Meli's voice came through steady and clear.

My knees weakened, and my weight sagged against Tag, tremors racing through my body.

"Hey, Meli, you doing okay?" Tag released my wrists and wrapped his arm around my waist as I buried my face against his chest.

"Yeah, I'm fine. Back at the villas. Where are you guys?"

"Just got out of the police station. We should be heading back soon."

"Sounds good, I'm just going to finish prepping the cabins for your friends' arrival tomorrow. Be safe on your way back."

"We will, thanks. Hey, do me a favor?"

"Sure."

"Stay inside and keep the doors locked for me. I can help with the villas when we get back."

There was a pause. "What's going on, Tag?"

His arm tightened around me. "Nothing, I just want to make sure you're staying cautious."

Another pause, this one a little longer. "Are you really okay?"

"Yeah, but Risia's a little rattled."

"I'll stay in with the doors locked. Flash your headlights when you pull in."

"Thanks, Meli."

"Keep her safe, Tag."

"I'm trying." He tucked his phone away. He ran his hand down my spine. "All right, Duchess. She's fine."

The emotional roller coaster ride was taking its toll, and I swallowed around a thick lump in my throat. "Thanks."

"What did you see?"

I pulled back, keeping my gaze locked on his chest. I gave a small shake of my head. "A flash. Nothing concrete. Maybe it's just nerves." Or my own insecurities and paranoia conjuring up horrible scenarios. Flashes, such as that one, could easily be happening now or years down the road. It's not like they came time stamped, because hey, that would actually be helpful.

"Better safe than sorry." He caught my chin forcing me to meet his gaze. "I know you want to head back, but we need to make sure we aren't bringing any tails back with us."

I gave a small nod, the best I could do with him holding my chin.

He studied me for a few more breathless minutes, probably trying to decide if my kind of crazy was really worth the hassle. Maybe, since he thrived on challenges. My life was nothing if not challenging. Walking in on killers, breaking into offices, high-speed car chases, meant normal steered clear. Of course, if normal appealed to either of us, we wouldn't be here, right? His lips twitched, and his eyes lightened. He leaned down and pressed a quick kiss against my lips.

I blinked a couple of times as he straightened. "What was that for?"

The lip twitch turned into a grin and he shrugged. "Let's grab something to eat."

"Not really hungry, Tag." I fell into step beside him. His grin stayed in place. "What's so funny?"

"Nothing."

Uh-huh. Wonder if they made couples' straitjackets.

Chapter Nineteen

TAG

I closed the hotel door and flipped the lock. After Risia's freak out about Meli, I decided against heading back tonight. She needed a break.

Instead, I told Risia we'd hole up in a hotel room, order room service, and hunker down until tomorrow's meeting with Rawlings. Then I called Meli to give her the heads up, before making a quick trip to a nearby mall for a clean change of jeans and T-shirt for me, and the shit ton of soap, lotion, and shampoo Risia seemed to need. I parked her bag on the floor by the bed. "You hungry?"

"Not really."

Taking in her pallor, I pushed, "Need to eat something."

Her hands went to her hips, her eyes flashing. "No, what I need is a shower." I opened my mouth but before I could say anything she added, "Alone."

Damn. I hid my grin by bending down to pick up the case and setting it on the bed. "Fine. You go shower, and I'll order us something from room service."

"Fine." She hip-checked me away from the bag so she could gather her things.

I watched as colorful bits of silk and bottle after bottle filled her arms. Finally satisfied with her haul, she turned to the bathroom. "Give me about an hour."

Recognizing her need for privacy, I said, "Take as long as you need."

She stepped into the bathroom, closed the door, and a few seconds later the lock clicked into place with a soft snick.

Blowing out a long breath, I moved to the side of the bed and sat down, resting my arms on my knees and keeping my back to the temptation occupying the bathroom. Right now, she needed a break. Today's events had run her ragged. Not to mention the number it did on me.

My head was pounding, my temper was a breath away from erupting, and the weight of Rawlings's depravity clung to me like a deranged monkey. The man focused on Risia to the point it took every ounce of will power I had not to spring across the table and choke the bastard. The cesspool of sexual hunger and twisted need to dominate seeped around the edges of my mental walls, rousing a dangerous fury and a fucked up primitive need to mark Risia as mine.

It didn't help when I touched her, and her fear and skin-crawling loathing joined in, even as her determination to play this dangerous game through rode alongside. There wasn't a damn thing I could do to protect her. I was forced to sit there and let the asshole taunt and touch her. It made me sick even as I calculated how to take him out of the equation regardless of how much it would screw with the mission. My demons were back in full fucking force. I didn't trust myself in this mood. If…when she pushed me, I'd snap.

Something she didn't deserve.

There was so much shit in my head and there was no way it wouldn't leak onto her. Sick shame made my skin itch. I dragged my hands through my hair as echoes of our earlier conversation joined the memory of her rare show of vulnerability and a fierce denial rose.

I like playing with you.

For how long?

However long you'll let me.

What I felt wasn't some damn game. No, this had nothing to do with using Risia and everything to do with wanting her. Hell, needing her for however long she'd let me. The urge to storm the bathroom and lose myself in her luscious body, in her heady taste, rode me hard. The image of her drawn face and bruised eyes held me in check, along with the volatile mix of protective rage, hunger, and something I refused to name that left me aching.

I hadn't lied to her. Something about her kept my demons in check and gave me breathing room. But how much of what I felt was tied up in that relief? This urge to keep her safe, to stand in front of her, was it all because of that relief or was it something deeper? Something much more real and lasting? Or was I using her?

Hell, I was still reeling over what happened this morning. It would be so easy to play the oblivious male card, but my intolerance of games wouldn't let me. Risia hadn't wanted to let me in. Not that I blamed her. It wasn't as if I gave her any real reason to open her heart to me. Yet she had, and that offering staggered me. She drew me like no other woman.

At first, I thought my fascination would fade, instead it grew claws and sank them deep. As much as I valued her gift, a bigger part of me worried I wouldn't be able to offer her the same, no matter how much I tried. The roiling mental conflict left me off balance. Something I couldn't afford if Risia and I were to survive this.

I blew out a hard breath. I needed to get my head together. In less than twenty-four hours, Wolf, Rabbit, and Jinx would be joining the party, and shit would get real quick. Because once they were here, I had every intention of making sure we got to the bottom of Rawlings's involvement.

As soon as Rabbit unlocked what was on that drive, we'd know what kind of scum we were dealing with. The black market for classified information tended to draw a specific crowd. If Rawlings was heading the sale, and my gut said he was, he was going in on the assumption his money and the information he held would keep him safe. Normally that wouldn't bother me, but because Risia was getting dragged along, I was worried as hell.

The sound of the shower coming on cut through my thoughts, and I got up and wandered over to the dresser stretched beneath the wall-mounted TV. On the glossy top was a collection of magazines and hotel information. Finding the in-room menu, I settled behind the desk tucked in the corner. Ten minutes later, order placed, I turned the chair to face the wide expanse of glass offering a glittering image of the Vegas Strip. Lights flashed and blurred, creating a surreal image.

It had only been seventy-two hours since Risia walked in on Hand Tooled killing Curtis. Now, not only was he after her ass, but she placed herself squarely in Rawlings's crosshairs. It was a calculated risk, letting him know she had the drive, but Hand Tooled was just the tip of the scum-sucking iceberg. Her chances of outlasting the horde remained high so long as Rawlings believed she was his to control. Tomorrow's meeting would be difficult to watch, but I had no doubts of Risia's ability to convince Rawlings he was better off with her beside him. Once he sent out word she was off limits, we'd have breathing room to formulate a plan.

We needed to figure out where the sale was going to take place, because sending Risia into a pit of criminals who'd slit her throat with as much concern as scraping shit off their shoes, gave me heartburn. It would have to be somewhere Rawlings felt safe and in control. Would he keep that information close at hand or would he hide it in plain sight in his office?

Recalling his superiority complex, I bet he had it somewhere in his office. He truly felt untouchable, and I had no qualms about shattering his delusion. In fact, I'd have fun doing it. Getting into Rawlings's office would be tricky. There was that key-card security to get to the top floor. An idea began to form, but Risia wasn't the only one running on exhaustion. Yesterday's accident left a dull reminder of its impact, and today hadn't exactly been conductive to rest. I let the half-formed idea roll around, knowing if I left it alone, it would come out and share when it was ready.

Pulling the curtains over the view, I went back to the bed, pulled my gun out, and laid it on the nightstand. Then I picked up the remote, kicked off my shoes, and stretched out. Flipping through channels, I stopped on the latest baseball game and zoned out under the drone of the announcer's voice.

A polite rap at the door jerked me from a light doze. Gun in hand, I was on my feet and halfway to the door when I realized the shower was off.

"Room service."

I stepped to the side of the door and checked the peephole. Seeing a lone male in his early twenties, with a covered cart in the hall, I called, "Just got out of the shower. Do you mind leaving it? I'll grab it in a second."

"I'd be happy to, sir. Please let us know if you need anything else." He disappeared out of the fish-eyed view.

I waited a couple of minutes before unlocking the door. Keeping my gun at my side, I pulled the door open, snagged the cart with one hand, and dragged it into the room. The hall remained empty. Cart safely inside, I relocked the door behind me.

The tantalizing aroma of grilled steak wafted from the covered dishes, waking my stomach with a vengeance.

Pushing it over to the table, I laid my gun down and began pulling off silver domes. Steak and potatoes for me. A pasta tossed with vegetables and shrimp for Risia. A salad, bread rolls, and drinks completed the offering.

"Food's here, Duchess," I called, replacing the cover on her pasta dish. No sense in letting it go cold. Leaving the salad for her, I added a roll to my plate and went back to the bed. I managed to get a couple of bites of tender steak in before the bathroom door opened, releasing a steamy scented cloud.

Jasmine and woman. It curled around me waking a completely different type of hunger. Shifting my plate to cover my obvious reaction, I tried not to stare as Risia stepped out of the bathroom. Woman made it damn hard. The piece of gold silk that tried to pass itself off as a nightgown ended mid-thigh on those long legs. Even the short robe she was tying close didn't help. Her spiral curls fell down between her shoulders, her caramel skin fairly glowed. My hands tightened on my fork and knife as I fought the urge to forgo dinner and satisfy a wholly different hunger.

She stopped by the dinner cart, her back to me. "Looks good." She bent over just enough to have the edge of her robe and gown ride up, lifting a lid.

More than good. Eyes trained on the possibilities, my breath hitched in anticipation.

When she straightened, I reached for my drink and knocked back a healthy slug.

Good lord the woman was dangerous. "It was the closest thing to that dish you had the last time we had dinner."

She finally turned; plate in hand, a curious look on her face. "You remember that?"

I shrugged. "Why do you sound so surprised?"

This time there was no mistaking the blush rising under her skin. She played with the silverware, avoiding my gaze. "You always seemed as if you couldn't stand to be around me."

"True." Her gaze jerked back up, eyes sparking. I cut her short. "You're hell on my control."

I shoved a now tasteless bite into my mouth. I hadn't realized how much my need to keep her at arm's length had hit her. Knowing it now, I couldn't be sure I wouldn't have done the same thing. She threatened me on so many levels. And now that I had a taste, my appetite had only grown, until I wasn't sure I'd ever get her out of my system.

Temper disappeared under her puzzlement. "I'm not sure how to take that."

I set my almost-empty plate aside, stacked my hands behind my head, and let my gaze roam over her. I took my time, not bothering to hide my reaction from her. My rising erection caught her attention and color washed through her face, her delectable chest rose and fell as her breathing deepened. The thin silk did nothing to disguise the rising points of her nipples. "Come here." My voice was husky and strangely enough my head spun.

Her plate rattled against the table as she set it down. She glided toward me, her hips swaying in temptation, her gaze holding mine and dragging me under. She stopped next to the bed.

Holding her gaze, I reached out and ran a fingertip over her collarbone, down the center of her chest, and along the plump side of her breast. Her breath sucked in, only to escape on a shaky moan when I gently circled the distended tip. "Like that?"

Nodding, she licked her lips and it was my turn to groan. I kept my touch light, moving to her other breast. She swayed toward me, and I sat up, the rush of blood to my cock leaving me lightheaded. But it didn't keep me from wrapping my lips around her silk-covered nipple. Her hands tunneled in my hair, holding me close as I teased and laved. My other hand continued its torment on the other side.

"Oh God, Tag." She arched closer.

Nuzzling the deep vee of silk aside, I found warm skin and laid soft, open-mouth kisses against it. Cupping her breast, I snaked my other arm around her waist, holding her close as I made my way up to the base of her throat.

She shifted and set a knee on the edge of the bed as she began to bend over me. Jasmine-scented curls fell around us as she tilted her head, giving me access to her neck.

A low growl escaped as the need to mark began to grow. Small, sharp nips alternated with gentle kisses until I found that sweet spot behind her ear. I sucked hard and she bucked against me, the feel of her, the heat of her, sent my blood thundering through my veins. I wrapped my arms around her and rolled her under me.

Unfortunately, the sudden change in position made my head spin. The unusual reaction set off faraway alarm bells. I swallowed the surge of nausea and under Risia's sweet taste recognized a bitter aftertaste. "Shit," I muttered, burying my face against her neck, fighting against the encroaching heavy darkness invading my body.

"Tag?" Hands framed my face, dragging my head up.

I tried to keep her features in focus, but it was a losing battle. My tongue felt thick, making it hard to talk, but desperation force the words free, "Run, Risia."

Her beautiful crystal eyes widened. "What's wrong?"

I tried to roll off her and couldn't tell if I was successful. Heaviness settled in my limbs, while the darkness crowded closer.

"Tag!" Risia's cry followed me down.

Chapter Twenty

Tag slumped next to me, while his slurred warning slid like ice through my veins. As if I'd leave him here, alone and unprotected. Panic had me in a stranglehold, but I managed to wriggle free. I knelt on the bed and ran my hands over him. *What the hell happened?* Under my palm, his chest rose and fell. "Oh God, Tag." I shook his shoulder, hard. "Come on, wake up, dammit."

Battling back the fear clawing for a foothold, I scanned the room, trying to put the pieces together.

A noise outside the door drove me to lunge across the bed and grab his gun lying next to the alarm clock. The overly loud sound of the lock sliding back sent me scrambling out of the bed until I could stand in between Tag and whoever was coming through the door.

The door began to swing open.

I raised the gun, barrel aimed, finger hovering over the trigger. If I pulled, the bullet would have no problems going through the wood of the door.

"Ms. Lacoste, please don't shoot."

The polite request made me pause. "Haven't you heard of knocking?" My voice came out surprisingly steady.

"My name is Liwei Bai. I have a business proposition for you." A young businessman in tailored shirt and slacks stepped around the door, his hands up.

Two other men came up behind him. One followed Liwei into the room, while the other waited until they passed the door, then pulled it closed, leaving him alone in the hall.

Two to one should be good odds, but I didn't feel confident about my chances. Maybe it was the way the one guy, Liwei's shadow, moved. Or maybe it was his flat-eyed stare. Then again, it could be because I was barefoot in a damn nightie with Tag passed out behind me. "You could have called first."

"Ah, but as this is our first meeting, I wanted to ensure you would agree to meet." Liwei stopped by the dresser. His dark eyes sharp as they took in my current attire and the man sprawled behind me. "I apologize if we interrupted at an inopportune time."

Refusing to acknowledge the discomfort of facing down two strange, probably violent, men in nothing but silk, I arched an eyebrow. "As this has been a hell of a long day, I'd appreciate it if you could get to your point."

"You've recently come into possession of a drive that belonged to Curtis Trammel. I'd like to make you an offer for it."

Dammit to hell. Someone was talking out of turn and it looked like Tag's hunch was spot on. The snakes were crawling out faster than expected, now that they thought I had a price. "You have my attention." The ache in my shoulders spread, a warning I wouldn't be able to hold the shooter's stance for much longer.

He dipped his head in acknowledgment. "I give my word, I am simply here to talk, Ms. Lacoste." He waved a hand. "If you would be so kind as to direct that elsewhere."

Stubbornly I held my position and took the time to study both men. Martial arts training was a given, considering the way they stood. Liwei's bodyguard, bully, whatever the hell he was, was out of my league. Staring down the bore of a nine-millimeter, he was too relaxed. Slowly, I lowered the gun.

Liwei's arms mimicked mine. He motioned to a chair. "Do you mind?"

A polite criminal. How refreshing. "Please."

He moved to the chair and left his man between me and the door, eliminating any foolish notion of escape. As if I was that stupid. I kept my derisive snort in my head. Only as he settled did I smooth the short skirt of my nightie under the back of my thighs as I perched on the edge of the bed, trying to block Tag from view.

Liwei's gaze didn't waver, but I caught the slight flare of his nostrils while the muscle along his jaw jumped, as he tried not to watch.

Gotcha, jackass. I readjusted my legs, slowly crossing one over the other. Laying the gun in my lap, I kept my hand wrapped around the grip. In keeping with our strange dance of manners, I waited, letting Liwei lead.

The professional smile gained an unusual edge of warmth. "You're a beautiful woman, Ms. Lacoste."

"Thank you."

"Please be assured your," he paused as his gaze flickered to Tag, "guard is only unconscious. He'll wake in a few hours with a minor headache. Nothing more. I wanted to ensure we could converse freely, without worry."

"You do realize drugging a military agent may bring trouble to your doorstep." Not to mention Tag was going to be one pissed-off male when he woke.

"It's a risk I was willing to take to talk to you."

Burying my nerves and fear under layers of ice and steel, I

let my lips curl up. "While I appreciate the effort, a phone call would've worked as well."

"Perhaps, but I've found personal conversations tend to garner better results. When someone sets aside time to meet face to face, it shows they are invested in the outcome."

"And what outcome are you pursuing, Mr. Bai?"

He gave a pleasant laugh. "A mutually beneficial agreement."

"Mutually beneficial indicates we both win in the end."

"Oh, I can assure you, Ms. Lacoste, we will both win in the end."

"Considering the information contained on the drive belongs to Aether Industries, I'm not sure that's a real possibility." I tilted my head to the side and threw out the first lure. "If you've done your homework, Mr. Bai, you know I am currently working with Mr. Rawlings. The last person to try and cross him ended up dead." I spared a moment to congratulate myself on not flinching. "I'm not eager to take his place. Besides, the files are highly encrypted."

"Valid concerns. I do not wish to discover you in such a state." He sidestepped the encryption aspect.

"Then you will understand if I must decline your offer?"

"But you've yet to hear it." The civilized veneer slipped, and the predator lurking beneath came out to play. "Aren't you curious?"

I let my gaze flicker and bit my lower lip. The picture of Eve about to nab the pretty red apple. Then I straightened my spine. "Curiosity killed the cat, Mr. Bai."

His smile gained sharp edges as the scent of blood hit the metaphoric waters. "Cats are notorious for their nine lives, Ms. Lacoste. I can offer you enough to live several, comfortably."

"Tempting," I murmured. "But I've discovered a taste for rather expensive things recently. Tastes Mr. Rawlings has no qualms accommodating."

"You strike me as an independent woman, one who'd prefer not answering to a male. Of course, I could be mistaken." His eyes went to Tag, then back to me.

"This?" I reached out and stroked a cold hand over Tag's denim clad leg and gave a light laugh. "This is merely to alleviate my boredom, Mr. Bai."

"So, your aggravation with my methods was merely for show?"

"No," I purred, adding a bite of fury to my words. "I immensely dislike being forced into situations where my actions are questioned. And this," I waved a hand over the unconscious man behind me. "Will require a great amount of finesse to smooth over."

"Ah, my sincerest apologies," he offered. "That was not my intent."

The urge to cough "bullshit" hit, but I stuffed it back. "Intent doesn't interest me."

"What does?"

"Security." I held his unnerving gaze. "Handing you the drive will result in me spending the rest of my life looking over my shoulder. Mr. Rawlings is not an enemy I want. Nor, should any of this come back to roost, would he hesitate to dangle me in front of the U.S. government as his patsy."

Amusement danced over his face. Anticipation sparked a baleful light in his eyes and added a cruel edge to his face. "But what if I could guarantee neither Rawlings nor the government would be any wiser to your actions?"

Unease tripped through my veins. "And how would you possibly be able to accomplish that minor miracle?"

"Because you aren't stealing the drive, merely copying it."

Narrowing my eyes, I tapped my fingers against Tag's leg. "And you would trust me to hand over a copy of these files?"

A real chuckle escaped as he leaned forward. "Trust? Oh

no, Ms. Lacoste, trust is overrated. I work better with guarantees."

My only warning was a quiet command in a Chinese. Before I could react, his bodyguard closed the distance between us and clamped his hands on my shoulders, his fingers digging deep. A wave of numbness rushed down my arms. My hands spasmed and the gun toppled from my lap. *Shitdamnfuck,* I was in trouble.

Liwei stood, walked over, and crouched in front of me. "Such stunning beauty," he murmured and then a pinprick sting against my thigh drew my gaze down.

"What the hell?" A small red bump rose against my skin. Fear held me still because sick knowledge pulsed through me in time with my panicked heartbeat.

"This is my guarantee, Ms. Lacoste." The combination of his pleasant smile with the flat, vicious light in his eyes reduced me to a reactive mess. An instinctive fear held me in place.

"Are you at all familiar with the latest advancements in nanotechnology in conjunction with viruses? It's amazing the leaps medical research can take, especially when your Defense Advanced Research Projects Agency steps in. For example, DARPA is touting the recent development of nanoparticles which can identify and trap invading viruses, aptly named nanotraps. Preliminary tests have demonstrated a high success rate with mainstream viral infections, especially multiple strains of the flu. But, I'm a curious man, and I wondered how effective these nanotraps would be against more aggressive, customized viruses."

Everything in me came to a screeching halt, icy horror freezing every reaction. But the bastard wasn't done.

"Do you know what I found? That with a little tweaking you can not only destroy the cell creating the virus, but pinpoint specific cell structures and create your own invading army, unique to the carrier. No one else can be infected by mistake, you can control the timeline of infection, or you can safely eliminate it from the host."

Liwei rose to his feet, pocketing whatever the hell he stuck in me, and sketched a polite bow. "I'd apologize, but I don't think you'd take my offering. However, as soon as you provide me with what I want, I will be more than happy to ensure you live a long, happy life. May I suggest you don't wait longer than ninety-six hours? It would be such a shame if we miscalculated our timeline." He waved his man back, and the pressure against my shoulders disappeared.

My mind spun in frantic circles and a familiar sensation of the world fraying around me crept in. To keep from melting into a screaming mass of fury and attacking Liwei, I curled my hands into the blankets and tried to hold on. Even if I could move without shattering my control, it would accomplish nothing.

He stopped by the dresser and laid a white business card on the surface. Then he continued to the door, pulled it open, and waved his bodyguard through, before turning to me. "I'd wish you a good evening, Ms. Lacoste, but…" He gave an elegant shrug. "However, I do look forward to our next meeting."

⸺⸺⸺ ••◆•◆•• ⸺⸺⸺

The suffocating silence of the room was broken only by my ragged breaths. Inside my head was a different story. A storm raged, punctuated by my screams. Fate, the vindictive bitch, was back, battering at my psyche with remorseless glee, and I was barely managing to hold on with a bloody grip. It was a pointless battle, one I was bound to lose.

I always did.

Still, something insisted I keep fighting. The future

wrapped around me, tore me away from my precarious perch, and tossed me into the chaotic storm of possibilities. For the first time, it was my futures I faced. And none of them garnered hope. The overriding theme was my death and the death of those around me.

The first wave hit, slamming me with options. Turning on Bai. Turning on Rawlings. Turning them against each other.

Altering my choices with each soul-battering hit still changed nothing.

Turn against Lawrence and my son would pay. Turn against Bai and my friends would pay. Even choosing to bail on the team cost more than my life; it endangered them, set them up for the unimaginable.

Unacceptable.

I may not have a traditional family, but these individuals were important to me and worth saving.

Barely staying above the cresting swells, there was no warning as the Cassandra's Spiral wrapped its arms around me, dragging me into the stygian depths. Soul stealing futures whipped around me, leaving behind scarring wounds etched by unforgiving claws. Then, a sudden, eerie silence fell, and the malicious winds pulled back. A form took shape in the eye of the storm.

Tag, his face carved in a merciless mask. There was nothing left of the man I shared my heart and body with, instead a hellish mix of fury and betrayal warred in his eyes.

"Tag," I couldn't stop the ragged half plea, half question that escaped.

"Damn you, Risia." His rage broke through the mask and his lips twisted. "Damn you."

He raised his arm and instinct had my hands rising in surrender as I faced the barrel of his gun. "What—"

He pulled the trigger.

Agony bloomed as the bullet hit my chest. Trying to staunch the pain, I clutched my chest, only to feel the warmth seeping in time with the slowing beats of my shattered heart.

The surrounding futures stilled into one crystallized moment, then fragmented with the last hard beat of my heart.

A screaming wind tore past Tag and whipped around me, gathering the various futures in its wake. A towering wave formed, only to crash down and drag the splintered pieces of me under. The broken futures howled, tossing me from one possibility to another. Glimpses broke through the storm.

Tag's agony-ridden face as he stood helplessly by, unable to do anything but watch as my virus-ravaged body shut down, piece by piece. Black fury eating him whole, eroding the calculating warrior. Blood-washed scenes dominated by pain and madness as he wiped out his enemies with singular focus, leaving his friends exposed to the circling threats.

A sickening spin, and the scene switched.

Tag's demons were in full control, allowing no one in to help, dragging him further and further down a road with no way back. No matter how loud I screamed or clawed to get his attention, he disappeared into the darkness, taking what was left of my heart with him.

A brutal gust tore me away.

Rawling's gloating face staring back as he handed out names of the government's most covert operatives to the never-ending line of shadowy figures, who left blood-soaked footprints in their wake. Chained to the wall opposite his desk I struggled against my restraints, sending barbed hooks deep.

Another surge.

Bai's sickening smile as he walked toward me through streets strewn with lifeless bodies. He crouched in front of me, and frozen in a body that refused to do anything but shudder in pain, I couldn't avoid his touch as he stroked the side of my face. "Such a beautiful waste. You could've avoided all this." A sad shake of his head. "I did warn you."

The crawling sludge of evil spread from his touch and

seeped into my soul. Guilt carved its own scars amid a chorus of skin-chilling wails.

Another surge hit, and familiar faces appeared twisted in agony or motionless in death. Another swell rose, then another, stronger, more brutal until my screams were nothing but harsh animalistic rasps. When the tide slowed and finally stilled, I barely noticed. The flood of nightmares had left a numbed horror in its wake.

A familiar touch cut through my antipathy and despair. "Duchess." Tag crouched in front of me, his emotional barriers stripped away, worry and that elusive emotion I once prayed I'd find evident on his face. "Let me help."

Weighed down with the endless, shitty possibilities, I could only shake my head. "No." I could barely get the word out around my battered throat.

The shadows around us rippled, and I jerked my gaze away from the temptation kneeling in front of me. Half-formed figures began clawing closer, their focus locked on the man so oblivious to their existence.

"Trust me." He held out his hand, waiting.

God, I wanted to throw myself into his arms so bad my body shook. A faint whisper offered one last breath of hope. *Maybe together we could figure a way out.* I raised a trembling arm.

He's going to kill you!

New forms joined the existing nightmares as they inched closer, red orbs glowing with malicious glee, while a curious tension hummed through them. One of the ones closest to us licked its lips, its gaze aimed at Tag's hand, then slid it to me, bright with eager hunger.

The few remaining pieces of my heart disintegrated under the knowledge carving fatal wounds across my soul. Tearing my gaze away from what lay in wait, I focused on Tag's beloved face. "I can't." My agonized whisper echoed around us, then changed into a hellish howl.

Unable to bear the disappointment washing through his face as his hand dropped, I could only watch as he rose, all traces of emotion disappearing under a blank mask. "You won't."

I didn't answer, couldn't answer. His lip curled as he spun on his heel and walked away, never once acknowledging the shadows around him. I covered my mouth, desperate not to call him back as his demons swarmed forward, intent on claiming their piece of me.

Chapter Twenty-One

TAG

A sense of urgency kept kicking me in the head, refusing to be ignored. My mouth felt like I'd been licking sandpaper and a strange heaviness weighed me down. It took a few moments before I could put the pieces together.

Checking into a hotel. Steak dinner. Risia. Gold silk. Damp skin. Dizziness. A bitter taste.

Dammit, I'd been drugged.

Anxiety cleared out the remaining cobwebs. *Where the hell was Risia?*

First get up, discover who or what I was facing. Hard as it was, I held still, eyes closed.

The soft glow hitting the back of my lids indicated a single lit lamp. Heeding the hair-prickling sense of being watched, I kept my breathing even as I strained to listen. The hum of the air conditioner. Faint sound of an elevator arriving. A burst of muted conversation cut short by a door closing.

The steady breathing from the corner by the desk.

I was lying on my back on the bed, a light blanket covering me. I let out a soft groan and rolled to my side, throwing an arm over my eyes. The rasp of material and creak of wood indicated my watcher abandoned their chair. Soft footsteps crossed the carpet, the tread light.

Only when I could feel them leaning over me, did I drop my pretense. I jerked my arm up, hooking my hand around a slender neck, yanking down and to the side, forcing them off balance. Slamming them face down into the mattress, I jackknifed into an upright position, and rolled over to trap them beneath me. The rapid change in perspective made my head whirl, but I gritted my teeth and rode it out.

"Dammit, let me up, Tag!"

With a soft curse, I jerked my arm back as if burnt and shoved up onto my hands and knees. "Son of bitch, Risia, don't fucking sneak up on me like that." Anger got up close and comfortable with the anxiety already cruising through my system, leaving me on edge and shaky.

Under me, she rolled over and brushed those curls out of her face, my Beretta cradled against her stomach. Her T-shirt-covered stomach. In fact, she was completely dressed. The gold silk was gone, and her curls didn't sport a drop of moisture.

I narrowed my eyes. "How long was I out?"

"Three hours."

Muttering another curse, I shifted until I could sit on the edge of the bed and dropped my aching head into my hands.

Behind me, I could feel her moving around. Her weight left the mattress and the dull thunk indicated she set the gun down on the table. The snap of plastic twisting preceded her offering of a water bottle. "Here, you could probably use this."

"Thanks." I grabbed it and began draining its contents.

She reclaimed a chair by the desk where the gun rested and tucked those long legs under her.

Wiping the back of my hand over my mouth, I asked, "What happened?"

She drummed her fingers against the desk as she watched me, the crystalline blue of her eyes carrying shadows that weren't there before my enforced nap. That they existed now pissed me off to no end. Guaran-fucking-teed, whatever story she gave me, I wasn't going to like. She finally broke the quiet. "You were partially right."

"About?"

"Other interested parties think I can be bought." Her carefully neutral tone meant serious shit went down during my enforced nap.

My hands tightened on the water bottle and the snaps of the collapsing plastic sounded overly loud. I set the bottle aside, more to give myself time to rein in my fury than anything else. "Who?"

"Do you know the name Liwei Bai?"

I combed through memories. "Liwei Bai? Doesn't sound familiar."

She held up a white business card between two fingers. "What about Zunjing Kashi Corporation?"

"Not ringing any bells, Duchess."

She blew out a breath and carefully set it back on the desk. "Figures."

"What did he look like?"

"Early thirties, five-seven, a hundred forty pounds or so, professional businessman, with a matching shadow proficient in martial arts."

A pretty general description and not much to use. Maybe I could get more once I accessed PSY-IV's database. "Why don't you start after I passed out."

She absently tapped the card next to my gun and shared the story of Bai's visit. As I listened, I watched her, fighting back frustration. She was hiding something, again.

Her voice was steady and other than the nervous drumming of her fingers, she appeared to be fine. But she scampered back behind her professional mask. Her gaze was guarded, her shoulders braced, and when she thought I wasn't looking, she bit her lip. "He assured me you were only unconscious, not dead. He said he wanted to talk freely." The little hitch in her voice made me wince.

Fury cooled to calculated anger, as I considered what I could do to this Liwei Bai for scaring Risia. And it wasn't just the threat to me that frightened her. Considering the bracing breath she dragged in and the quick glance from under thick lashes, the real reason behind Bai's visit was coming.

"He wants me to copy Rawlings's files and hand them over to him. Assured me no one, not Rawlings, not the government, would be the wiser." She fell quiet, her hand absently rubbing her thigh.

"And you would do this for him, why?" Shoving my roiling emotions back, I kept my tone gentle. She didn't need me adding to the shit raining down on her.

She bit her lower lip and despite the conversation, or maybe because of it, the urge to take her mouth and sooth the small injury flared. Remembering the results of my last attempt to assuage my hunger threw ice over it. We weren't safe here, and until we were, there was no room for indulging in the ultimate tension reliever. I didn't move from my position, simply held her gaze and gave her something solid to hold on to. No judgment, no pressure.

Those long lashes fluttered down, brushing the bruised skin under her eyes and highlighting the pale undertone dulling her skin. God, I needed to get her back to Meli's. Exhaustion and stress were wearing her down. She drew in another breath, straightened her shoulders, and met my gaze, her lips curling into a cynical twist. "Because he offered to match Rawlings's price, multiple times over. He also tossed in a few extras."

"Multiple?"

She nodded.

Old habits had suspicion whispering ugly insinuations. I

stared at her, wondering, even as I tried to shut it down. I caught her wince before I succeeded. "An offer that big means there's something more than just names on that drive." I ran a hand through my hair, trying to erase the moment. "What extras?"

"A new identity and a removal of any lingering threats. His words, not mine." Her voice was as bland as her expression.

Obviously, my mental slip was going to cost me. Nothing to do but move forward. "Tempting," I drawled, injecting a wry note into my voice.

That stopped her nervous tapping and garnered a tiny thaw in her expression. "Seems a woman like me requires a lifestyle of a certain caliber."

"And if you don't manage to hand him a copy of Rawlings's files?" Because offers like that always carried a catch.

"He'll eliminate me."

The brutal words fell into the room, slicing into me like a hot knife. I took the sting, but couldn't stop my rejection, "He won't get to you."

"He already did."

Her soft accusation brought me to my feet, guilt and anger churning into a seething storm. I was across the room and standing in front of her, hands on either side, trapping her between the chair and me. "He won't touch you."

Her chin jutted forward, and anger sparked hectic color along her cheekbones. "Look, stuff the macho bullshit, we knew this would happen. I don't need your reassurance. You're just pissed he caught you off guard."

Macho bullshit? Was she fucking serious? "You think I'm pissed because he took a swipe at my ego?"

She leaned forward, close but not touching. "Isn't it? It's not like you're some romance novel hero, is it?"

What the hell was she talking about? "My ego has nothing

to do with this. And I can't even begin to understand what books have to do with this."

She slammed her hands against my chest and shoved hard. "I don't need fucking rescuing, Tag."

Rearing up, I took a step back, retreating from the temptation to shake her until she made some goddamn sense. "I never said you did." The conversation had jumped tracks and I didn't have a damn clue on how to get it back on line. "Where the hell is this coming from?"

She sprang from the chair and paced in the other direction, keeping a shit-ton of space between us. "I was so stupid to think this would work." She dragged her hands through her hair and glared at me. "There's no way you can keep our jobs separate from whatever this is between us." She looked away, her gaze dancing over the room. "You're going to get me killed."

She stomped over to the chair tucked in the corner where the flash of gold silk barely registered through my shock. She kept her back to me and snatched it up. "If you can't trust me to do my job, then you need to step out of this. Let Wolf handle it when he gets here." She stormed to the end of the bed, grabbed the bag, and heaved it up. Opening it, she threw the handful of material inside.

My mind reeled as she raged around the room throwing shit in the bag on the bed.

She disappeared into the bathroom, still talking. "I'll call Delacourt and explain, tell her it's my fault."

Fury edged out shock, and I stalked forward, blocking her in the bathroom. She turned, armful of lotions and bottles cradled against her chest. "What the fuck are you talking about?" I bit out each word, holding my control by the thinnest of margins.

"We can't work together."

"The hell we can't. We've been doing just fine."

Her arms tightened, hugging her beauty collection closer. "Maybe, but it won't last."

"Why not?"

"Because you don't trust me. Not really, not where it counts."

The absolute certainty in her answer left me reeling. "Are you fucking serious?"

"Yeah." She took a deep breath. "Look, I get it. I do. Earning your trust takes time, and time is the one thing we don't have right now. We're about to enter into a dangerous game. If you hesitate because you can't decide if I'm playing a part or if I'm considering betraying you or the team for real, it will cost me more than I'm willing to pay." She watched me with a strange intensity.

Every word landed with a devastating accuracy I had trouble recovering from. "That's not going to happen."

"Really? Then look me in the eye and tell me you didn't just wonder if I had taken Bai up on his offer?"

Unable to lie to her, I could only stand there and endure the glimpse of torment she was quick to hide behind a brittle smile. "That's what I thought."

"Duchess," I grated out, but she was shaking her head.

"Don't, Tag, please. Just..." she swallowed. "Let me pack. Let's go to Meli's and wait for the rest of the team to arrive. I can't deal with this right now."

"And if that doesn't work for me? If I want to fix this before we leave the room?" The need push, to corner her and show her why walking away from me wasn't an option had the words tumbling out. The craving for her taste, her touch clawed my heart raw, while my demons cackled in delight, slithering from doubt's shadows. She was slipping through my fingers, leaving me exposed and desperate. Two states I had trouble handling.

"It's not going to happen." She stepped closer. "Let me go."

Instincts demanded I ignore her, but logic warned it would cause irreparable damage and drive her further out of reach. Uncurling my grip on the doorframe, I reached out to touch her, needing the connection touch would give.

"Don't!" She flinched back.

The agony of her sharp refusal whipped across my ragged emotions, yanking me up short with brutal effectiveness. Hearing her deny my touch buckled something in my chest. Unable to take any more, I straightened and locked every piece of anger, hurt, and disappointment behind familiar walls.

Fuck this and fuck her.

She wanted this to be about the job, then that's what she'd get. "Finish packing. We'll leave in ten."

***

A couple of hours later, caught between the warring need to fuck her or shake her, I left Risia in the villa. I figured we were safer that way.

On the ride in, she pretended to sleep. Hoping to get a handle on my mental mess, I let her. Unfortunately, trapped next to her while her scent invaded every inch of the interior and reminded me of things better ignored, my mental mess had graduated to a full-blown disaster.

My head ached as much as my body and trying to untangle the confrontation at the hotel seemed to make matters worse. Lying next to her in the dark would not end well, which is why I was currently parking my ass on the bench on the porch.

Hell, I'd probably spend the rest of the night out here. Not like sleep would be joining me any time soon.

The moon was bright and shone across the quiet clearing. A slight breeze washed through the leaves of the surrounding trees. The sound mimicked the hush of falling water over rocks. Utilizing old habits, I sank into the quiet, until the night's patterns became familiar and the whirling chaos in my mind began to slow, then settle. Only then did I unlock the door holding my emotions back, letting them leak out where I could figure out what the hell had happened. Because something about the confrontation with Risia was off.

I couldn't pinpoint exactly what was making me think that, but the certainty of it grew with each passing minute. The argument looped through my mind as I tried to view it objectively. Guilt at being caught with my pants down didn't do a damn thing for either of us. Worried about Hand Tooled, it never occurred to me that other scum, like Bai, would scuttle out of their pits so quickly.

So, the bastard managed to drug me. Now that I was aware of the methods he would utilize, I'd take precautions and make sure Risia wasn't left hanging in the wind. Once Wolf, Rabbit, and Jinx showed up, my odds increased. The more eyes on this, the better.

Those three hours must have seemed endless for Risia. The games your mind could play in that amount of time could be crippling. Normally, she'd be able to face down whatever life threw her, but in the last three days, she'd been blackmailed, shot, subjected to brutal vision after brutal vision, and running on fear and adrenaline. Add in the drastic change in our relationship and there was no doubt her emotional footing was no more stable than mine.

Hell, much like me, she knew how to hide her emotions.

Even from me.

Her sharp rejection of my touch replayed with crystalline clarity and something clicked into place. "Son of a bitch," I muttered, wiping a hand over my face, as realization seared through the tangled mess, leaving a clearer picture in its wake.

She hadn't wanted me to touch her because she knew it would let me see beneath her mask. The mask she wore whenever she was scared or pissed. I was betting on scared this time, which meant she was hiding something big. The question now was what was it, and how would it impact our job?

Of course, asking her would get me nowhere, especially since she deliberately derailed our conversation. Smart of her, since it guaranteed I'd be too pissed to look beyond the obvious.

Damn her. I needed to come up with a way to get the truth from her, without touching.

And wasn't that a bitch? Because sure as shit, if I took that route, I'd lose her and that wasn't an option I was willing to accept.

Chapter Twenty-Two

I finally peeled my eyes open to find sunlight dancing across the twisted covers and Tag nowhere to be found. The headache that followed me home was joined by the weight of a sleepless night.

The drive in had been uncomfortably silent, Tag's anger riding shotgun, while I tried to reassure my bruised heart that this was for the best. We arrived at the cabin late last night and I headed straight for the bathroom trying to keep the distance between us. I heard the front door close and safe behind the bathroom door, finally gave into the tears.

I was really beginning to hate Meli's bathrooms.

Once the waterworks slowed, I washed my face and crawled beneath the covers. The hours ticked by as I fought the urge to go outside and spill the whole sorry mess to Tag. Every time, flashes of what I saw served as pitiless reminders of why that would be a bad idea.

Somewhere near dawn, I finally fell into a light sleep, riddled by the images still dogging my psyche. Now, I drew back the covers and sat up slowly, brushing my hair out of my face. Staring at the skin exposed by the oversized T-shirt I slept in, my gaze caught on the irritated redness surrounding the injection mark. Anger and fear churned inside me, making me sick. I dashed to the bathroom and dropped to my knees in front of the toilet. Dry heaves wracked my body. *Damn Liwei. Damn Rawlings. Damn me.* There were no more tears to shed.

My body ached as I pushed to my feet and turned to the sink to splash cold water over my flushed face. Hectic flags of color stained my cheeks, indicating a low-grade fever. Staring at my reflection, I knew I had to hold it together, otherwise Tag would dig, and I didn't think I could keep him out if he decided to be relentless.

Once the others arrived tonight, I'd get some breathing room, but first I had to get through this morning and the meeting with Rawlings. Which meant I couldn't afford to wallow in the disaster the rest of my life was currently in, so I began tucking it away, piece by piece. As soon as I managed to shove it all away, I concentrated on the things I could control.

First up, get rid of the nuisance headache. I went through the medicine cabinet, found some aspirin, and popped two tablets. Next, I began reconstructing the woman Rawlings expected.

An hour later, I stepped from the bathroom dressed in heels, pencil skirt, and a silk blouse I salvaged from my condo. Carefully applied makeup hid the circles under my eyes and disguised the pale undertone of my skin. Curls were tamed into a simple twist, and I was slipping the last earring in when the door opened.

I froze.

"Meli sent over bagels." Tag raked a glance over me, set a cloth-covered bowl on the table, then turned to close the door behind him.

Caught off guard, I could only stand in silence, waiting to see which way he'd attack. Instead, he continued, with no sign of last night's confrontation in sight, "She threw in a couple of orange juices."

He pulled a bottle out of each front pocket and set them next to the bowl. Then he emptied the bag and set small paper plates next to each drink.

"Thanks, but I'm not hungry," I offered cautiously, not trusting this Tag.

He looked up. "You didn't eat dinner last night, and I can't remember the last time you actually ate something. You're running on empty. Sit down and we'll head out once you've eaten."

All righty then. Not wanting to step into another argument, I slowly walked over and took the seat he pulled out for me.

He finished slathering cream cheese on a toasted bagel, then set it in front of me. He doctored another bagel and then took the chair across from me.

I watched, mesmerized, as his white teeth bit into the warm bread.

He caught me staring and something in his eyes flashed too fast to catch, but his face remained relaxed, revealing nothing. He chewed slowly and waved his bagel at me in silent encouragement to eat.

A blush rose under my skin, hotter than the fever, as I looked down at my plate. The warm, yeasty smell rose and instead of the expected nausea, my stomach gave a quiet growl. I broke off a piece and chewed.

Tag continued to eat, all the while watching.

Not a comfortable experience, but my determination not to react left me with nothing to do but finish my bagel. So, I did. I was taking a sip of juice when Tag broke the silence, "You look beautiful."

The juice went down the wrong way and I broke into a coughing fit. Grabbing a nearby napkin, I managed to save my blouse without further embarrassment. Once I could breathe, I looked up and caught the small twitch of his lips and glared at him. "That wasn't funny, Tag."

"Wasn't meant to be, Duchess, just stating a fact."

What the hell was he up to now? "What are you doing?"

"Having breakfast with you. Is that not allowed?"

With no way to answer that wouldn't make me look like the mental case I was, I drummed my fingers against the table. He raised his arms, laced his fingers behind his head, and leaned back in his chair, tilting it until he balanced on the back legs.

"You're going to fall over and hit your head," I muttered.

He grinned. "Nah, this is one of my many talents."

Unable to stop myself, I snipped, "So is being a pain in the ass."

"Ah, but you like my ass, don't you?" he drawled.

More than was smart. I squashed the thought, our byplay snagging against the rough edges of my heart. "I can't play games right now." The confession tumbled from my lips, part anger, part hurt.

His grin faded to be replaced with a tender seriousness. "I'm not playing games. I'm just trying to give you a break before you tangle with Rawlings."

The implication behind his answer brought a lump to my throat and I looked down, unable to hold his gaze. There would be no break from the danger lining us up in its crosshairs. Rawlings and Liwei; individually they were enough have me quaking in my Jimmy Choo's. Together, they upped the pucker factor, an apt term the team tossed around when things were about to go south, by twenty. I fiddled with the plate in front of me.

"I know you're hiding something." Tag's quiet statement yanked my head up and panic surged hard before I could lock it down. He resettled the chair and leaned forward, arms on the table. The instant denial hovered on the other side of my teeth, but before it could escape, he continued, "I don't know what it is, but considering how hard you're shoving me away, I'm thinking whatever really happened with Bai won't make me happy."

I bit my lip. Oh, that was the understatement of the year. Ballistic. Crazy. Protective. Overbearing. Foolish. Murderous. Those words were much better options, but none would help take this conversation anywhere I was comfortable with, so I kept quiet.

He studied me and the sense of him seeing far more than I wanted had my ass dancing in my chair before I could think better of it. The gold green deepened, and he gave me a tight smile. "I thought so," he murmured.

I stilled. "Don't."

Don't push? Don't keep digging until I break? Hell, I couldn't decide if I wanted him to back off or force me into spilling my guts. One would cost him, the other, me, either way it could cost us both more than we could pay.

The tightness in his face faded until his smile was a mix of male exasperation and wry humor. "You know better than to throw down the gauntlet like that, Duchess. It's too hard not to pick it up."

And maybe that's exactly what I wanted. Right? No. Yes. Damn him, he was driving me insane. "It wasn't a challenge."

"Uh-huh." His smile widened into a grin.

Unable to sit still, I used one of the napkins to wipe my fingers clean and pushed the paper plate aside. "I thought you were going to give me a break?"

"I am." He got to his feet and stretched.

Not fair! The internal whine came from the part of me still reveling in tactile memories of heated skin under my hands and mouth, fueling an addiction I had no desire to break. Tearing my gaze away, I brushed invisible crumbs from my lap and rose, proud when my legs remained steady.

But before I could test out my balance, he spoke, "How are your pickpocketing skills?"

The unexpected question had me tilting my head in inquiry. "What?"

"I need access to Rawlings's office. Preferably by tonight."

Needing a bit of breathing room, I stepped around him and picked up my clutch from the foot of the bed. "Why? Think he's going to have 'illegal sales' penciled in his calendar?"

Tag gave a soft snort. "No one keeps an actual calendar anymore, it's all on their phone."

The pieces began to fall into place. "You want to clone his phone?"

"And his ID badge."

Because he needed to get both items to Rabbit. Either one would be more than enough for the team's electronic genius to gain access to Rawlings, having both guaranteed it. I dug in my small clutch, nabbed a familiar tube of no-smudge lipstick, and thanks to years of practice, applied it without a mirror. "Ballsy move."

His shoulders hitched in a shrug. "Necessary, actually."

"And how do you plan on cloning these without Rawlings realizing he's missing his phone and badge?" I tossed the lipstick back into the bottomless pit every clutch or purse seemed to generate.

"The phone is easy. I had Rabbit ship me out a new phone, which we'll pick up on the way into your meeting. According to him, all you have to do is run an app while you're sitting next to him and we'll have access to his calendars and contacts."

"An app?"

He grinned. "One of Rabbit's personal inventions."

Sounded simple enough. "Glad he's on our side."

"The badge is a different story."

Of course it was. I turned to face him. "Hence the pickpocket question?"

He nodded.

I folded my arms. "You know he wears his badge on his belt clip." Which made it much easier to snag, but also meant I had to get close, very close. "You understand what that means, right?"

Gold flashed in his eyes and a slight frown marred his forehead. "Yeah."

Dropping my arms, I smoothed out the material of my skirt and took a step, closing the distance between us. "And you're okay with that?"

His throat worked as he swallowed, his gaze darkening as he watched. "No, but it's not like we have much of a choice."

Inches separated us, and I tilted my head back a bit to look into his face. I ran a hand down his arm and placed the other right above his heart. "True, but I need to know you can handle it."

"Is this where I say, trust me, I'm a professional?" His hands landed on my hips and pulled me closer. "Maybe the better question is can you handle it?"

To answer him, I let a slow smile grow and leaned back just enough to raise my hand, complete with his wallet, to eye level.

He blinked, looked at the wallet, then back to me, his lips twitching. "Guess that answers that question." He snagged the wallet. "Can you do that in reverse?"

"What do you think?"

"I think we're good." Much to my disappointed relief he stepped back. "Once you have his badge, you can slip away to the bathroom, hand if off to me, then pick it up on the way back."

Doable. Still, like a grain of sand caught underfoot, worry

scratched at me. "You're not planning on going into his office alone, are you?"

"Backup's on the way, remember?"

I nibbled on my lower lip. "Doesn't mean you'll wait for them. Rawlings tends to pop into his office during odd hours." Something I discovered in the weeks I watched him. "You should take Rabbit."

He shook his head. "I need him working on the files. I'll take Wolf or Jinx."

"Good." I checked the digital display on the alarm clock on the nightstand. "We need to go. I don't want to be late."

"Let the ass wait. Might do his ego some good."

My lips twitched despite my best intentions. "No sense in pissing him off more than necessary. I need him in a cooperative mood."

Heat wrapped around me as he came up behind me. "He'll be more than happy to cooperate with you looking like this," he growled.

Warning bells blared, and I struggled to wall off my traitorous emotions and block his Peeping Tom touch the only way I knew how. The soft brush of lips over my bare neck generated a delicate shiver and my clutch fell to the bed. I fought not to lean back and barely won the desperate battle, slipping to the side and out of his reach. "That is kind of the point of this exercise."

"The point is to keep you breathing, any way I can."

The ruthless edge to his answer served as a balm to my battered heart, but it also made me nervous. *How far would he really go? At what point would that change?* I took a chance and turned around to face him. "Which means what, Tag?"

We were so close, one breath away from touching. I studied his face, memorizing every detail. Did he not understand that the feeling was mutual? Knowing how bleak my future was, I finally admitted the truth, if only to myself.

I loved him.

Not with some sweet simplicity, but with the searing intensity of a lightning strike, one that would burn long after the flash of light seared the world away. But it wasn't enough to keep his demons at bay. The only way to keep him safe was to torch any chance he had at realizing how much power he really held over me. With cruel intent, I began slicing through the fragile ties between my heart and hidden dreams, taking something precious and smearing it with distrust and disillusionment. "Are you trying to seduce me to fuck me, or fuck with me?"

My jab bounced off, leaving behind a wicked smile, filled with equal parts of heat and danger. "Either would work for me right now, Duchess."

His volley found its mark. Anger and need tangled into a hot, bright mess. I brought my hands up, palms flat against his chest and leaned in. "You sure it's just me who'd be fucked?" Brushing the lightest of kisses against the underside of his jaw, I followed it with another. Under my hands, his heart picked up speed, and mine chased it. I took my time, laying another kiss against his hot skin.

This was so dangerous, because it could reveal more than I was willing to show, but caught in my own web, I didn't want to stop. I tilted my head back, my voice husky with desire. "I'm not the only one with something to lose here."

It didn't take much to go on tiptoe, bringing me level to that mouth that haunted too many of my fantasies. This close, I couldn't mistake the rigid proof I was getting to him. Problem was, I was just as ensnared. A delicate flick of my tongue traced his lower lip, and our breaths mingled.

With an almost-audible snap, his impressive control broke. He captured my mouth, ravaging it with a wild hunger. My anger morphed into craving and a desperate need to lay a claim I couldn't keep. We fought for dominance, a rough tangle of tongues and breath.

I clutched his shoulders for much-needed stability as the riptide of emotions rocked the world under my feet. I fought back, stealing strength from him, hoarding it against what waited for me on the other side of the door. Caught up in my own needs I missed when he gentled the kiss, making it more, taking it deeper than anticipated. I arched closer, encouraged by the heat of his hands as they cupped my hips and pressed me closer.

My heart and body waged war against my better judgment, taking the battle to the edge of my unraveling control. The ground crumbled underfoot and I slipped over. Memories dowsed my rising desire in frigid horror. Tag surrounded by his demons, their hungry gazes focused on me, their lips curled in cruel anticipation. I yanked against his unyielding hold, gasping for breath, and scrambled for emotional purchase.

Tag's gaze narrowed on my face. "What the hell was that?"

Shitdamnfuck! What had I been thinking letting him in that close? *Stupid, stupid Risia.* Might as well just kill him now and call it good. Agony lanced me and with a harsh sound, I broke free, my eyes burning. "Damn you, Tag." Damn me and my delusional heart.

His stunned confusion changed into steely-eyed determination. His hands curled into fists as he glared at me. "Don't worry, Duchess, your secrets are safe."

He walked to the door, yanked it open, and stepped to the side, waiting. Unable to form a single word that wouldn't end in a frustrated scream, I gathered my clutch and forced my stiff limbs to cooperate. I made it to the door and tried to ignore Tag's silently perusal. I stepped even with him. His arm shot out, blocking my way, trapping me in front of him.

Struggling to keep my badly damaged emotional shields in place, I gave him my haughtiest princess-to-the-peon look.

And, frustrating male that he was, he smiled. A smile that held nothing nice and set off every warning bell I had. "Haven't you learned yet?"

"Learned what?" I snapped.

He leaned down until my entire view was his face. "I live for secrets."

Beautiful, arrogant ass! "Adrenaline junkie."

He laughed. Laughed! "Damn straight. Better lock 'em down tight, Duchess, because some things are worth the risk."

Chapter Twenty-Three

I waited in front of the wrought-iron doors of The Spires while Tag handed the valet the keys to his rental. The spiraling architecture was a breathtaking addition to Vegas's skyline, more a sculpture than hotel, similar in style to those in Dubai, but that was the only resemblance.

Here the heat was a solid wall, with no chance of humidity and the line of cars waiting to park was a mishmash of luxurious indulgence and practical family mobility. Even the milling humanity represented the eclectic mix unique to Vegas. A group of college-age kids waited for a taxi, hands weighed down by overpriced plastic cups complete with their alcoholic drink of choice. A sleek two-door number slid up to the curb, disgorging an attractive thirty-something couple, while childish laughter came from the family waiting patiently by a stack of luggage.

Tag came to a stop in front of me, cutting my people watching short. "Ready?"

I gave him a nod, turned on my heel, and headed in. We threaded our way past the casino and into the heart of the hotel where shops spread along the wide walkways. We arrived at

The Attic, its facade a re-creation of a posh private club situated in the cobbled streets of London, which looked strangely out of place among the well-known shops surrounding it. An attractive woman dressed to the nines manned the hostess station outside the door and after getting my name, led us inside.

It took a few moments for my eyes to adjust to the low lighting. Heavy wood paneling and padded leather, interspersed with brass, completed the experience of stepping into an actual private club. Burnished tables perched amidst high-backed, cushioned benches, giving diners a private niche.

A few feet inside, the din of shopping crowds disappeared, replaced by the soft murmurs of conversation and the muted clinking of silver on china. We followed the hostess as she wound her way further into the restaurant. A highly polished bar top ran the length of the room. Leather-padded barstools, some full, perched in front of the brass foot rail, with views to the strategically placed TVs tuned to various sporting events.

Our hostess continued until she stopped in front of one of the semi-secluded booths and with a polite smile said, "Enjoy your lunch."

Rawlings slipped out of the booth, holding his hands out and giving me no choice but to take the offering. He closed his fingers around mine and pulled me forward until he could kiss my cheek. Weeks of his presumptive behavior made it easier to ignore the shiver of revulsion his touch created. "Risia, looking lovely as always."

I stepped back with a polite murmur and tried to ignore the uneasy feelings settling in for a visit as he studied me. "Lawrence."

He looked behind me to Tag, and his charming smile gained a sharp edge. "Agent."

"Rawlings."

"Feel free to make the most of the bar."

Staying true to character, I set my clutch on the table and ignored the testosterone-studded exchange. With my back to Tag, I couldn't see his response to Rawlings's not-so-subtle hint, but I didn't miss the merest brush of his fingers against my back. A reassuring touch hidden from Rawlings's avid gaze. He walked away, and I slipped into the booth.

Rawlings watched Tag, something sly and crafty sliding through his face before his carefully constructed mask fell back in place. The malice in that one revealing glimpse left a sickening dread curling through me. Before I could determine if it was a touch of prescience or just paranoia, he turned back to me, his smile firmly in place as he re-took his seat. "So glad you could make it, dear."

The benevolent-leader shtick set my teeth on edge, but I managed to curl my lips up. "Wouldn't dream of missing it, Lawrence."

A waiter glided up to our table. "May I get you a drink?"

"Booker Noe neat." Because right now, the burn of a damn good whiskey couldn't hurt.

"Make it two," Rawlings echoed our initial meeting that kicked off this whole nightmare, deliberately, if the cruel amusement in his tone was any indicator.

I suppressed a shiver and the waiter dipped his head in acknowledgement and left.

Rawlings prattled on with meaningless pleasantries as we waited for our drinks.

I managed to respond appropriately, all the while fighting the urge to look to Tag.

Our waiter returned, delivered two smoky amber drinks in heavy cut crystal, took our order, then slipped away.

"You seem a little nervous, Risia. Has something happened?"

Rawlings's drawled question shoved me face first into a

reality check. If I didn't get my head in the game, Liwei's little concoction would be the least of my worries.

I lifted my glass and murmured, "You could say that." Taking a small sip, I set it back down with careful precision. "Your little project seems to be attracting all kinds of interesting attention."

Behind the wire-frame lenses his eyes glinted. "I did warn you not to play the game if you couldn't win."

I let a cold smile twist my lips. "I never play to lose. Especially considering the stakes."

"You think you hold enough to keep the wolves at bay?"

I circled the edge of my glass with a nail. "I think I hold enough to be able to keep you between me and them."

"I'm curious at how you arrived at that conclusion." He picked up his drink.

I gave him a delicate shrug. "Experience."

He paused, studying me over the rim of his glass, took a sip, and set it back down. "Experience? My, my, Risia, you continue to surprise me."

"Really? You don't seem like the type to be surprised."

"Hmm, but you haven't responded quite the way I predicted."

Fury burned away my nerves. "Did you think you could issue such a threat and I would, what? Crumble and beg?"

His hand whipped out, locked around my wrist, and squeezed until bones grated. "Begging is a much more productive move than trying to out maneuver me."

Ignoring the bruising pain of his grip, I leaned forward, until I could reach his thigh where a very sensitive nerve lay. Digging my nails in deep, I could feel his muscles jump under the pressure even as I tried to ignore the unsettling spike of lust darkening his face. It took effort to keep my polite smile in place. "I don't beg any man."

Message delivered, I let go, knowing it would take a good

thirty seconds for feeling to resume in his leg. As I drew back, I brushed against the plastic edge of his badge, but left it alone.

For now.

For a moment, I thought I'd pushed too hard, as his fingers tightened until I thought my wrist would snap under the pressure. "I love challenges," he murmured, then slowly released his fingers one at a time.

What the hell was it about men and challenges? God save me from men out to prove themselves. "That was a statement, Lawrence, not a challenge." I pulled back my arm, absently noting the red marks, which would graduate to bruises. Tag was going to lose his shit when he saw this.

Our waiter returned with our food. Rawlings waited until he left to ask, "Why should I risk my skin for you?"

I concentrated on cutting the steak into bite-size pieces I had no appetite for. "Because you're first and foremost a businessman, and competition is barely tolerated."

He chuckled. "You think you're competition."

I stabbed a piece and held it on the tines of my fork while I met his gaze. "I'm not competition, I'm much worse. I'm the one who could undercut your price. I'm sure I could find a price considerably more reasonable than yours." I raised an eyebrow as I took my bite.

His gaze flicked to my mouth before coming back up. Lust was overshadowed by reluctant respect edged with calculation. "Beauty and brains make for a tempting combination."

I simply smiled and took another bite.

He picked up his cutlery and began cutting his steak into uniform bites. "I'm curious."

Swallowing, I reached for my drink and took a sip before I replied. "About?"

He stabbed a cube and raised it, the light glinting off his lenses as he studied me. "These interested parties you mentioned. What did they offer you?"

I shook my head. "It's poor business practice to share such information. Suffice to say, it was considerably more than expected."

His lips twisted into a smirk. "So, you do have a price point?"

I leaned back, letting the simmering rage and disgust he evoked rise and seep around the edges of a brittle smile. "It wasn't so much the price point, as the extras they suggested."

He raised a mocking eyebrow. "Extras?"

My smile grew into a baring of teeth as I picked up my glass. "They promised to remove any obstacles I may encounter."

Red rose along his cheekbones, his mouth thinned, and his voice was frigid. "Is that so?"

Instead of answering, I tilted my glass toward him in acknowledgment and tamped down my vicious satisfaction.

"I'm surprised you didn't accept."

I affected a careless shrug. "Truthfully? I was tempted."

"Unfortunately, that's understandable."

"Mmm." I took another sip, then set the heavy glass down carefully. Time to up the ante. "But after witnessing how intense your colleagues can be and seeing how you already have an exit plan, I think my chances of enjoying my return on investment may be partnering with you." I slid him a heated look from under my lashes even as my stomach turned. "Besides, some things are worth a little danger."

"You think our partnership could be dangerous?"

Picking up my fork, I leaned over, one hand balanced on his thigh, and speared a piece from his plate. "Perhaps," I murmured, slipping the bite into my mouth.

He watched, his eyes brightening, and the muscles under my hand tensed. Offering him a small, knowing smile, I slowly leaned back, nabbing the badge on my way.

"Perhaps," he repeated. Then he took his bite and chewed slowly.

For a few blessed minutes, silence reigned. The occasional considering look told me behind that blank mask his mind was running through options. Finally, he spoke. "I could easily force your hand."

The implied threat to my son sent fear spiraling through me. I choked it back and held his gaze. Absolute fury burned a ruthless bite to my voice, "Do you really want to know what I would do with nothing to lose?"

He gave me a tight smile. "I'm highly aware, Risia, of how vindictive the female persuasion can be, but I would be a fool to trust you."

"Who said anything about trust? I'm only interested in a one-time partnership. You get what you want, I get what I want. Afterwards, we both walk away." If this proposition was for real, I'd ensure the only one walking away would be me.

Our attentive waiter made a stop, offering refills. "Could you bring me an espresso?"

"Of course, ma'am."

Giving him a brief smile, I took the opportunity to slide out of the booth. "Where is your ladies' room?" He pointed me back toward the bar even as Rawlings began to slide out, but I waved him back. "No, I'll only be a few moments."

I didn't give him a chance to insist but walked away. I could feel him watching me. Near the bar, I brought my clutch up and pretended to dig through it, angling too close to a booth where another waitress was currently handing out drinks. Absorbed in my search, I stumbled into the poor girl.

She valiantly tried to save me and her drinks, but I still managed to get splashed. I dropped my clutch and grabbed her arms, trying to help. "I'm so sorry," I said. "Are you all right."

"I'm fine," she murmured with a professional ease, even as irritation tightened her smile. "Are you okay?"

I gave a half-hearted swipe to my skirt. "Nothing a little water won't clear up."

"Ms. Lacoste, your purse?"

Behind the waitress, Tag straightened and offered me my clutch. With a murmured "thank you", I took it and continued to the bathroom. Alone behind the closed door of the ladies' room, I stood before the mirror, hands braced on the counter and concentrated on breathing through my nerves. By the third breath, my hands had stopped shaking.

Using the thick, disposable towels folded in a neat stack on the counter, I began to blot away the remnants of my klutzy run-in. I just finished reapplying my lipstick when the door swung open, letting in two young women in skin-tight sheaths and heels. I relinquished my spot in front of the mirror and headed back out.

As I drew even with the bar where Tag sat hunched over a glass, ostensively watching the soccer game, I changed direction and stepped up to the bar, keeping two empty seats between us. Deliberately ignoring him, I opened my clutch, pulled out my plastic and then laid my open clutch on the top. Catching the bartender's attention with a raised hand and smile, I called, "Excuse me."

Early thirties, neatly trimmed mustache, and dressed in the same black and white style as the waiters, he asked, "What can I get you?"

I leaned forward. "Actually, I'd like to cover whatever that table would like." I handed over my card, then turned and angled so I could offer a smile to the occupants of the booth. "An apology for my clumsiness."

The older couple smiled back.

I turned back to find the bartender's polite smile had turned into a grin. He ran the card; I signed off, then reclaimed my clutch and made my way back to Rawlings. My espresso was waiting for me, and I slid back into the booth, feeling the weight of Rawlings's gaze as he looked up from his phone.

"Are you all right, dear?"

I gave a small grimace. "Purses are the bane of all females. No matter how small, you still manage to lose your lipstick." I set the clutch between us and reached for my little cup of heaven. I took a sip, making a soft hum of appreciation. When I looked up, I caught him staring and raised an eyebrow. "What is it?"

"Are you free tomorrow night?"

I blinked at the unexpected question. "Tomorrow night?"

He lifted his phone. "I have a black-tie affair which requires my attendance. My companion just canceled, seems she's not feeling well. Join me?"

I just bet she canceled. "Rather short notice." I popped open the clutch, rooted around, and finally pulled out my phone. A little sleight of hand and Rawlings's badge was in my lap. Touching the screen, I hit the specialized app, then quickly pulled up the calendar. "What time?"

"I can pick you up around eight."

I shook my head, adding an unnecessary reminder, and laid the phone face down on the table between us. "My little shadow won't allow that. Let's meet at the office instead."

Distaste flickered across his face. "This is an invitation only event, Risia, leave him behind."

"I'd love to but ditching him will bring too much attention to me." I leaned over and braced a hand on the leather between us. "The last thing either of us can afford is the attention of my employer."

Undaunted, he leaned in and caught my chin, pulling me off balance. I gasped and recaptured my balance when my hand landed on his thigh. "The last thing you can afford is me questioning your intentions."

There was no hiding my spike of anxiety, so I didn't try. "I told you what I want," I whispered, unable to break from that cruel gaze. Even as every feminine warning bell clamored for attention, I managed to return his badge to its proper place.

"Information and protection," he answered softly, exerting pressure on my chin.

Against his thigh, my fingers curled, sinking my nails deep as I reacted to the sting.

His lips tilted up and his head dipped down until we were a breath apart. "I like your claws, Risia, but mine are sharper." He closed the distance and covered my mouth.

My heart pounded in my chest as I fought to keep still, fought not to struggle. He bit down on my lower lip, slowly increasing the pressure, and bringing tears to my eyes until I had no choice but to gasp. He took advantage with savage intensity. My stomach churned, my muscles locked, and inside my head I was screaming in rage. I clung to the reminders of why I had to play this game with him, of what hung in the balance, who hung in the balance. Then, when I thought I'd reached my breaking point, he lifted his head.

His gaze was bright with lust and deviant hunger. A knowing, malicious smile spread across his face. He brushed his thumb over my swollen lower lip, pressing on the exact same spot he'd bitten. "I think a partnership is an excellent idea."

With as much composure as possible, I pulled back out of his reach. "Limited partnership," I hissed. "Very limited." I couldn't stop my hands from trembling as I shoved my phone back into my clutch. I wasn't sitting here any longer. If I did, I wouldn't be responsible for my actions.

He laughed. "We'll see. Make sure you bring your bargaining chip tomorrow night." He shifted his weight, pulled out his wallet, and tossed some bills on the table. "Thank you for the entertaining lunch." He slid out of the booth and held out his hand. "Let's get you back to your guard dog, shall we?"

For a moment I considered grabbing the sharp knife off my plate and proving to him how sharp my claws could be, but I caught the knowing glint in his eye. Instead, I tucked my clutch under my arm and slid out from the other side, pointedly ignoring his hand. With chin up and spine straight, I walked ahead of him toward Tag, who was still watching the damn game.

In moments, I felt Rawlings's hand at the base of my spine. My skin crawled. We drew even with the bar. "Agent," Rawlings called, "I'm returning your charge."

Tag turned in his seat and watched us approach, his face giving nothing away. He rose to his feet, set some bills on the bar top, and rose to his feet.

Much to my relief, the weight of Rawlings's hand disappeared as we stopped in front of him. It took every ounce of training to turn and face the monster behind me. "Until tomorrow night," I offered, my voice cool and composed.

"Until then," he murmured, raising my hand to his lips.

I stifled the shudder at the feel of his lips. My answering smile felt stiff and awkward.

His was bloated with satisfaction. He turned on his heel and walked away.

Tag shifted closer, still not touching me. "Are you okay?"

Unable to answer, I simply led him out of the restaurant.

Chapter Twenty-Four

I settled into Tag's rental sedan as the valet closed the door behind me. I waited until Tag slid behind the wheel before I blurted, "Do you have a tux?"

He pulled away from the curb. "Do I need one?"

"Yes, and I need a dress." And a shower, preferably with scalding-hot water. "Seems Rawlings needs a date for a black-tie affair tomorrow night."

"Guess Delacourt's paying for a tux then." He merged with traffic. "Where do you want to shop?"

Normally those words would thrill me to no end. Not now. All I wanted was to get as far away from this mess as possible. Since that wasn't an option, I'd go shopping. "We can hit the shops at the Plaza." One thing about Vegas, no matter what you needed, you could find it, so long as you could afford it.

"The Plaza it is," he murmured.

The rest of the ride passed in silence. Not the uncomfortable kind, but as if Tag was giving me a chance to get my shit together. I should've been grateful, instead I was angry. Angry at Tag. Angry at Rawlings. Angry at Delacourt. Angry at me.

And under all that emotional crap, I was scared to death.

Rawlings was a whole new bag of twisted. Add in the nightmares my vision shared and the white jacket with buckles and padded room began to look better and better. Needing an escape from my own neurosis, I finally broke the quiet. "Were you able to clone the badge?"

"Yep, did you copy the phone?"

"I think so." I dug through my clutch and pulled out my phone. "Followed your directions, but I'm not sure how to check." I handed it over, careful not to touch him.

He took it and tucked it into a pocket. "We'll find out tonight when we give it to Rabbit." He passed a taxi and pulled into the right lane to turn into the parking garage for Roman Plaza. "This black-tie affair, any details?"

"He didn't give any. His date got sick and canceled."

"That's convenient." He pulled to a stop behind the line of cars waiting to disgorge their passengers.

"Isn't it? He wanted to pick me up, but I told him I'd meet him at the office around eight. With you." I didn't want Rawlings anywhere near Meli. She had enough horrors haunting her.

"Bet that went over well." He inched forward as the taxi in front pulled away.

"Not really." I rubbed my wrist. The marks from Rawlings's fingers had darkened. "Not that I gave him much choice." I lifted my head to find Tag staring at my wrist, his face etched in stone, his door half opened. "Tag—"

A valet appeared in the open door. "Hello, sir, welcome to Roman Plaza. Are you checking in?"

Tag lifted his eyes until he could hold my gaze. I sucked in a breath. Fury, bright and savage, stared back, carefully held in check. A heartbeat passed, then another. Finally, he bit out, "We're shopping."

He handed the keys to the valet and came around. My door

was yanked open with such force I was surprised it didn't come off the hinges. He held out his hand. As much as I didn't want to touch him, I didn't dare refuse. Sucking in a bracing breath, I locked every emotion down and placed my hand in his.

His mouth tightened, but he didn't say anything, simply helped me from the car. As soon as I stood beside him on the sidewalk, he lifted my hand. His thumb rubbed feather soft over the marks. He lifted his head and his gaze roamed over my face and lingered on my lips. I knew the bottom was still swollen, I could feel it. His eyes darkened. "I'm going to kill him."

It wasn't the words so much as the utter lack of emotion behind them that sent a shiver down my spine.

* * *

One sky-blue evening gown and pair of decadent stilettos courtesy of Manolo Blahnik later, I was curled up in one of Meli's overstuffed chairs, a cup of chamomile tea cradled in my hands.

Meli, world's best friend that she was, took one look at my pale face and shooed Tag out of her house, banishing him to the villa. When he tried to protest, she told him, "Go, do whatever it is you need to do before your friends show up."

Tag stomped off, grumbling.

After he left, she took the other chair. "You don't look good, girl."

"I just need this to be over with," I muttered.

"This being the situation or the mouth-watering guy you've been shacking up with?"

Despite the gentle teasing note, Meli knew me too well. I looked down at my cup. "Both."

"Hmmm, I wouldn't be too eager to shake Tag off your heels, if I were you."

That earned her a squinty-eyed glare. My headache was back in full force and my temperature had spiked. At the rate things were going, I'd be too sick to do Rawlings or Liwei any good. "Tag isn't relationship material."

She gave a delicate snort. "And you are? You go through men like you do shoes. Wear 'em once, then on to the next sparkly pair."

"That's not fair!"

Her expression softened. "I get the whys behind not wanting to connect with the opposite sex, but Tag's not like the rest. You wouldn't have brought him here if he was."

No, he wasn't, which is why pushing him away was my only option.

I don't know what she saw, but she gave a little hum. "I'm not telling you anything you don't already know, am I?"

Color that had nothing to do with fever rose. "Shut it, Meli."

She ignored me. "What are you doing here, Risia?"

"I'm trying to stay alive."

"That's not what I'm talking about and you know it. Something's got you running scared, which means there's more at risk here than what you shared, isn't there?" For someone with no psychic ability whatsoever, those vivid green eyes always saw too much.

I lifted my head and met her worried gaze. "Yeah, but I can't share, so don't ask."

"As if that's going to stop me." She set her cup on her knee. "You saw something, didn't you?"

If I didn't love her so much, I would shut her down with a cutting response, but this was Meli. "Yeah."

"If I were to guess, I'd say it wasn't pretty."

"It never is." I fiddled with the cup, not comfortable with her conversational direction.

She blew out a soft sigh. "Sweetie, you know I don't trust the whole woo-woo thing."

Which is why I didn't bother explaining exactly who I worked for or what they could do. I gave her a small grin. "That's putting it mildly."

She flushed, but continued undaunted, "If you hadn't kept at me, I wouldn't be here." Her delicate face darkened as old ghosts rose. "So, I know there's truth to what you see."

"I hear a but in there."

She gave me a faint grin. "But, have you ever considered that you're self-fulfilling your own prophecies?"

I shook my head in weary denial. "We've been through this before. I can't truly change the future. The best I can do is influence a person's choice and nudge them to the best possible outcome. But this…" I looked away. "This is different. The only good choice is the one I'm making."

She slipped out of her chair and came to kneel in front of mine, hands on my knees. "Risia, you know I love you. You're the closest thing I have left to family, but don't be such a martyr."

My eyes narrowed.

Undeterred, she kept going. "You are so focused on taking care of yourself you don't let anyone else help. No one can make it through this world alone. Who's to say that what you're seeing isn't because it's fated, but a result of your standard go-to response to kick everyone out and go at it alone? You tried to tell me over and over that the future is dependent on an individual's choice. What happens if you change your choices? Throw a kink in Fate's plans. Do the unexpected and stop trying to shoulder this alone. Look around, sweetie." She threw out a hand. "Whether you want to admit it or not, you have friends. Me. The man you just kicked out. His friends who are coming to help. Use them."

If I didn't know how much courage it took for her to confront me, I would never pick up on the slight tremble in her hands. Closing my eyes against the press of tears, I freed a hand and dug my fingers to the bridge of my nose. "I'm trying to keep them safe." I blinked my eyes open, refusing to fall apart. "I need to keep him safe."

Her smile was wistful. "Don't you think he feels the same about you?"

Unable to bear the emotion in her gaze, I looked away.

"Do you love him?"

I gave a miserable nod.

"Does he love you?"

"I don't know." Getting that out around the lump in my throat hurt.

"I hate to break it to you, but Tag isn't hanging around just because you're hot. Although I'm sure it helps." Her sneaky dig made my lips quirk. She shifted in front of me until I couldn't avoid her gaze. "When are you going to forgive yourself?"

"For what?"

"For giving up your son." The soft words fell with devastating weight.

I jerked as if absorbing a body blow.

Her hands tightened on my knees. "You are not a horrible person. You let him go so he could be safe."

"And that's working so well right now." The words were ripe with bitterness, giving her accusation weight.

"Nothing lasts forever, and you and I both know you can't stop life from taking swings at you. You gave him a beautiful family who loves him. You've done everything you could to keep him happy and safe. You made an impossible decision in a difficult situation. Stop punishing yourself."

Is that what I was doing? Punishing myself?

Once I tucked my baby away where my life couldn't touch him, I embraced the opportunity Delacourt offered, finding an outlet for my anger and resentment. The superficial world I played in didn't demand much emotionally, but the constant proof of humanity's depth of depravity left its mark. Flitting among the powerhouses, ferreting out their secrets without getting caught, and manipulating the manipulators kept me from focusing on the gaping hole in my heart.

But somewhere along the way, that hole got deeper and darker, swallowing me whole. My anger and resentment turned inward until the snide, cruel words of my guilt became truth.

What kind of person gives away their child? You should've fought harder, been better. You failed. You don't deserve to be happy.

Taking unnecessary risks couldn't shut it up. Even the deliberate distance I put between myself and everyone around me couldn't muffle its whispers. I met Meli's steady gaze and uttered the brutal truth. "I don't know if I can."

"How's that old saying go? You won't know until you try?" She cupped my face, pulling me down until our foreheads touched. "If you really love Tag, try."

⸻ •◦❖◦• ⸻

Between Meli's impromptu counseling session and the number the virus was doing on my body, I was wiped. She let me crash in her bed and I took full advantage, hoping against hope the combination of rest and more aspirin would keep the feverish aches under control.

When I woke, the sun was gone, leaving behind a dusky twilight. Faint clatters of pans and the aroma of baked cornbread drew me out of the room and into the kitchen. Meli stood by the stove, hair in haphazard ponytail, her petite frame swallowed by the overly large T-shirt.

"What are you making?" My voice emerged rough and scratchy, scraping along my raw throat.

She looked over her shoulder, concern shadowing her face. "You look like crap. Sit down before you fall down."

Since everything hurt, I didn't argue. Shuffling over to a stool parked under the counter, I sat with a soft groan.

Meli tapped the serving spoon against a bubbling pan, then set it aside. "It's chili and cornbread. It's almost done." She looked at the clock. "Tag said they'd be back around now."

"Airport?" I croaked, trying to stick to one-word questions.

Fortunately, she was fluent in sick speak. "Yep, they got in safe and sound." She leaned back against the counter next to the stove and studied me. "Do not give me whatever crap you picked up. I can't afford to be sick right now."

It was tough, but I managed a wan smile. "I'll make sure not to kiss you anytime soon."

She rolled her eyes and began rummaging in a nearby cupboard. Within minutes she set a steaming mug of tea and plopped a heaping spoon of honey inside. "Stir and drink."

"Yes, ma'am." As I drank, I worried about giving Meli a head's up on who was coming, regardless of her professed skepticism.

Techie guru, Rabbit held a special affinity with electronics, one that defied logic. The dark haired, deceptively slender man lent a whole new meaning to electric personality. Anything boasting an electronic heartbeat bowed to him, one way or another.

But not Jinx. A tough cookie wrapped in a pretty, college co-ed package, she wove illusions so realistic they became truth.

Then there was Wolf.

I once heard a woman describe him as big, bald, and

beautiful. Tall as Tag, but built like a linebacker, Wolf made an imposing first impression, but he was a hell of a friend once you earned it. A powerful telepath, he spent time teaching me how to strengthen my mental barriers, giving me a semblance of control over my visions. During that time, I realized that seeing the future wasn't the worst ability a person could have.

Of the three, I was worried about Wolf's ability the most. Not that he'd intentionally eavesdrop on Meli's thoughts. No, the depth of integrity inside him was staggering and solid. But explaining his ability meant Meli would be uncomfortable in her own home. This was her haven, and I couldn't take that from her. So, I'd have to trust Wolf to lock himself down. I heaved a quiet sigh as Meli finished up her chili.

We both heard the crunch of tires on gravel before the flash of headlights bounced across the large front window. Meli wiped her hands on a towel and sucked in a deep breath. "Okay, here we go."

I followed her to the door and out to the porch. The sun had settled behind the horizon allowing shadows to creep in, dragging the night's darkness in its wake. The rented sedan's lights flicked off and doors began opening. Tag's familiar lanky form emerged from behind the wheel. Standing by the open driver's door, he stretched, twisting at the waist.

From the backseat, Rabbit's wiry frame popped out, his soft southern drawl drifting across the yard. "All I asked was why we couldn't stay at one of the casinos, sugar."

"Because we're here to work, not play. You do know the difference, right?" Jinx emerged from the other side and headed to the trunk.

Rabbit got there first, lifted the lid, and reached inside. "I'd be happy to demonstrate my understandin' any time you want."

"Now, children, do I have to put you both in time out?" The

sound of Wolf's raspy voice chiding with deceptive patience from the other side of the car made me smile.

"He started it." Jinx hefted the nylon strap of a duffle bag on her shoulder and waltzed past Rabbit.

"So long as you finish it," he drawled as he watched her walk away.

My smile morphed into a grin as Jinx flipped him the bird without looking back.

"Don't encourage him," Tag advised falling into step with her as they headed to the porch.

Next to me, Meli whispered, "Are they always like this?"

"Worse," I kept my voice low as I answered. "Bets are going around when the two will end up in bed together."

Wolf stepped out of the shadows to join Rabbit in collecting their bags, and I heard Meli suck in a sharp breath. "Lord have mercy."

Hearing the strange mix of fear and awe, I looked over my shoulder. She was staring at Wolf and Rabbit as they made their way over, her face pale. Concern had me turning toward her, worried she was about to pass out. "Meli?"

Slowly she switched her wide gaze to me. It took a moment to recognize the panic darkening her eyes because it had slowly disappeared during the last handful of months. That it made a comeback now wasn't good. "Melisande, breathe."

Her gaze skittered behind me, but I shifted, blocking her view. Even focused on my friend, I still caught Tag's raised hand, a silent signal to hold. The easy banter fell quiet as the three behind him held still.

"Meli," I softened my voice as she worked to drag in shaky breaths. "It's your place, you're safe. They're safe."

She blinked, and my heart broke a little as I watched her come back from the nightmares that obviously weren't as faded as I thought. Color and shame stained her face and she shifted back, trying to hide in the shadows.

I reached out to stop her. "It's okay, Meli." Dammit, I should have considered what having a bunch of strangers would do, but caught up in my own shit, it didn't even register.

She stopped pulling back. "Okay," she whispered. Her spine straightened, her hands curled into bloodless fists at her side. "I'm okay." Reassuring herself or us, it didn't matter because this one came out stronger.

"Okay," I repeated. Then, because I knew how mortified she was, I let her go and turned around to the face the three behind us, using my body to give her what privacy I could. "Welcome to Vientos Salvaje. Tag why don't you take everyone inside. Meli just finished making chili and cornbread. We'll join you in a minute."

"Sure thing, Duchess." Tag didn't hesitate but picked up my unspoken volley and herded the other three inside.

The door clicked shut, and the muted conversation resumed inside.

A weight fell between my shoulder blades, then proceeded to thump twice more as Meli literally knocked her forehead against me. "Holy smokes." Muffled but clear, her unique form of cursing indicated she was wrestling free of her fear. Embarrassment and frustration stained her voice as she stepped back. "I'm such an idiot. How about I just stay out of the way while your friends visit? Say, maybe, in Mexico?"

"No can do, girlfriend. This is your place, and I'm not cooking for three men who can put away more food than an entire high school football team." Turning around, I studied her drawn face. "I'm sorry, I should've warned you."

She was already shaking her head and waving her hand as if to wipe away my apology. "No, sweetie, not your fault. It…it happens sometimes. The strangest things will bring it back."

I wanted to ask what triggered it this time, but part of me was fairly sure it was a who that flipped my friend's trigger.

She managed a shaky smile. "I just need a few minutes, okay? Then I promise I'll come in and try not to embarrass you."

Wrapping her in a tight hug, I whispered, "You could never embarrass me."

She returned the hug, gave a watery laugh, and stepped back. "Go, I'll be in soon."

Chapter Twenty-Five

A couple of hours later, Meli was cleaning dishes in the kitchen with Jinx, while Wolf and Tag huddled around Rabbit as his fingers flew over the sleek laptop. I concentrated on cleaning the massive stove and tried not to admit that the sweat on my brow had nothing to do with the chills coursing through my aching body and everything to do with the lingering heat from cooking. Liwei's guarantee was taking its toll.

Worry blocked out the highly technical discussion at the table and the female chatter at the sink. The clock was ticking. Maybe I could duck out before Tag emerged from his quest to crack the encrypted files. My vision swam, and I braced against the counter, breathing away the sudden bout of light-headedness.

"Son of a mangy one-eyed bitch," Rabbit's distinctive accent layered the curse in honey.

The faucet where Meli rinsed the last of the dishes turned off. She handed Jinx the plate to dry.

When the guys tried to kick Meli out with stern words about security clearances and need to know, she shot their protests down with a steely, "I'm already involved, so suck it up." They grudgingly did so and gave her the bare bones of what we were facing.

"This isn't good," Wolf's husky timbre echoed in the sudden quiet.

Guess they cracked the files. I dried my hands on the towel slung over my shoulder, then took care to leave it neatly folded on the counter.

"What are we looking at?" Jinx asked with remarkable calm as she set the plate on the counter.

Certain I wouldn't face plant, I managed to turn around and found all three men sporting grim looks. My stomach, already rocking, sank. *Oh, shit.*

Rabbit ran a hand over his short black hair. "A massive cluster."

"So Delacourt was right?" I was pleased when my question came out calm.

Tag looked up and his gaze narrowed. "You okay?"

I took a chance and let go of the counter behind me to wave a hand. "Tired, but fine. What did you find?"

"It's worse than Delacourt suspected," Wolf answered. "It's not a one-time list. It's an actual backdoor into the government's communication lines."

"An undetectable backdoor that can be opened or closed as needed," Rabbit qualified as he frowned at the computer screen. "Rawlings is a sneaky bastard for sure."

Understanding dawned. "He can sell the list over and over again, updating it each time."

"Wouldn't the government clue in and stop the leak after the first break?" Meli asked. When everyone's attention settled on her, she lifted her chin. "I'm sure they have programs and such that can catch more than the standard anti-virus program, right?"

Rabbit grimaced. "They do, but because Rawlings can open

or close the breach at will, it makes the current protections reactive, as they wouldn't catch it until after the fact."

"We'd always be a step behind," Wolf added, his attention on Meli. Something in his face gentled as he watched her, but his voice remained unchanged. "Deep cover operatives would be at risk, special teams would be walking into traps, not to mention the number of operations that risk losing their targets as they scuttle back into the shadows."

He turned to Rabbit, shared a silent look, and I wondered. Tag, pacing along the far side of the table, caught the exchange. "We need to let Delacourt know the game's changed."

Wolf dipped his head in acknowledgement. "Roger that."

Something more lay under their conversation, but there were other things to worry about, especially when Tag said, "We can't afford for this sale to happen."

"We don't even know when it's happening," I pointed out. "Or who all the players are yet."

"Do the files contain the actual program?" Jinx broke in, directing her question to Rabbit.

"Haven't found 'em yet, but there's a couple more layers to dig through."

"Anything on Rawlings's phone?" Tag came over and stood next to me.

"Some interestin' numbers in his contact list, but not much else." Rabbit's fingers didn't stop moving.

"He have one for a Liwei Bai? Or Zunjing Kashi Corporation?"

"The biomedical research company?" Wolf joined in.

Tag turned to me. "Biomedical?" The dangerous heat in his question put me on the defensive.

I squirmed. "What?"

He continued to pin me in place, which meant I wasn't having much luck with my innocence act. "Something you want to tell me?"

Beyond Tag's shoulder, Meli, too damn smart for her own good, wiggled her eyebrows in a silent command to share. But I didn't need an audience when Tag lost it. "Maybe later," I muttered.

"Change of plans," he said without looking away. "Jinx, you up for a late-night visit with Wolf? We need information on Rawlings's black-tie shindig scheduled for tomorrow night. I want to know where it's happening." He finally turned his attention back to the rest of the team. "Once we have that, Rabbit can work on getting us invited."

"Love me a fancy *fais do-do*," Rabbit murmured, going back to his computer. "Give me fifteen to duplicate the badge and pull up the office layout."

Wolf stood up, looking to the kitchen where Jinx and Meli stood. "I'll gear up and we can head out."

Jinx nodded.

He then turned his attention to Meli. "Do you mind showing me where we're bunking?

A delicate blush rose as Meli brushed her hands over her hips. "Sure, let me grab the keys."

She hustled out of the kitchen in the direction of her office nestled on the other side of the living room. Jinx followed, probably wanting to get a few things from her bag in the living room.

"Leave my bag here, if you don' mind," Rabbit said without looking up.

Wolf gave him a short nod of acknowledgement.

"Hit me up when you're back," Tag said, then wrapped a hand around my upper arm, eliminating any possibility of escape.

Guess later was now. Huffing out a breath, I didn't protest his hold. Instead, I told Wolf, "Be careful, Rawlings tends to pop by at the oddest hours."

"I've got Jinx with me, they'll never see us."

And if they did, he'd make sure they forgot all about it. "Still."

His gaze sharpened and that dangerous edge all of the team carried peeked out. "You getting a feeling?"

Instead of an automatic response, I gave his question serious consideration, finally deciding that my unsettled feeling had its roots in my upcoming conversation with Tag and the virus crawling through my body more than actual premonition. "Not yet."

He flashed a gentle grin. "Works for me."

"Ready when you are," Meli said from the doorway.

Wolf moved toward her, careful not to crowd her.

She held her ground, the only sign of her nervousness the quick dart of her tongue as she wet her lips.

Tag began to follow and thanks to his hold, I had no choice but to go along.

Jinx knelt next to an open bag. She tucked a sleek, matte-black number into her back holster, then zipped the bag closed. Standing, she tugged her shirt back into place and looked at Wolf. "Ready when you are, big boy."

"Give me ten. Want me to take your bag?"

"Sure, I got what I need." She ambled back over to Rabbit. "Thanks," she threw over her shoulder.

As Wolf picked up a bag and slung it over one broad shoulder, Jinx's drawled, "Dazzle me, gator boy," drifted back.

"Girl likes playing with fire," Wolf muttered, snagging the second bag.

"*Mouche a mielle*, I can blind you for all others." Rabbit's unhurried response had Wolf shaking his head.

I leaned against Tag's shoulder, nabbing his attention. When he looked down, I mouthed, "*Mouche a mielle*?"

"Honey bee," he murmured. With a frown, he laid the back of his hand against my forehead. His mouth tightened, but he didn't say anything.

Grateful for the brief reprieve, I kept my focus on the entertaining puzzle of Jinx and Rabbit. Listening to the two continue to razz each other, I figured Jinx liked the burn of Rabbit's fire.

Meli waited by the open door. When Wolf drew close, he waved her through. "Lead the way."

Another one of those blushes stained her face, but to my surprise, she gave him a tiny, but very real, smile. Something in that shared look sparked a brief, bright glimpse. An echo of Meli smiling up at Wolf as he gazed down at her, light chasing away the shadows. A snapshot of them, but not them. Not yet. Too tentative to be truth, just a possibility, but enough to make me smile with hope for my friend. At least one of us was strong enough to reach beyond our fears.

"What's that smile for?" Tag asked.

"Nothing." Looking up into his face, my heart ached. What I wouldn't give to have that with him. To be enough to hold his demons at bay.

My earlier words circled back. I needed to keep him safe.

Don't you think he feels the same about you?

The answer to Meli's question was staring back at me. Maybe he deserved better, but I was here for now, and I wanted a chance.

If you really love Tag, try.

Her wisdom tugged at me, daring me to step outside my self-imposed cage.

What was the worst that could happen?

An image of Tag with his gun aimed at me flashed through my mind, quickly followed by him standing before me with his hand out, 'Trust me?'

I swallowed hard. Time to throw Fate a curveball.

Tag didn't give me much time once he closed the villa door behind us. "Sit down before you fall down." He followed his gruff order by tugging me over to the bed, yanking back the covers, and pointing.

I didn't bother arguing. Besides, the bed looked damn inviting. Toeing off my sneakers, my balance wobbled. I caught myself against the bed, my head hanging down as I waited for the world to righten. One breath, two, then three, before I was steady enough to continue. My fingers were thick as I tried to undo my jeans.

Tag's patience was non-existent, and he gently brushed my hands out of the way, taking over. He got the button undone and the zipper down, then knelt. His big hands drifted over my hips and pushed the material to my ankles. The warmth of his palms left chills in their wake.

Using his shoulders for balance, I shifted from foot to foot so he could pull the jeans completely off. From his kneeling position, he looked up and the red, angry welt on my thigh caught his attention. When he finally raised his head, I got tangled in the gold-shot green depths. I lifted a hand from his shoulder and cupped the side of his face, rubbing lightly against the bristle of his five o'clock shadow. "Thanks."

Under that wild hair, his serious gaze roamed over my face. When his hand rose to cover mine, I didn't draw back or use any of the mental blocks Wolf had drummed into me. Determined to follow through with my recent resolution, I didn't hide a damn thing.

Anger at being played, sick fear of running out of time, determination to keep those around me safe, and through it all a bright, hesitant offering meant only for him, it was all in reach of his touch. I watched his eyes darkened with knowledge, a fierce determination edging out concern. I swayed, and he switched his hold.

"Sit, Duchess."

I sank down.

He stayed crouched in front of me.

In my lap, his hands held mine. I gave him a small half smile. "Impromptu lie detector?" I teased.

He didn't smile back, but some of the tension in his face eased into gentler lines. "I'm finally making progress with you, not about to lose any ground. You're a wily woman."

"Wily, uh?"

"Wily," he reiterated. His hands tightened on mine, a weighted reminder he was holding on to me. "How bad?"

I couldn't hold his gaze, so I looked down. "Bad," I choked out.

"What happened?"

The story came out in halting pieces, filling the gaps I deliberately left out the first time. During my recitation, he pulled me from the bed and into his lap. I didn't mind. I burrowed closer and mumbled, "I'm not infectious."

"As if I'd give a damn if you were." Under my ear his chest rumbled. "Dammit, Duchess." Resignation and frustration echoed in his voice.

Not the expected anger, but still, I closed my eyes and a single, hot tear spilled free. It was quickly followed by more, until all I could do was bury my face against his chest and hold on. When the tears finally passed, I felt curiously empty as Tag continued to stroke a comforting hand down my spine. Finally, he broke the quiet with a low, vicious curse. "The drive for the antidote."

"Yeah," my voice was rough.

"One of the extras Bai promised?"

I nodded and tucked a hand against his chest, under my chin.

"You deliberately picked a fight with me."

"It was the only thing I could think of to keep you out of my head." But there was one thing I needed to address. I lifted my head so I could watch his face. "I wouldn't betray you or the team. Not even for the antidote, Tag."

He brushed a thumb over my lower lip, while his pressed together with a slight grimace. "I know that, Risia. I do, but…" he shook his head.

"But demons are hard to shake." Because experience had damaged his ability to trust and damage like that took time to fix. Time we may not have. It hurt, but there was nothing else I could do.

"Yeah," he muttered.

Shifting a little, I laid a soft kiss against his mouth. A silent indicator that I got it. What started sweet grew heated, gained depth and left us both breathing hard.

He drew back and rested his forehead against mine. "We'll figure this out and get the antidote."

"Liwei's not the only reason I pushed you away." As much as I wanted to believe him, reality could be a brutal bitch. Gathering the tattered remnants of my courage, I said, "I had a vision, only this time it was about me."

He frowned. "You said you never see your own future."

"I don't." I winced and rubbed my eyebrow as I gave a small shake of my head. "I didn't, until I did. Every choice, my choices, resulted in death. The team's, all those undercover agents, hundreds of innocents." The images replayed in my mind, bringing back the horror and suffocating guilt. "You, me," I choked out. "I couldn't stop any of it. I tried."

For a moment, he studied me, his jaw set, gaze steady. "I know it's not fair, but do you trust me, Duchess?"

I gave a shaky nod.

"We'll make it through this."

"Don't make promises—"

"I'm not playing anymore." He cut me off. "We will make it through this, because I'm not losing you."

Even though his words soothed the ragged edges of my heart, I tried again, "Tag—"

This time he didn't use words, but a devastating kiss, to stop me. When he finally raised his head, I could only blink up at him in a daze. "I'm not losing you. You're mine, Risia."

"Because I keep the demons away," I murmured.

"No," his denial was sharp. "No," his voice roughened. "Because you make me laugh, even as you drive me crazy. You let me see you, strong, soft, cracked, solid, all of you with no apologies and you're fucking beautiful. I know you deserve better, but I'm a selfish bastard. Dressed in silk, jeans, or a white jacket with buckles, you're mine, always. You make me want to fight free of the shadows and take a shot in the light. I don't know how you dug yourself into my heart, and I really don't give a damn, because even battered and scarred, it's yours."

Unable to escape the truth in his declaration I could only sit in his lap while he tied me to him with unbreakable chains. My mind whirled, old insecurities screaming obscenities as I stared at the man who'd taken the biggest risk of all.

For me.

As that sank in, that nasty little voice choked off.

Tag loved me. Even knowing my future could hold more nightmares than dreams, he wanted me. With a sob, I threw my arms around his neck and held on tight and stepped over the edge, as I whispered fiercely, "I love you Thomas Anderson, just don't let me go."

His arms tightened around me, squeezing me tight. "Roger that, Duchess."

Chapter Twenty-Six

TAG

"Your best bet is to keep her hydrated. Water, broth, whatever she can keep down." On the other end of my phone, Doc's steady voice rose above a muted din of beeps, dings, and garbled intercom announcements.

"She's running a low-grade temp, just under a hundred."

"Chills?"

I stood over a sleeping Risia and noted her lips were no longer tinged with blue. "Earlier, but I've got a wet washcloth on her head and she's resting easier."

"Good. Have her take some acetaminophen or ibuprofen. Tag—" A wailing siren cut him off and we both waited until it faded. "Look, man, without knowing the nanotraps' design, I'm flying blind."

I ran a hand through my hair, then wrapped it around the back of my neck and squeezed. "I know, Doc."

"There's no way I could get to you guys in seventy-two hours." Frustration was rife in his voice. "Hell, I'll be lucky to make it back in a week. I'll reach out to my contacts stateside, see what I can come up with."

It wasn't a rousing reassurance, but I'd take it.

"In the meantime, see what Rabbit can dig up on our mad scientist and have him share info."

"Will do."

I hung up and resisted the urge to throw my phone against the wall.

The first call I made after getting Risia in bed was to Doc, our team's corpsman who managed to keep most of us alive until the better-equipped professionals could step in. Normal medical personnel tended to scratch their heads, or asses, according to Rabbit, when a psychic presented unique health issues, which meant Doc tended to be our first stop.

The fact he was a healer was bonus. Problem was, utilizing his services meant the only one paying the bill was Doc, and not in a good way. Healers could only heal by taking on their patient's injury, then healing themselves. Sometimes Doc thought he was invincible. We made sure his kryptonite didn't take a lethal toll. As much I wanted to drag his ass out of whatever third-world cesspool he was tossed in and have him heal Risia, I couldn't. Choosing friend or lover, either way the cost was too damn high.

Seventy-two hours.

Three days.

My thoughts spiral down dark corridors and only my phone's sudden vibration kept me from slipping into a murky darkness where morals sat on the sideline while necessity took the field. "Go."

"Get Rabbit running the name Des Carter." Wolf didn't waste time.

Checking Risia one last time, I left the light on in the bathroom and locked the villa's door behind me. "What happened?" I beat feet to the main house.

"Rawlings's office seems to be the latest Vegas nightspot."

"You found company."

"And had a nice little chat before leaving him all trussed up for the local police. He bears a striking resemblance to the sketch you shared, so I'm sure they'd like a word, or four, with him regarding Trammel's death."

"Hand Tooled," I muttered. "Fucker's been on Risia's ass like a damn tick."

Wolf gave a dark chuckle. "Tell her to consider herself tick free."

I hit the front porch and caught sight of Meli's shadow against the drawn blinds; I pulled up short and clued Wolf in to the latest cluster. No need to scare Risia's friend, girl was skittish enough. "She's racing a clock, Wolf. Seventy-two fucking hours. Bai infected her with a customized virus and he's holding the antidote for a copy of Rawlings's files."

"Shit," Wolf hissed. "Hang tight, Tag. We're heading back now."

I slipped the phone into my back pocket, dug deep, and shuttled away the fear and worry gnawing at my gut, focusing on what needed to be done. Without the luxury of time, there was no choice but to wade through shit and find the pieces, then slap those bitches together so we could light it up. Risia may believe the future was set, but I didn't. The universe was a moody bastard that'd flip a situation from sugar to shit and back just because it could.

Not this time.

Whatever it took, I'd make sure Risia walked away from this, because if she didn't, I'd burn the world down with me.

⁌●⸙●⁍

Three hours later, a sigh cut through the dining room and dragged my attention from the laptop screen where files that shouldn't exist, existed. Meli, holding a tray with empty dishes, stood next to a wan-looking Risia, both women eyed the mess of papers, laptops, and half-empty coffee cups.

Risia's eyebrow arched. "From the mess, I'm guessing your trip to Rawlings's office paid off?"

She wandered over and stopped next to my chair, while Meli headed to the kitchen. Shoving the laptop back to make room, I wrapped an arm around her waist and tugged her onto my lap. She half fell, half sat, her spine stiff, her expression caught in some strange cross of embarrassed and pissed. Ignoring it and the surrounding gazes of speculation, I grinned. "How are you feeling, Duchess?"

Her gaze searched mine, softened, and heat touched her cheeks. "Better." She covered my hand at her waist and wove her fingers with mine. "What did you guys find?"

Across from us, Jinx slid a mug shot across the table. "Meet Des Carter, a little fish who's currently swimming in a chum-filled pool of sharks."

Risia twisted around and I stifled a groan as someone came rocketing to attention. She caught my grimace, winked, and settled deeper in my lap with her back to me.

"Tease," I growled under my breath.

The shimmy of her ass was my only answer as she leaned forward and snagged the photo. "You found Hand Tooled?" Her curls danced between her shoulder blades as she looked at Jinx.

"Had an enlightening conversation," Wolf added. "Right before the locals showed up to a tripped alarm at Aether Industries." Light glinted off his head as he gave a mockingly sad head-shake. "Poor clumsy fool, really should have paid attention to where he was going."

"What was he doing there?" Risia tapped the edge of the photo against the table.

Unable to resist the lure of her curls, I wrapped one around my finger with a gentle tug. "Waiting for you."

She looked over shoulder, those crystal blue eyes puzzled, and her brow furrowed. "Me? At Aether's office? Why?"

I shrugged. "Don't ask me to unravel the mysteries of the stupid, it's outside my skill set."

Next to me, Wolf pushed back and rose from his chair, an empty mug in hand. "Fear will do that to a man." He headed to the kitchen. "He was hoping someone would show, hopefully you. Instead he got us."

Passing Jinx, he half turned, his back to the kitchen, and ruffled her hair. She batted his hand away with a grin, and he took another step backward, never seeing Meli behind him.

"Whoa!" Her yelp had Wolf doing a rather graceful spin, as he avoided stepping on her. Barely.

He managed to catch his balance and her in one smooth move. "You okay?" he asked, holding her close.

Her hands had landed on his chest, her head tipped back, and a wave of red washed over her face. "Yes."

"Sorry about that." He held her for a few more seconds and then finally stepped back. He lifted the cup in his other hand. "Was heading back in for more tea."

Meli grabbed it. "I can get it." She disappeared back into the kitchen so quick I was surprised she didn't leave a smoke trail, but she did leave a very bemused Wolf in her wake.

Unable to resist, I drawled, "Smooth move, Casanova."

Unsurprisingly, I got a full-bird salute in response.

"What spooked Des?" Risia got the conversation back on track.

"His boss." Rabbit sat back from his sleek laptop and rubbed a hand over his face. "Our friend had a very particular set of skills, skills he acquired over a very long career."

Rabbit's half-assed nod to a popular action flick left me shaking my head, while next to him Jinx groaned. "Not again."

Undeterred, he grinned and continued, "Any guesses as to our career track?"

"I'll take debt collection for two hundred," Wolf offered as he leaned against the entryway.

"And we have a winner." Rabbit turned his laptop around so his screen was front and center. "He was contracted," he drew out the word, "by one Mihailo Jovanovic, a nasty piece of work."

He tapped the edge of the screen where grisly images filled the screen proving how monstrous humans could be. "Jovanovic is the head of one of Serbia's up-and-coming crime syndicates. He's been nippin' on the big dogs' tails and managed to get on every alphabet watch list for the evil trinity."

"Drugs, weapons, and flesh," Jinx clarified.

Meli stepped back into the room with a steaming cup of tea in hand. She handed it to Wolf, who gave her a nod as he accepted it. Normally, Rabbit would be all over his ass about his unusual drink preference, but tonight the grim tension riding through the dining room quashed any lighter inclination.

Rabbit touched his nose. "I'm thinkin' if Carter knew who hired him, he would've thought twice about acceptin'."

In my lap, I could feel Risia growing more and more tense. I rubbed small circles over her back.

"He's not the brightest crayon in the box." Jinx shifted in her chair so she could look at Wolf and Rabbit at the same time. "But he did do us one favor."

Wolf's jaw tightened. "Because he let his ego do the thinking." He looked at Risia. "He didn't tell his boss about his run-in with you. Which means Jovanovic has no idea who you are."

The line of her shoulders sank. "Thank God."

"Don't thank Him just yet." I hated to burst her bubble of relief, but… "When we dug into Rawlings's contact list, we had a couple of pops. Zunjing Kashi Corporation and EuroNet Industries. Rumors surround both companies, but nothing has ever stuck."

She stood up and as much as I wanted to drag her back to my lap, I let her, recognizing her need to burn off nerves as she began to pace.

Rabbit took over. "The fancy do you're going to tomorrow? It's a charity auction at Hotel Italiana sponsored by One World, a humanitarian organization that provides paid education to kids around the world. Lots of art and other la-la type things will be going for big bucks. Their guest list reads as a who's who of the global corporations."

Risia wrapped her arms around her stomach. "Let me guess, Liwei is on the list."

"Along with Adam Pendleberry, board member of EuroNet who, if you can find your way through seven degrees of separation, has some sticky connections to Jovanovic. Most of the guests are straight up movers and shakers but weed 'em out and there's some names that make me go hmmm."

He pulled the laptop back around, hit some keys, and showed us the screen. "Goin' left to right, our entrepreneur of shady deals, Rawlings." The familiar face popped up.

"Bidder numero uno who obviously isn't happy with the askin' price, Liwei Bai." An obvious press shot showed a Eurasian male, late thirties, early forties, professional smile firmly in place.

"Next up with a proper stick up the ass is Jovanovic's representative, Adam Pendleberry." Despite his receding hairline, his dark hair was buzzed close to the scalp and didn't detract from the forty something's air of seriousness. Or maybe it was the permanent frown etched on the clean-shaven, angled jaw.

"After him, Sunil Bavin, a global investment banker who prefers sunnier climes where extradition laws don't apply. While our departmental friends like to watch, they've managed to get shit all to stick, which means the world remains his oyster, business wise." Late forties, early fifties, dark hair sprinkled with gray, dark eyes, olive skin, but nothing that screamed corruption.

Risia had stopped to study the pictures. Her fingers were tapping on the table. "You think Rawlings plans to hold his very own private auction tomorrow?" Although she directed the question to the room at large, she looked at me, her eyes dark with rioting emotions.

I gave her a nod.

Her lashes lowered for a moment, then rose, and my pride in her swelled. All that fear and anger was replaced by grim determination. "I suppose you have a plan to stop this, right?"

"We're going to try," Wolf answered, making no promises, because we all knew some promises couldn't be kept. "But we're working against the clock with limited intel."

"Seems you have quite a bit," Meli spoke up and lifted a set of printed floor plans of Hotel Italiana's Grand Ballroom, where the charity ball was going to be held.

Wolf came up beside her and plucked the paper out of her hands, then set it on the table. "DMP for any op requires days of meticulous planning, glass houses, triple checking facts, and ensuring you have COAs in place before you green light it."

She folded her arms across her chest and gave Wolf a puzzled glare. "Plain English, please."

"DMP," Jinx chimed in. "Decision making process."

"Glass houses, mock layouts of structural targets," I added, nodding to the diagram Wolf had taken from her. "In this case, the Hotel Italiana."

"COAs, courses of action, or as I like to think of them, SNAFUs A, B, and C," Rabbit continued with the acronym lesson.

Meli's lips twitched. "I know SNAFU; situation normal, all effed up." She glanced around, and her brief flash of humor faded as she looked back to Wolf. "How dangerous is this?"

He didn't bother lying. "Very."

"Right," she breathed out. Her jaw firmed, and she turned to Risia. "You can't go in alone. And, no offense, Tag," she turned to me. "But I don't think you'll be enough to keep her safe from the International Villains' club."

Obviously Meli had been paying closer attention than expected tonight. Under that skittish demeanor hid a damn fine friend. "None taken, but she's not going in alone. Right, Rabbit?"

"Snagged us two extra invites to the party." He grinned and kicked back in his chair, hands linked behind his head, his eyes dancing with mischief. "Just one tiny problem."

"How tiny?" Wolf growled.

"We only have the makin's for one couple." He wiggled his eyebrows at Jinx. "I know who I'm askin'." He raised his gaze to Wolf. "But who are you takin'?"

Wolf frowned, and his jaw worked, only to have Meli's "I can go" drop into the room like an IED.

"No." Wolf set his mug on the table with a sharp crack.

Unruffled, she faced him down, rising to her feet with a casual deliberateness. "You going with Tag?" she asked with such saccharine sweetness even my teeth ached.

Wolf's brow lowered, his arms crossed over his chest, and he aimed a steely-eyed glare at her. None of it seemed to be working, since she held her ground.

Jinx braved the silent standoff. "Let her come. She's involved now whether we like it or not. Besides, you going stag will stand out like a sore thumb. She'll offset your bad-ass factor."

Wolf blew out a hard breath and took a couple of steps away from Jinx and Meli.

Jinx kept at him. "Instead of looking like the hard-ass you are, you'll look like a possessive date."

Focused on the drama, I noticed Meli pale. Next to me, Risia jerked. Not much, but enough.

I looked at her.

She slid a glance at me and frowned. Interpreting her silent "not now" warning, I held my tongue.

Finally, Wolf turned back around, his face set. "You can come, but you'll do everything I say, when I say. We clear."

"Clear," her voice broke a little, but steadied. "Just make sure Risia stays safe."

"That's the goal."

With that possible glitch out of the way, it was time to set the last pieces in place. I diverted attention away from the reluctant couple. "Rabbit, where are you at on the drive?"

"Got two copies." He held up two flash drives, one silver, one black, both resembling pens. "This one," he lifted the silver one to Risia, "you're going to give to Rawlings before the party. Even if he checks it, it will read like the real deal. Same goes for the one for Bai." He lifted the black drive. "Both require an access code, because you don't want to hand either over free and clear until they cough up what they owe you."

"No, I don't." Risia took them. "You sure they won't be able to tell the difference?"

"Nope, it's good all the way through the program until it comes to translating the actual information. Say Rawlings or Bai decide to provide a test run, it will look as if they're in like Flynn, gatherin' info. It'll even download the data. But, thanks to my little somethin' extra, when the data is opened, the info is scrambled. Names will be changed, coordinates altered, key phrases compromised. It's not a complete fix, but it's a duct-tape solution until the powers that be can get to it." An evil grin spread over Rabbit's face. "And once it's hooked up to a network. Ohh baby, then comes the fun. I nested a nice little virus that'll make a Saturday-night bar fight look like a tea party. Y'all can thank me later."

"I'll thank you once Bai hands over the antidote," Risia murmured. "Maybe even give you a big, sloppy kiss."

My muttered "over my dead body" was drowned out by Meli's sharp "Antidote?"

Guilt and remorse flooded Risia's face as she stared at her stricken friend. "Meli, I'm sorry, but I—"

"Couldn't tell you," I cut in, forcing Meli to focus on me. Risia had enough shit on her plate; she didn't need the added weight. "Bai injected her with a virus to force her to hand over a copy of the files. Once she does, he'll hand over the antidote."

Doubt clouded her face. "What if he doesn't?"

"He will." Or I'd rip the information from him, one bloody piece at a time.

She looked to Risia, then back to me. "Promise."

"Promise." My voice was rough, I knew there were some promises you couldn't keep, no matter what you did. This one, though, I would do everything in my power to fill.

Chapter Twenty-Seven

"Are you ready, dear?" Rawlings's falsely solicitous question had me gritting my teeth as my stomach roiled.

Not that there was much in there. I managed to keep down broth and toast throughout the day but fought through another bout of fever and chills earlier, until Tag got a hold of stronger antibiotics and poured them down my throat.

We were in Rawlings's limo on our way to the Hotel Italiana. On the other side of the privacy glass, Tag shared space with the driver, at Rawlings's request.

"For?" The question came out husky thanks to my scratchy throat.

"To step into the game with me," he drawled, and lifted a slender flute filled with champagne.

"Is that what I'm doing?"

His gaze roamed over my bare shoulders, lingering on the ice blue topaz pendant dropping into the daring neckline of my gown. "I certainly hope so. You did bring what I requested?"

I curved my lips and tilted my head as my fingers tightened on the small clutch in my lap.

His flat gaze focused on the telling movement, and his smile surpassed charming and went razor sharp. "Lovely," he murmured and took a sip.

While he watched, I unsnapped the clutch and withdrew a small piece of paper. Holding it between two fingers, I offered it to him.

He frowned as he picked it up. "What is this?"

"The account where my finder's fee may be deposited."

"Finder's fee?"

I gave a small hum. "You did promise to exceed existing offers."

He nodded and tucked it inside his jacket.

"Good," I shifted and turned to watch the passing scenery. "Your competition seemed especially eager to meet today, so I'm assuming tonight's affair should be rather beneficial to us both." It was a risk to push, but I couldn't afford to appear weak.

The atmosphere in the limo grew edgy with suppressed danger. Finally, he chuckled, and the tension scaled back a notch. "I'd forgotten how much fun it is to work with someone so intelligent." The way he said the last word made my skin crawl.

Thankfully, the limo pulled up outside the ornate exterior of the Hotel Italiana forestalling further conversation. I allowed Rawlings to hold my hand as we rode up the elevators to the Grand Ballroom. Even managed not to shudder when that same hand dropped to my lower back. Only Tag's silent presence kept me from bolting. The virus left me a mess. I fought to ignore the lingering ache settling deep in my bones and concentrate on the dangerous waters I was wading into. Exhaustion and lack of food made me shaky, but my mind remained clear.

We stopped outside one of two entrances to the ballroom, both manned by security who were checking the embossed invites. Rawlings handed over his invitation. Behind me, Tag kept a polite distance.

"Thank you, Mr. Rawlings, ma'am." The man at the door looked to Tag.

"He's with us," Rawlings said.

Security considered us for a moment before nodding. "Enjoy your evening." He waved us through.

As we stepped inside, I caught sight of Rabbit and Jinx coming through the other door. They made a stunning couple, him all dark and dashing in a black-on-black suit, with her vibrant in sparkling gold. Laughter competed with conversations, while the chime of crystal accented the music. The party was in full swing.

As we made our way along the edge of the dance floor, Rawlings stopped to acknowledge various people, while Tag hung back. I managed to keep my smile firmly in place, even as the names and faces began to blur together.

A flash of color caught my attention. Out on the dance floor, Meli, in a jeweled tone emerald sheath, moved with natural grace in Wolf's arms. As they waltzed passed us, he gave me a quick wink before moving on. Having them here helped. The odds were still crappy, but much better than going at this alone.

I managed to play my part of Rawlings's date without a hitch, until he stepped into a small group peppered with newly familiar faces. Liwei Bai, Adam Pendleberry, and Sunil Bavin, plus a few unknowns.

"Ladies, gentlemen, so good of you to come tonight." Rawlings flashed his smile. "May I introduce my lovely partner, Risia Lacoste."

Subtle though it was, I didn't miss his emphasize on the word partner. Neither did the men of the group, and their speculation sharpened into something much more dangerous. Sheer force of will kept me from shuddering under the combined weight of their stares. "Gentlemen," I murmured.

"Alexander Spires," one of the two strangers held out his hand. Brown hair, brown eyes, he had one of those faces that made you wonder where you'd seen him before. "Lovely to meet you, Ms. Lacoste."

I took his hand. "Risia, please."

His smile grew, almost changing my polite twist of lips into something more real. Little fissures tickled my mind, but next to him, Liwei stepped forward and sketched a polite bow, stealing the stage.

"A pleasure to meet you, Ms. Lacoste, I am Liwei Bai." A cruel spark of amusement lingered in the dark depths of his gaze.

My smile tightened as I imaged stabbing him in the eye with the ragged edges of a broken crystal flute. "Mr. Bai." I inclined my head.

Pendleberry and Bavin stepped up next, both taking the time to introduce their wives. They were followed by the final member, Mateo Besora, who's arm was wrapped around the waist of a long-legged model type. Introductions fulfilled, the men began to chat. The two wives began a side conversation as they sipped their drink of choice.

I caught Besora's date silently judging my outfit and smiled. Obviously not used to that reaction, she sniffed and deliberately looked out into the crowd.

Within minutes, a petite blonde stepped up next to Alexander and gave a gentle tug to his hand. "Darling, dance with me?"

He gave the other men a "what can you do" shrug and turned to look at her with an indulgent smile. "Of course, if you'll excuse us?"

As he turned away, the little blonde gave me a wink and

stepped into his arms. They whirled away into the crowd. As if Alexander's departure was some sort of signal, the group began to dissipate. Rawlings waved a hand toward the dance floor. "Shall we join them?"

Refusing wasn't an option, so I set my drink aside and took his hand. It took thirty interminably long minutes to finally free myself from him. I made a beeline for the ladies' room. As I passed in front of a long mirror, I caught sight of Tag keeping pace. Relief took the edge off my tension.

Two chattering women left as I slipped inside. Blessed silence greeted me. The bathroom was empty. With a grateful sigh, I sank down on the small couch nestled in front of a mirrored counter. I pulled out my phone and checked the dummy account to see if Rawlings had fulfilled his part of our little bargain. A one followed by a long string of zeroes stared back. Relief of clearing the first hurdle shuddered through me, and I buried my face in shaky hands.

Okay, things were falling into place the way Tag and Wolf predicted. It boded well. Right? I sucked in a deep breath, hoping to still my tremors. My fever was back and combined with the constant strain of keeping up appearances, it was taking its toll. Exhaustion and over-strung nerves did not make for a fun evening. Nor did the very unpleasant company I was keeping. A few more minutes and I'd be ready to go back in.

I managed to steal five before the door swung open, letting reality and a giggling trio in. Lifting my head, I took a few more minutes to repair my makeup and reapply my lipstick. Dragging in a deep breath, I set my shoulders and headed back out.

I took my time, wandering around the outside edges of the dance floor where various pieces of art were displayed, each with a discreet white card tucked to the side, waiting for bids. It was a toss-up on who would find me first, Liwei or Rawlings. My money was on Liwei.

In the meantime, Tag hovered in a nearby alcove, hands clasped in front, his normally wild hair tamed into some semblance of order and a stoic mask firmly in place. It helped having him close by, helped steady me, because as my body deteriorated, so did my confidence. Trusting Liwei was like trusting an air mattress to break your fall from the edge of the Grand Canyon. Moving to the next art piece, I stood in front of a framed wood carving depicting a panther prowling through a field of lotus blossoms, while warriors rode in the background.

A movement beyond the display caught my attention. Tag shifted, his focus on something or someone behind me. Head bent toward the burnished carving, I fought not to stiffen as I felt the presence of another come up behind me.

"An exquisite piece, isn't it?" Liwei stepped to my side, crowding close. "A beautiful example of Dongyang wood carving. Do you know why this piece is so unusual, Ms. Lacoste?"

"No," I played along.

"Dongyang carvings were meant to serve as home and furniture decorations. Their main subject matter tended toward galloping horses, lotus flowers, cranes, and humans. This one." He reached out and brushed a finger against the ebony frame. "This one was requested during the last imperial dynasty, by Nurhaci, father of the Qing Dynasty. He also founded the Eight Banners, and elite military backbone which brought about the defeat of the Ming dynasty."

Seemed the mad scientist was a bit of a history buff. "Will you be bidding on this piece?"

"Perhaps," he murmured. "Are you enjoying your evening?"

"It has possibilities," I answered, then turned to face the room. A waiter drifted by and I snagged another champagne and its accompanying napkin.

Liwei claimed another. He let a few minutes tick past, both

of us watching the crowd drift by, blissfully unaware of the evil in their midst. Finally, he said, "Have you given my offer consideration?"

Keeping my gaze on the crowd, I answered, "I have."

"And?" he prompted, the eagerness in that one word setting my teeth on edge.

"And I find your terms acceptable."

I turned to the side, set my drink down on the edge of the table, and retrieved the pen-shaped drive from clutch. My fingers tightened around it, knowing this is where it could all go so horribly wrong. If Rabbit's electronic wizardry failed, I was signing my own death warrant. "However, I'd like to ensure our future business relationship."

I took a second to scribble a phone number along with a second string of numbers on the napkin. Turning, I handed the napkin and pen to him.

He took both, with a raised brow.

Reclaiming my drink, I lifted it. "Not everything is what it seems."

He reconsidered the pen, then a slow smile curved his lips. "Clever." He pocketed the pen. "Your number?" He lifted the napkin.

It didn't take much to tap into the banked fury lurking so close to the surface. I let it seep into my face and fill my eyes. "When I have my payment and antidote, you get your access code. Until then, enjoy your pen." Without waiting for his response, I strolled away.

I barely got my hand to stop shaking when Rawlings caught my elbow. "There you are. I've been looking for you."

I looked up and caught harried exasperation, but no anger, as he studied me. "I went to the ladies' room and then got side-track by the art. Are you all right?"

"Fine." He shifted his grip and began guiding me along the floor.

Yeah, he didn't look fine, in fact, he looked rattled. I kept my voice low, "Lawrence, what's going on?"

"Did you check your account?"

I gave a short nod.

He slowed but didn't stop. "Time to ditch your shadow, Risia."

My heart picked up speed, and my mind raced. "We can't leave, he'll get suspicious." Around us, the crowd swelled and waned.

"We aren't leaving, we're simply going upstairs." Rawlings turned to check behind us. I did too. Tag was trying to maneuver through the crowd without much success. "Move it, Risia," Rawlings hissed as his grip tightened.

He set a determined pace. After we slipped through the far entryway, he headed straight to the elevator, where he swiped an electronic keycard.

Seconds ticked by.

I caught a flash of gold as Jinx and Rabbit emerged from the ballroom. Jinx was giggling as if she'd had too much to drink, and Rabbit had his arm around her waist, pulling her in tight and whispering into her ear. They wobbled toward us. I caught Rabbit's eye, wrapped my free hand over the pendant embedded with a micro-tracker, and gave the tiniest shake of my head, warning them off.

The elevator dinged, and Rawlings tugged me after him. Once inside, I turned back in time to see Tag hit the entryway, frustration on his face, his eyes dark with anger and worry. The elevator doors slid shut.

I was on my own.

Chapter Twenty-Eight

I followed Rawlings down the plush-carpeted hallway on one of the restricted floors. I sent up a brief prayer Rabbit would be able to override whatever security existed, because I didn't need my ability to know being here alone was not a good thing. Rawlings stopped in front of one of the doors, knocked twice, paused, and knocked once more.

Pendleberry answered. "Rawlings." He stepped aside. "Ms. Lacoste."

Not trusting my voice, I nodded, and stuck close to Rawlings.

A dramatic wall of floor-to-ceiling windows showcased the Vegas lights, but it was the other occupants of the room that held my attention. I expected Liwei, Bavin, and Pendleberry, but the forth addition standing by the bar? Nope, hadn't seen that one.

Alexander Spires stood next to his little blonde. She gave me a finger wave as she crossed her legs on the barstool.

I smiled, not sure what the hell she was doing here. As non-threatening as they appeared, my internal warning bells were screeching their little throats out. *Who were they representing?* A puzzle for later, maybe. For now, I needed to concentrate on the known dangers. Behind me the sound of the door's lock latching echoed like a hammer hit.

"Drink?" Alexander asked me as I made my way to the expansive living room.

An overly large sectional surrounded a low table, which held a pad of paper, pens, and a laptop. A large cut-crystal vase with exotic birds of paradise stood in the center, directly in front of the fireplace.

Who the hell needed a fireplace in Vegas? The irrelevant thought crossed my mind.

Focus, girl. The need for a mental slap could mean the virus was well underway.

Or you're scared shitless.

Or that.

Trying to ignore my mental schizophrenia, I went to answer Alexander, but didn't get a chance, because Rawlings stepped in. "Booker Noe neat."

I caught Alexander's raised brow as we walked by and nodded. He turned back to the bar.

"Welcome to Vegas," Rawlings addressed the room at large and took up a position in front of the fireplace, ever the benevolent businessman. "If you all would make yourselves comfortable, we can get down to business and return to the auction downstairs before we're missed."

Not really wanting to share space with anyone else, I picked the single chair to Rawlings's left. The symbolism was not lost on me, but hey, when in Rome… Besides, it backed to a wall and gave a great view of the door, which happened to be my only exit.

If I got past everyone else. Shoving the mess of nerves, worries, and fears into a box, I locked it tight and prepared to enter the arena.

Liwei picked the seat closest to me and settled on the sofa. As he passed between me and the sofa, he said, "I'd like to return in time to hear the auction winners, Rawlings." His dark eyes met mine, shining with shared knowledge. He ran a hand over his pants and gave Rawlings a smile. "There's an exquisite carving I'm hoping to acquire."

"And I would not want my wife to worry," Bavin chimed in, taking a seat on the center section.

Pendleberry held his tongue and simply perched on the armrest to Rawlings's right. Alexander handed me my drink, and I murmured my thanks. He lifted his glass and returned to the bar to stand next to the blonde. He leaned back, and the couple seemed to settle in to enjoy the show.

"Since we're all anxious to return, let's begin with the opening bids, shall we?" Rawlings leaned over the table and picked up the pad of paper and a handful of pens. "Please write down your offer," he instructed, tearing, then handing out a blank sheet and a pen to the three men on the sofa.

He walked over and handed one to Alexander. I found it interesting the blonde didn't warrant a piece. "Fold your offers in half and Risia will be happy to collect them."

I would? I took a sip and tried not to glare at him.

"Rawlings, not that I don't believe you, but I'd like to see that this does what you claim." Alexander's relaxed position didn't change, but the atmosphere in the room gained an edge. "Before I decide my price."

Rawlings's smile didn't slip, but it did sharpen, bringing to mind a predator baring its teeth. "Of course." He turned to me. "Risia? If you please?"

Time to take the stage. My heart skipped a beat, but I set my drink on the small table next to the chair, proud my hand didn't shake. I opened my clutch and withdrew the silver pen. Handing it to Rawlings, I tried not to think about what would happen if Rabbit was wrong.

He hasn't been yet.

My inner cynic chimed in, *There's always a first time.*

Great, not only was I dying, I was cracking under the pressure. I rubbed my temple where a dull ache had started.

"Just hold it together, Risia."

It took a second to process that the unexpected voice in my head wasn't mine. Startled, I froze in my seat. Thankfully everyone else was watching Rawlings as he popped in the drive and pulled up his program.

"Can you picture the room?"

My mind clicked into gear. I held my breath and sent the mental question out. *"Wolf?"*

"You were expecting someone else?"

"I wasn't expecting anyone." I tried to stop that last thought by re-creating the room and everyone's position.

"Just hang in there. We can't reach you via stairwell, you're too high up. Rabbit's working on bypassing the elevator's security."

It was strange to function on two levels, but multi-tasking was nothing new. I kept my attention on Rawlings, who finished typing and was now standing back from the laptop.

"Feel free to check it out," he invited the room.

A cold sweat broke over my spine as each man rose and spent a few minutes reading the information scrolling over the screen.

Please.

I had no idea who I was talking to—Wolf or that bitch, Fate.

Alexander crouched down, his gaze fixed on the screen. The seconds ticked by before he slowly stood and moved away. Bavin took his place, then Pendleberry, and finally Liwei.

"Satisfied?" Rawlings asked Alexander.

Alexander flashed another one of those smiles. "Quite."

Rawlings withdrew the drive and handed it to me, sardonic amusement dancing in his flat gaze. "If you would be so kind as to hold this, my dear."

I reached out and gingerly took the drive from him.

Then all hell broke loose.

The door flew open and bounced off the wall, bringing everyone to attention. *"A little warning next time,"* I sent to Wolf.

"For what?"

Standing in the doorway was Mateo Besora, flanked by two men holding guns.

"Shitdamnfuck."

"Risia, talk to me!"

"Unexpected company." It was all I could manage.

"Señor Rawlings, I seem to be missing an invitation." Mateo strode forward and motioned one of his men to close the door. "Perhaps it got lost in the mail?"

Rage ripped away Rawlings's businessman persona, and he glared at Mateo. "You were unable to meet the minimum qualifications for this event."

Mateo stopped on the other side of the white couch and clicked his tongue. "Well, let's see if we can't renegotiate, shall we?"

He flicked his hand and the thug on his left put a bullet between Bavin's eyes. Stunned shock left me blinking at the red ruin spattered across the couch's center section. Well, this wasn't going well.

"You seem to be down a buyer." Cold and utterly unmoved, Mateo met Rawlings glare for glare. "Do I meet the minimum qualifications now?"

Rawlings stepped out from behind the laptop, his hands curled into fists. "Do you plan on killing everyone here?" Disdain dripped from his words.

"If you're coming, Wolf, now would be good."

Mateo shrugged.

"Drop!"

I hit the floor just as the door flew off the hinges. The

hollow sound of metal hitting the marble floor echoed, then was wiped out by a loud bang and a flash of heat. The air filled with acrid smoke and my ears rang. Muted yells rebounded through the haze. Then came the soft pops of bullets.

A quick slice of pain along my arm quickly disappeared under a burning need to stay alive. The soft pops gained speed and the yelling became a confused din of sound as the smoke got thicker.

In front of me, something heavy hit the floor.

Then the screaming started. Agonized and terror-stricken.

Lifting my head, I cracked my eyes open the tiniest bit, only to widen them in horror as Mateo was engulfed in a blue-white flame. He stood in the center, his mouth opened wide, his screams cutting through the ringing of my ears.

I couldn't look away.

The flames danced over him with a strange silence, but their destructive nature was graphically in evidence. The image of him burning alive would haunt me forever. A curtain of heavy smoke cut the nightmare short and made me cough with harsh, rasping gasps. My eyes teared and burned. Needing an escape route, I looked blearily around.

The hellish screams and resulting chaos surrounded me, but movement by the bar caught my attention. Alexander sent me a mocking salute before he and the blonde faded into the heavy smoke.

Mateo's screams achieved a new level of agony.

Voices started shouting, and I thought I heard my name.

"Here," I tried to call out, but ended up in another coughing fit.

Another burst of gunfire sent me scrambling back in a lame attempt to escape what I couldn't see.

Something tangled in my hair and pulled me up short. Crying out, I dropped the drive and reached up, only to have my head yanked back. I rose to my knees trying to get free and Liwei's furious face filled my vision.

"Traitorous bitch." He raised his hand and off balance, with no way to avoid the hit, he slammed his fist into my temple.

The world wavered as I tried to fight. Another hit and everything went black.

Chapter Twenty-Nine

TAG

Standing over Rawling's dead body in the bullet-ridden shambles of the penthouse should have brought a sense of relief. Instead, all I could see was Risia's pale face as she stepped into the elevator.

Don't let me go.

Fury and fear made for a toxic combination and my demons were laughing their asses off. The little fuckers.

The smoke from the flash bang was drifting away, revealing a scene that would do a horror flick proud. Besides Rawlings, the storm of bullets took care of Bevin, Pendleberry, and two John Does. The burnt remains of the asshole who'd FUBARed the whole op lay on the floor.

No sign of Risia or Liwei.

"Where is she?" I gritted out when Wolf stepped up next to me.

"I can't reach her." Under the ashy residue, Wolf's face was stony.

My heart dropped, and my world shuddered. A hand gripped my shoulder as I swayed.

"Tag, dammit, stay with me here. She's probably unconscious. Give Rabbit a second to get the tracker up."

The small tracker Rabbit insisted Risia wear on the back of her pendant was the only thing keeping me in place. Without it, I'd be tearing Vegas apart despite my training.

"GPS has her moving at a fast clip to the west," Rabbit said, focused on his phone.

"Let's go." I turned, only to come up short when Wolf imitated a damn boulder. "Move."

He shook his head. "Get your head out of your ass first."

Rage wiped my vision to red. When it cleared, my cheek ached, and I could taste blood on my tongue. Muscles screamed along my arm currently twisted along my spine, trapped there by Wolf's hand. His thick arm was wrapped around my neck, pulling my spine into a painful arc.

"You done?" It took a few seconds for the rough growl next to my ear to penetrate.

The pain of his hold snapped me back. *What the hell was I doing?*

We didn't have time for me to lose my shit. Risia didn't have time. I managed a tight nod. Slowly, he let me go. I stood there breathing hard and pulled my shit together.

Wolf stepped in front of me, blood seeping from a split lip, his green gaze serious and focused despite the beginnings of a shiner. "You good?"

Rubbing my neck, I coughed, winced, then managed, "Yeah."

He watched for a few more seconds, then turned to Rabbit. "You still got her?"

"Yeah," Rabbit looked up, worry etched across his features. "You better get moving, I think she's heading to an airfield. I'll stay with Jinx and handle the cleanup."

"Meli?" Wolf asked.

"Got her covered." Rabbit handed him the phone. "Go. I've got this."

We left.

Just hang on, Duchess, I'm coming.

I wove my way through the traffic, ignoring the horn blasts and shouted curses, while Wolf barked directions. We left the Strip in minutes and hit an industrial area. The steady blink of lights to my left had me asking Wolf, "Is that McCarran's air tower?"

"She's not there, but she stopped. It looks as if they're just beyond the airport."

I shoved my foot harder against the gas and the sedan leapt forward.

"Left in fifty…thirty…twenty…ten…"

I yanked on the wheel, and the sedan shimmied over the rough road. A chain-link fence kept pace on my side, but I couldn't find a break in the barrier. "Opening?"

Wolf kept one hand on the chicken handle. "Make one."

Without slowing, I angled and followed orders. The screech of metal on metal met with Wolf's steady curses. Tires found traction on pavement and I followed Wolf's curt directions.

"Left." Then, "Three hundred yards out, right."

A dark building loomed on our left. "Park it."

I killed the lights and let up on the gas, letting the battered sedan roll to stop in the shadow of what looked like a small office. The outline of a hangar sat just beyond it, lights shining from inside. I shut off the engine.

Next to me, Wolf pulled up his pant leg and withdrew his H&K, cleared his slide, and chambered a round.

I pulled out my Beretta and followed suit. "Anything?"

"I can't get a clear hold," he answered. "It could be a concussion or her fever."

Both choices had me clenching my jaw. "We need Bai alive."

Wolf cocked an eyebrow. "You reminding me or you?"

"Me," I gritted out. "Ready?"

We left the car and made our way to the hangar, using silent hand signals. Coming up on the nearest wall of the hangar, I set my back to it. I held my gun ready, ignoring the heat still radiating from the corrugated metal surface.

"I want the access code, Risia." A lightly accented male voice drifted through the opening.

"Funny, Bai, I want the antidote."

I barely acknowledged the relief of hearing her voice, slurred though it was, and waved Wolf forward. The sound of flesh meeting flesh and a feminine grunt of pain had me fighting for the slippery leash on my control.

"Do you really think you're in position to negotiate?" Bai snapped.

I blocked out the rest of the conversation, freezing out everything but logic. If I kept listening, I'd forget why keeping the dickless bastard alive was so important. I waved Wolf forward.

He crouched and inched closer, then popped his head around the corner for a quick recon. He pulled back, held up two fingers, and made a quick motion.

Two targets. One in front of Risia, the other to the left.

I gave a nod.

Wolf did a quick countdown. At one we moved.

A quick bark from Wolf's H&K and the man standing to the side of Risia went down. Risia was on her feet with her arms bound behind her, bruised and bloodied, but breathing.

Unfortunately, Bai was using her as a human shield, keeping her between me and a clean shot. With a gun in one hand and her curls wrapped in the other, he was backing toward a door in the far corner, dragging her with him.

A dark bruise spread from temple to chin and under it her skin was almost translucent. The overhead light glinted off the damp sheen on her face. Tears or sweat, I wasn't sure, but it sent dangerous fissures through my concentration.

"Stop!" Wolf barked. "Let her go!"

"I don't think so," Bai shot back, shuffling back a few more steps.

Risky though it was, I sighted to the right of Bai's position and pulled the trigger. The bullet kicked up concrete but brought Bai to a halt. His sudden movement jerked Risia's head at an impossible angle.

She cried out in pain.

My finger flexed, the need to put a bullet into Bai dug in with cruel heels, trying to spur a reaction. "You want to negotiate? Access codes for her."

Bai paused, his black eyes staring straight at me, flat and evil. He leaned in to Risia until his lips touched her ear. He whispered to her. Whatever he said had her eyes widening and she began to struggle as he began dragging her backward again.

"You want her?" His voice carried through the hanger. "You can have her." He gave her a brutal shove forward and raised his gun.

Time slowed to a crawl.

I aimed and pulled my trigger, even as I lunged forward.

The deafening sound of simultaneous shots echoed through the hanger.

Risia jerked, her terrified gaze locked on mine, her lips moving, "Tag!"

Her body twisted to the side.

Another shot echoed in the hanger.

Just out of my reach, she sank to her knees, her hands still bound behind her. Panic held oxygen hostage in my chest as she swayed.

Behind her, Bai stumbled back and raised his hand again.

Another deafening report.

Fire ripped along my hip and barely registered.

Bai stumbled into the wall and slid down.

As Risia tumbled forward, I dropped my weapon and went into a desperate dive. "Risia!"

I dove the last few feet, my hands outstretched. My knuckles scraped across the rough floor, but I managed to get my hands between her head and the concrete. Silky curls buried my shaking hands, twining around my wrists as my chest burned. I dropped my face against my outstretched arms. My fingers flexing against her skull, as relief turned my muscles to water.

I shifted the weight of her head to one hand, then used my other to brace as I got to my knees. "Open your eyes, Duchess. Come on." I turned her over and cradled her against my chest, feeling the lump behind her ear. I brushed her curls away from her face.

Her lashes fluttered. "Tag?" The skin above her temple was marred by a darkening bruise. A concussion. Just a concussion.

Wolf's voice snapped through the freezing paralysis crawling through me. He knelt next to me, his gaze fierce. "Sit her up, we need to get the zip tie off her wrists."

I cradled her against my chest, giving him room to cut her bindings free.

Wolf made quick work of slicing through the plastic tie.

My recent relief died a quick death and my heart stuttered. Red stained the sky-blue silk below her ribs along her lower back. Against my chest, she groaned as her arms fell free.

Pressure. I need to put pressure on the wound. I pressed my free hand against her, trying to staunch the bleeding.

Wolf knocked my hand away. "Move your hand."

I growled.

His gaze iced, and he snapped, "I need to see how bad it is. Hold her still." Wolf didn't wait, but bent over her, muttering to himself. After what felt like an eternity, he lifted his head, relief evident on his face. "Looks like a deep crease. No entry wound."

I shifted my hold, cradling her close, shaky with relief. When I was sure my voice wouldn't break, I asked. "Bai?"

"Dead."

The prison restraining my demons fractured and the echo of their hellish delight was drowned out by an agonized howl of denial.

"Tag," the husky whisper brought my attention to the woman I had just killed. Her eyes were glassy bright with fever, but a strange intensity kept me from looking away. She raised a trembling arm and cupped the side of my face. Her touch sent my demons scrambling back. "Tag, find me the Tiger."

"What?" The question escaped with a harsh rasp.

But she lost consciousness, her body shuddering in my arms. Chills visibly raced across her bare arms, even as her skin burned under my touch.

I lifted my head, trying to find solid ground as my world crumbled around me.

Wolf stared at her, his brow furrowed. He blinked twice, then looked at me. "Was there a wooden carving of a tiger in that penthouse?"

Some image tugged at me. I tried to set aside my guilt to pull it closer. Finally, I dragged it forward. "At the auction, a framed carving. She was talking to Bai in front of it."

Wolf was on his phone talking to Jinx, but all I could hear was demonic laughter as my heart bled out in my arms.

Chapter Thirty

The rumble of a familiar voice sounded above me, bringing me closer to awareness. I swam through a confused jumble of memories.

Elevator doors closing on Tag's frustrated face.

Following Rawlings to the penthouse.

My heart pounding as Rawlings ran the program.

Crimson exploding over white leather cushions. Choking smoke. A rain of metal.

Hellish screams. Alexander's salute. Liwei's furious face.

An empty hangar, Liwei demanding the codes.

Tag and Wolf bursting in. Liwei's man falling to the ground.

Tag, his face carved in fury, aiming a gun, then pulling the trigger.

At me.

I jerked upright. "Tag!"

"Shh! Duchess, I got you. I got you." Solid arms wrapped around me and held me tight against a familiar, bare chest. "You're okay."

"You shot me!" My voice emerged on a croak. I tried to push against him.

His hold loosened, and he shifted back until he could see me. "What?"

"You. Shot. Me." And I didn't know if that pissed me off or not.

He dropped his head until his forehead rested against mine. "I shot Bai. Not you."

It took a minute for me to process.

A hysterical mental voice piped up, *Appearances can be deceiving.*

The vision of Tag killing me took on a whole new meaning. "Well, damn," I muttered.

Guess Meli was right. Maybe I was self-fulfilling my own prophecies.

Swamped by giddy relief, some unseen chain snapped as my heart swelled. Needing an anchor, I lifted my arms, wound them around Tag's neck until I could bury my hands in his hair. My fingers felt clumsy, but he didn't seem to mind. Pieces of my surroundings began to filter through. He sat with his back to a familiar headboard. We were in the bed at Meli's. I was wearing on oversized T-shirt again. Next to me, Tag's chest was bare, raw patches decorated his skin. Noticing the wounds, I jerked back. Then hissed as the move caused pain to erupt across my back.

His hands tightened on my arms, not letting me get far. "Careful, Duchess. You don't want to reopen the bullet crease along your back."

That would explain the pain. But I frowned at the ugly scrapes on his chest.

He raised an eyebrow. "What?"

I lifted my gaze. "Why didn't you tell me I was hurting you?"

He grinned. "You weren't."

His nonchalant manner left me glaring. "Right, because you're a super hero." I sat up, the move causing the sheet to pool over my lap. I lifted it and pulled it away. My legs were bare, and Tag was wearing boxer briefs. Normally that would be enough to distract me, but not this time. White bandages covered his knees. "What happened?"

"Bai shot you. I shot Bai." His raw answer said so much more. A painful darkness seeped into his eyes, and I swore I heard demonic giggles.

I tangled my fingers with his and held on, offering what protection I could.

His grip tightened, then slowly lessened as the darkness slunk away. "You were falling forward, your hands bound behind you." He tried to grin. "Figured better my knees than scraping up your pretty face."

I could hear the frustrated helplessness wrapped in panic under the forced lightness of his tone. I curled around him, careful of his battered chest, and wrapped my arms around his waist. His arm curved over my shoulders, staying above my waist and drew me close. I felt the press of his lips against the top of my head.

Listening to the reassuring beat of his heart, I traced a fingertip over on old scar. Silence settled between us. Now that I wasn't moving, my body provided a catalog of injuries. The fire along my back dimmed to an ache. My knees felt stiff and my head hurt. Other than that, I felt good. My breath caught, and my pulse spiked. "Did you get the antidote?"

His arm tightened. "Bai tucked it behind the wooden carving at the auction."

A trembling wave of relief washed through me. "I'm not going to die?"

"Nope, sorry." His voice was curiously gruff.

Curling closer, I whispered, "I'm not."

And I wasn't.

"Rawlings is dead."

I lifted my head and braced my hands against Tag's chest. "What?"

"Rawlings is dead."

Hope unfurled in a bright, burning light, chasing back my worries. "My son?"

He smiled at me, wrapping a curl around his finger. "Safe, I promise."

A strangled laugh escaped, and I dropped my head to his shoulder. My son was safe. Tag was safe. "What the hell happened?"

"I was hoping you could tell me," he rumbled, his hand cradling my head. "The coroner's report on Rawlings indicated he was shot at close range, execution style."

I lifted my head to meet his gaze. "It wasn't me."

He grinned. "Didn't say it was." The grin faded into seriousness. "Who all was in there with you?"

I shifted until he let go, then moved so I could lie next to him. I took care to roll to my side, wincing as the wound at my back protested. Finally settled, I answered, "Rawlings, Liwei, Adam, and Sunil." I bit my lip. "Sunil was shot by Mateo."

He rolled to his side, so we could face each other. "Mateo?"

"Mateo Besora. He was the one that crashed the auction." I flinched remembering his agonized screams. "The one who was burning alive."

Tag's brow furrowed. "Anyone else?"

I nodded. "Alexander and his little blonde. Why?"

"Because we think Falcon may have taken out Rawlings and Besora."

That didn't make sense. "Why?"

He shrugged. "Don't know."

I remembered Alexander's mocking salute and the blonde's finger wave. That kind of arrogance would fit. "Alexander and the blonde," I muttered. "But if Falcon was involved, I'm surprised they didn't take me out."

"You're too valuable and complicated."

Oh, he was right about valuable. As a seer, my services could demand ludicrous sums of money, but, "Complicated?"

He studied me. "How easy do you think it is to kidnap someone who can see your every move?"

"But I can't. If I could, we wouldn't have to worry about Falcon."

"Maybe they don't know you can't, but I'm betting they don't want to risk it. Better they figure out a way to lure you to their side, rather than using force." His lips twitched. "Especially seeing how well threats worked for Rawlings."

I gave an inelegant snort. "Whatever, but they'll be waiting a damn long time." I paused, thinking about Rawlings. "I need to talk to Delacourt."

The ever-insightful man in front of me asked, "About your son?"

I nodded. "I need to make sure no one else can touch him."

"How are you going to do that?"

"I'm going to ask her to burn my connection to him." Saying it out loud hurt, but the quiet sense of certainty soothed the sting.

He traced a line along my jaw. "You want to make him think you're dead."

"It's better for him that way."

He frowned down at me. "What about you?"

I covered his hand and pressed a quick kiss against his palm. "I need him safe. He has a family that loves him and he's happy. I'd like him to stay that way." I searched his face for judgment. "I'll be okay."

His smile burrowed deep into my heart. "Yeah, I know."

Something shifted deep inside, leaving me unsteady. I needed to change the topic. "Did they get the drives?"

He shook his head. "Rabbit found it under the couch and we got the one off Bai."

"So, we're safe."

"For now."

Quiet fell as we hid in a villa that felt more like a home than any other structure I'd been in. Or maybe that had more to do with the man holding me. I indulged in the unusual well of peace, reluctant to disturb it. But outside the door, life waited. "What now?"

A strange tension ran through him. "What do you think about San Diego?"

"For?"

"A new start?"

"With you?" My heart stumbled over the realization he really wanted me.

"If you're willing to take the risk."

"How long?" I whispered, daring to hope.

"How long will you give me?" Fierce and bright, my battered soldier bravely handed me his heart. The flash of uncertainty on his face meant I wasn't the only one taking a risk here.

If you really love Tag, try. Meli's words whispered through my heart.

Trying sounded good. "As long as you want."

He kissed me, long, slow, sweet, and fierce. His love seeped into the wounded cracks of my soul.

I gave as good as I got, willing to stand guard against his demons. I was breathing hard when he drew back.

His gaze searched mine, hiding nothing. "You good with a lifetime haul?"

Tracing his lips, I handed him my dinged up heart. "Yeah, that'll work."

———————•◦●◦•———————

What happens when a woman on the run from a stalker's obsession dares to trust a man who sees deeper than her heart? Find out with Meli and Wolf in MARKED BY OBSESSION. Now available at your favorite bookseller!

———————•◦●◦•———————

PSY - IV Teams Books

Welcome to a world where facing danger requires the unique skill set of the men and women of Jami Gray's PSY-IV Teams. As sparks, and bullets fly, love, action, and adventure will target these unique couples as they race through each breath-stealing operation.

Binge the series today at your favorite bookseller!

HUNTED BY THE PAST

Cyn & Kayden

To escape a killer from their past, can a reluctant psychic trust the man who walked away?

TOUCHED BY FATE

Risia & Tag

A seer's secrets become her only bargaining chip in a high-stakes game of lies and loyalty determining her fate.

MARKED BY OBSESSION

Meli & Wolf

A woman in hiding. A telepath who sees deeper than her scars. Can they forge a bond stronger than the obsession stalking them before time runs out?

FRACTURED BY DECEIT

Megan & Bishop

After a brutal attack by a telepath, Megan turns to Bishop for help, but how does he keep her safe when she's threat?

LINKED BY DECEPTION

Jinx & Rabbit

Forced to play intimate criminal partners, will Rabbit & Jinx risk turning illusion to truth as they race to untangle a web of conspiracies and lies?

About the Author

Jami Gray is the coffee addicted, music junkie, Queen Nerd of her personal Geek Squad, Alpha Mom of the Fur Minxes, who writes to soothe the voices crammed in her head. Her series combine high-stakes urban fantasy and edgy paranormal romantic suspense into books you don't want to put down. Buckle up and get ready for a wild ride through the fascinating worlds of the Arcane, the Kyn, the PSY-IV Teams, and the Collapse.

Come visit Jami's website at **https://www.jamigray.com** and stay up to date on what kind of trouble she's getting into and when you can expect to join in.

amazon.com/author/jamigray

instagram.com/jamigrayauthor

facebook.com/JamiGrayWriter

threads.com/@jamigrayauthor

goodreads.com/JamiGray

bookbub.com/authors/jami-gray